JILL MAR[...]

S·W·A·G·G

BOOK 1

SPOOK

SWAGG

Book 1: SPOOK

Jill Marshall

Jill Marshall Books
First published by Jill Marshall Books 2020
Copyright © Jill Marshall 2020

A CIP catalogue record for this book is available from the National Library of New Zealand

ISBN 978-1-99-002400-9 Paperback

Cover Design by Katie Gannon
Illustrations by Madison Fotti-Knowles

Deep undying gratitude to Levana, Madison and Katie G for your amazing talent and for stepping into the breach; to friends and family on both sides of the world for putting up with me and putting me up; to K and JJ for inspiring me always, and to all those JB fans who told me they wanted to be or even are Jane Blonde, and wanted to see her again. It's been a long time, but here you go.

For the young readers of the world who might need something new to chew on in these strange locked-down times. Stay safe, stay well, and enjoy.

Prologue

Gideon Flynn watched from the shadows.

The machine dominated the room completely, as brooding as an armoured tank sitting in a garden shed.

Beyond its cylindrical surface, at the distant end of the tube, Simone Varley was being ushered into a chair – a simple, plastic garden chair, as if she was at a barbeque. It seemed unbecoming for a woman of her age and status, but there was a special reason for not offering her anything more substantial to sit on. Any hint of metal on the chair - even a tiny amount in the castors - would cause chaos. Because, basically, the machine would eat it.

Now, though, it was about to devour a whole man.

Head first.

The MRI specialist positioned Trent Varley, Simone's husband, on the machine's sliding flat-bed. He smiled efficiently at the woman. After all, he must have done this procedure a thousand times. Probably as straightforward a process as running his Audi through a car wash, thought Gideon.

Of course, all the other times the doctor had done this would have been in an open hospital environment, while this was in a private facility. The set-up was flawless, however, and no doctor in the world would have had a bad word to say about it. Nor would they be complaining, of course, about the bonus in their pay packet.

HOST really was an extraordinary organisation to work for.

The MRI consultant spoke in his calming, airline pilot, "everything's fine here" voice. 'Now, Mrs Varley, at this point we normally tell our patients that they're going to have to keep very still for up to an hour,' he said. 'But I gather that won't be necessary in your husband's case?'

Simone Varley shook her head, her neck flushing as she swallowed back tears.

'That's precisely why we're here, Doctor Barnes,' she said. 'Nobody has been able to explain this paralysis that's taken over his body. The nausea. The muscle spasms. We're really hoping ...'

She stopped, overwhelmed, clutching a handkerchief to her face to hide her grief.

Doctor Barnes held up a hand. 'Don't upset yourself, Mrs Varley. Your husband's in the best possible place, with the finest brains and expertise right on hand.' Behind the glass in an enclosed office from which the Magnetic Resonance Imaging scanner would be operated, a row of familiar faces nodded to Simone. 'We'll get to the bottom of this, I promise you.'

'And you'll be here the whole time?'

'Right there, just the other side of that panel.' Doctor Barnes smiled confidently. 'Trust me. This is very routine.

Now it will be extremely noisy, so we'll put plugs into Mr Varley's ears - assuming that he can still hear anything.'

Simone Varley gulped furiously, stemming the flow of tears. 'I don't think he can,' she whispered. 'He hasn't responded to any sound for days. Oh, do make him better, Doctor Barnes. He's my rock. My lodestone.' She gulped back a terrible sob.

From his secret hiding position, Gideon Flynn could have sworn he saw a tiny flicker of movement across Mr Varley's eyelids, but his wife was gazing imploringly into the doctor's placid face and didn't notice.

'It's all right,' said Doctor Barnes, looking a little alarmed at Mrs Varley's increasingly emotional outbursts. 'Let's get it over with, shall we?'

Ripping two sterile ear plugs from their packaging, the doctor stuffed one into each of the patient's ears and then proceeded to tweak Trent's gown, checking he was in a comfortable position on his back, with no danger of anything getting caught in the machine's innards.

Satisfied, he tore a second set of ear plugs from the paper strip. 'The noise is incredibly loud even if you're sitting outside the machine, so you're going to need these.'

'Thank you. You're very considerate.'

'Not at all ... oh!' As he handed over the small packet of ear plugs, the doctor stopped short. 'We mustn't leave that in here,' he said. 'The magnetic force of the MRI is immense. It can pull oxygen tanks right out of their

housing and into the scanner, so it would make very short work of that little piece of jewellery.'

He pointed to the offending article.

It was a ring – not Mrs Varley's wedding ring, which she'd obviously remembered to remove, but a larger signet ring on the middle finger of her right hand. The stone in its centre glowed like a sunset - some kind of ruby – while the band itself was chunky, dark and heavy, like something a Viking might wear. It looked oddly out of place on Mrs Varley's slender finger, especially as she appeared to be wearing very fine latex gloves beneath them, as if she possibly had some issues with her skin.

She started out of her chair, spreading her hands wide as she twisted at the band on her finger. Once more, Gideon thought he saw Trent Varley's eyelids squeeze tight.

'Goodness,' the woman exclaimed. 'How could I have forgotten? I ... I'm so sorry. Do I need to leave the room?'

The doctor smiled. 'Not at all. I'll just take it outside for you now.'

'Thank you.'

'All set?'

'Yes.'

Doctor Barnes slipped the ring off Mrs Varley's shaking finger and into the pocket of his white coat. She returned his pleasant smile, her eyes drifting across the faces behind the glass partition.

Finally, thought Gideon.

'Okay. We're ready for lift-off,' said the doctor with over-the-top chirpiness. 'We've checked all Mr Varley's clothing, so he's good to go. And you're quite sure there's nothing internal that's made of metal? No clips from heart surgery or brain aneurysms?'

This time he was sure. From his dark hiding place in the furthest corner of the room, Gideon caught a flash of white as Trent Varley's eyes edged apart the tiniest fraction.

'No.' Mrs Varley shook her head. 'Nothing.'

'I think that's a bit of a lie, Simone Varley,' muttered Gideon under his breath.

In fact, he didn't just think it. He knew it. There was definitely metal in Trent's body.

And his wife knew it too.

As Doctor Barnes exited the room to install himself among the Varleys' associates in the glass cubicle, the woman scratched at her finger where the ring had been sitting. Then, under her breath, she whispered something.

The sound was overshadowed by the deafening noise of the machine thundering into life, so Gideon couldn't work out what she'd said. Instead he heard the doctor speaking to Trent Varley who lay trapped in the belly of the MRI machine. Like Jonah inside the whale, thought Gideon with the tiniest burst of satisfaction. What was that song he'd sung at school? 'Go down, Jonah, deep in the ocean. Go down, Jonah, far from the shore.'

Dr Barnes was fiddling with something in the other room. 'Okay, Mr Varley, not sure if you can hear me, but we're going to take a number of images. Each cycle will take about six minutes. Nothing to worry about. It will all be over before you know it.'

With a clunk and a screech, the scanner started its routine in earnest, beeping with the regularity of an oversized heart monitor, blasting sound even to the corners of the room where Gideon crouched, hidden from sight. Derrrm dem derrrm dem dem. What was that? Dub step, he realised. The rhythm was as infectious and tuneless as the drum and bass music of the nineties and noughties.

He almost felt like dancing, until he realised he could hear another sound.

Laughter.

Only for a moment, and more like an escaped breath than a full giggle, but it was definitely laughter.

And the only person it could have come from was Trent Varley's own wife.

He'd expected to feel very differently about Trent Varley, but suddenly, he felt a huge pang of sympathy. The woman was a monster, just as he'd thought.

What was it she'd said? He was her rock, her lodestone. Well, he knew exactly the kind of rock Simone Varley liked, and poor Trent wasn't it.

But at long, long last, Gideon Flynn finally knew what he was searching for, and that he had to make his move now.

With a violent shudder, he sank back into the shadows and waited for his moment to escape. The last time had been an accident. This time was ... too awful to think about. But think about it he must, because the plan had to go into action. Now.

Chapter 1 – A Chilling Message

Janey Brown ambled home after double English at Everdenn, trailing a stick along the fences down her street and wondering just what on earth had happened to her life lately.

She knew the answer. Precisely nothing. *Nothing* was what had happened to her life lately.

And she was starting to tire of it.

It used to be an adventure, her life, to rival anything that Huck Finn and Tom Sawyer or Harry, Ron and Hermione could ever come up with, and now it was … well, fine. Ordinary, and fine. Ordinary and fine and kind of flat, if she was honest. Rather like Janey's hair.

She grabbed the end of a tendril of said hair as it floated past her in the breeze, attempting to analyse the colour. Sort of dark blonde. Maybe honey on a sunny day. There was nothing wrong with that – she remembered a time when it had been just dull, mousey brown, all the time. She'd learned to combat that herself with a toner from the pharmacy, so that at least it was glossy and healthy-looking and shot through with natural highlights. And she could always use straighteners, curling wands, rollers, trips to hairdressers, and any number of tricks and treats that her family had given her for Christmas to make her hair more interesting if she wanted.

Not so long ago, though, her hair had been blonde. Blonde with a capital B. A gleaming, platinum ponytail, thick and lustrous and useful, whenever she took a trip through the Wower which spat her back out into G-Mamma's lab as sensational spylet, Jane Blonde.

There had been many amazing missions with her crazy, wanna-be-gangsta SPI Kid Educator and her growing network of spy-friends, and none so amazing as the adventure that placed Janey Brown firmly in the heart of her staggeringly great family: Mum and Dad; Uncle James; Uncle Sol and Aunt Maisie; and her irritating but brilliant cousin, Alfie. After years of it being just Janey and her mum, this was an adventure in itself.

And for a long time, that had been enough. Over many, many months, she'd got to know them all both individually and as a strange and wonderful group. She'd gone to a normal school doing normal things with her normal friends and her normal (ish) cousin, and for the first time, Janey Brown had been IN - not a member of the totally in-crowd, as such (and she didn't think she'd really want to be) but with a set of close friends including Tish and Leaf and Alfie, who were fun to be around and made her feel like she herself was fun. They didn't remember at all how wild they used to be when she knew them first, but they were still great company. There were good grades to enjoy, wins for the athletics team even without her Fleet-Feet super-powered spy-shoes, and a growing sense of just being at one with the world – no, not just with the world, but at one with herself. No longer two people, Blonde and Brown, but one strong individual, with all the best parts of both and the sum of the parts being bigger than the whole and all that deeply philosophical stuff they were being taught about in their 'mindfulness' classes at school.

Meanwhile G-Mamma, AKA Rosie Biggenham, had been leading an interesting double-life as a singing octopus called The Bigg Squid, at the same time as keeping Janey supplied with enough gadgets (homemade) and training (home spun) to single-handedly thwart the next world war, if it ever came about.

Which, of course, it didn't.

Which, of course, was great. Nobody wanted war.

But a little tiny bit of fighting somewhere … a miniscule morsel of some kind of skirmish or combat to deal with … well, right now, thought Janey, that wouldn't go amiss. Even just some in-fighting between different spy organisations would be welcome. After all, it was the kind of thing she used to do in her sleep – or rather, when she was meant to be asleep but was instead SATISPIing her way around the globe, battling baddies.

These days, the most mysterious thing to happen was that her new jeans had been lost among the laundry just when she'd intended to wear them for 'own clothes' day at school. Dull. Really dull.

It was ironic, really. Before her spying time, she'd been pretty much afraid of everything. Janey Brown was rather afraid that *not* being afraid of anything might be even worse.

She stopped short as her trailing twig caught in the fence and the silliness of her own internal discussion smacked her between the eyes.

'You're afraid not to be afraid?' she asked herself aloud. 'That's ridiculous.'

'No. Talking to yourself,' said a newly deep voice that had only just broken, and still came out with the odd squeak that made her giggle. 'That's ridiculous.'

Alfie popped up from behind the fence, still holding the stuck end of Janey's twig. So that was why it had got caught.

She swatted him around the head. 'You maniac. Were you lying in wait for me or something?'

'Yep.'

Swinging his long legs over the fence, her cousin shoved Janey across the path so that he could fit onto the pavement beside her.

'The parents are all going to some concert or other, if you remember,' Alfie said, 'so I'm keeping you company until they're back. Aren't you the lucky one?'

Janey sneered, although she was actually very pleased not to be spending the evening on her own. Now she'd have an *actual* distraction from finishing her English poetry assignment, instead of getting herself into a tizz by leaving her homework to the last minute - for no good reason other than to feel some mild buzz of excitement at doing something even a tiny little bit reckless.

'Aw. Do I have to babysit for you?' she said airily.

'I think I'm the one who has to babysit.' Alfie hunched over till he was down on Janey's level, then performed a very insulting and startlingly accurate imitation of her voice. 'Ohhh, I'm afraiiiiid! I'm afraid to be home on my oooooown even though I'm totally old enough. I'm afraiiiiiid to be all alooooone in a big dark house with –'

'Alfie,' said Janey sternly, 'you've got that completely wrong. I was saying the opposite of that. I'd love to be in on my own, all alone in a big dark house with no electricity and nasty noises coming from the basement. I'd love to be scared out of my wits, to be perfectly honest.'

'I've said it before, and I'll say it again.' Alfie stared down at her from his great, lanky height – he must have shot up by a whole half-a-body in the last year. 'You're very strange, and I can't believe we're related.'

Neither can I, thought Janey. However, she didn't bother to explain to him that for a long time, he'd been first an enemy and then her co-spylet and buddy, until she'd done some creative looping of time and he'd turned up as her cousin. After the crazy looping, she'd spent many hours trying to catch him out, seeing if he really remembered *anything* about their past activities working for Solomon's Polificational Investigations (SPI). Even though he'd always been a very good spy and wouldn't have given anything away easily, she knew that by now she'd have found some tiny Achilles heel, some chink in his armour to get him to confess if he had any recollections of his spy past. He never did. It was definitely sad but true: Alfie was no longer an agent. He was just a tall, irritating, sarcastic relative who happened to be in her class and was also a very good friend. Her best friend, in fact.

And that was great. Really great. Would she go back to the old days though? Just at that moment, she wasn't at all sure …

As if to prove how flat her life was and how annoying he could be when he really tried, Alfie spent the evening skulking around the house after her, turning out lights and flicking the curtains to try to scare her. When that didn't work, he upped his efforts, disappearing outside and scratching down the windows with a garden fork while he made wailing noises and shouted, 'No, no! Don't murder me!' When even that failed, and Janey just carried on eating the pizza they'd been allowed to order, he rummaged through her parents' DVD collection until he got hold of the scariest film he could find, and switched off all the lights so it was pitch black.

'Alfie, it's not going to work,' said Janey, laughing. 'Even the child catcher in Chitty Bang is not going to terrify me.'

'But he's hideous,' hissed Alfie. 'I had nightmares about it for years! And anyway, your family doesn't have –'

There was a thud, and his words cut off abruptly.

'Doesn't have what? A DVD horror collection?'

Silence wafted around the sofa like a chill wind. Even the child catcher had ceased his monstrous mewling search for hidden kids, so the film must have gone off too.

Okay, so maybe that was a little bit more effective.

'Alfie, dearest cousin of mine, you are not going to scare me by being quiet because that would, of course, be the answer to my prayers.'

Still nothing.

Absolute and total nothing.

In fact, it was the kind of *nothing* she'd experienced before – when she'd plummeted through space or down time-twisting helter-skelters; when it felt like the world had collapsed in on itself and nothing existed beyond her own skin.

How had he done that?

Suddenly a voice sliced through the darkness in a way that froze her to the core. It was hollow – a dark, hacking noise that sounded like someone speaking from the deepest pit of their own body, amplifying the horrible rasp through their stomach. It was vile. Cold.

Frightening.

'Are you afraid now, Jane Blonde?'

She tried to laugh into the darkness, but the dank, soul-less air around her swallowed the sound. 'Don't be silly, Alf.'

'You are afraid,' said the voice. 'Very afraid. That is good.'

'Why … why is it good?' said Janey, rather than admitting that she was actually getting a smidge freaked out. Very freaked out. 'Alfie,' she added for good measure.

'I am not your cousin,' croaked the voice.

'Course you're not,' said Janey, trying not to let nervousness creep into her voice. 'You would say that, wouldn't you?'

There was a long pause during which she tried to remember where the light switch was, pulling her school cardigan around her against the ever-decreasing temperature. This was getting a little weird.

Then suddenly the voice growled, 'This is your cousin,' and the frozen white face of Alfie was thrust into her vision, illuminated by a sickly green glow. His head was turned away as if in horror, his eyes screwed tightly shut in fear.

Then the voice continued, and it definitely wasn't coming from Alfie because his dead-looking white lips didn't even twitch.

'So do you believe me now, Jane Blonde? Are you afraid?'

Her chest was so constricted with terror that she could hardly speak. Why was she still in her uniform? At least in her spysuit she'd have had some chance of finding out who was talking. And saving Alfie. What had happened to him? Was it really as bad as it looked?

As anger at this … this thing that had hurt Alfie vibrated through her, Janey recalled the power that used to pour into her from the Wower. There was strength in anger, she remembered - a force in turning fear outward against the enemy.

'Yes, I believe you,' she said, stalling for time and wishing beyond all else that she could still see Alfie's face. It had floated back into the black vacuum surrounding her. If she reached out to attack the voice, she might damage Alfie in the process.

Then she remembered the first rule of spying that she had ever been taught by G-Mamma: surprise, surprise, surprise.

'And yes,' she said, dropping her voice to a whisper.

As silently as she could, she hunched down towards the sofa and groped for the one thing she knew was in arm's reach and might possibly save her and Alfie.

'Yes,' she repeated, even more quietly. 'I'm very, very afraid.'

A small sob escaped from her lips, and another and another, until soon she was gently crying.

The voice started to laugh. The icy air around Janey pulsated with the dreadful sound as the voice's owner drew breath to speak. 'I knew it–'

'Kidding!' shouted Janey, and in that same moment she grabbed the DVD remote control and pressed all the buttons at once. Even with the TV off, the DVD player might do something helpful – and it did, opening up the DVD drawer to spit out the film, flashing a vibrant blue beam across the lounge …

There was just enough time and sufficient light for Jane Blonde to grab Alfie by the collar and whirl the dead weight of his body round onto the sofa, then leap on top of who or whatever was crouched behind him like some diabolical puppet master. She flung herself onto the creature, not sure if it was human or some spy-created abomination such as she'd witnessed in the past. She felt fur beneath her palms and a soft, yielding presence like a … like a trampoline. Or a sprung mattress.

Had she misjudged and fallen onto the sofa? Hoping she hadn't, as that would mean Alfie getting even more injured, Janey bent her leg and skewered her sharp knee into the side of the body.

The grating, hacking voice erupted into shouting. In the same moment, the air got distinctly warmer, and the lights all came on at once.

'Get your bony bits off me, Blonde!' screamed the voice – only now it was a voice that Janey recognised all too well, with nothing sinister and chilling about it (although it was certainly someone of whom she could, from time to time, be very afraid).

'G-Mamma! What are you doing? You've killed Alfie!'

With Janey still straddling her SPI:KE's well-upholstered ankles, Rosie Biggenham heaved herself over onto her back on Janey's living room rug. 'I have not killed Alfie, tempting though it is. He's neither use nor ornament these days, since you de-spied everyone.' She flipped her hands at Janey. 'Get off me, and I'll show you.'

Janey obliged, and then helped lever G-Mamma to her feet.

The spy pointed to the gadget in her left hand. It resembled a small torch, and looked completely unremarkable. 'It's just a stun gun. Sort of a Taser, only gentler. He'll be up in about seven minutes when the effects wear off.'

'Good. I'm glad he's okay.' Feeling suddenly weak-kneed, Janey sank onto the sofa. 'But what was all that about? And how did you do that voice? It was … scary.'

There it was again. 'Are you afraid, Jane Blonde?'

'That was me.' G-Mamma sniggered as she waved the instrument in her right hand in Janey's face. It was a megaphone – the same megaphone she had employed to shout at office workers in London during Janey's first ever mission, several years ago.

'We-- I put a voice refrigeration module onto it,' G-Mamma explained, pointing to the large white cube bolted onto one side. 'I call it a vox-pop. Freezes my words and the atmosphere around it.' Behind fluttery fake eyelashes in virulent yellow, G-Mamma's large blue eyes sparkled merrily.

It looked like she was really enjoying herself - which led Janey to her next question.

'So did you seriously just want to try out a new spy-buy? Because knocking Alfie out and invading my living room with both our parents due back any minute is a bit mental. Even for you.'

G-Mamma stared at her, and Janey experienced that same chill-and-thrill she got whenever something exciting was afoot.

It was as she thought.

Hoped.

Dreamed ...

'I was just making sure you're really as ready as you've been saying. Luckily, you passed the test. On your feet, Blonde,' snapped G-Mamma.

25

She got up warily, half-expecting to find her socks secretly transformed into Fleet-Feet without her knowledge. G-Mamma grabbed her by the shoulders and pushed her big moon face up to Janey's.

'It's what we've been training for, all this time,' she said breathlessly.

'Not a … It can't be …'

She could hardly believe it, and yet her gut instincts were fizzing madly. Janey knew for sure that something huge was about to happen.

G-Mamma nodded. 'We have a mission, Blonde. We meet tomorrow.'

'Oh!' squeaked Janey, delighted. 'That's brilliant!'

'You bet your Blonde booty it is.' G-Mamma's eyes snapped left as Alfie began to stir on the sofa, and she tapped her watch. 'Spylab, this time tomorrow. Be there or be no longer a spy.'

'Try stopping me. I'll be there!' said Janey.

A key turned in the front door. In her usual fluid and surprisingly agile manner, G-Mamma scooped up her gadgets, hastened Alfie's recovery by giving him a tiny zap in the neck with the stun gun in reverse mode, and disappeared out through the back door to flit across the garden and back to her own house.

'What happened?' moaned Alfie plaintively.

'You passed out, I think. Afraid of the child-catcher in Chitty Chitty Bang Bang.'

'Was not,' he replied, although he didn't sound entirely sure.

It was only later that Janey realised she hadn't had time to ask what the mission was going to be.

Or how it was that, an hour or two after she'd gone to bed, her bedroom suddenly grew very cold and still, and a voice as brittle as perma-frost whispered to her.

'Are you afraid, Jane Blonde?'

But G-Mamma had taken the Vox-pop with her as she left.

Oh yes. She was terrified.

And it felt fantastic.

After a long period of flat-lining, Janey Brown – and Jane Blonde - finally felt alive again.

Chapter 2 – Lips with Tips

By nine o'clock the next night, Janey could barely contain herself. Two hours earlier, she'd made her excuses to her parents and disappeared upstairs. They'd never known her to be so fond of chemistry homework. For the entirety of those two hours she had perched on the edge of her bed staring at the fireplace, hardly breathing, hoping the weird chilly voice would whisper in her ear and wondering if – no, wishing that – the back of the hearth would slide up. Up and up, to reveal G-Mamma's roller-booted feet and the shiny floor of the Spylab.

Not that the Spylab was much of a Spylab any longer. Most of their gadgets still languished behind dusty panes of glass in the cabinets that lined the lab walls, but for years they had either hung in tatters or lain broken into pieces for experiments, like a kid's old, unwanted Christmas presents. Without the backing of the SPI organisation, there had been no money to keep the spy-buys active or replace anything that was no longer working. It just wasn't like the old days at all, no matter how hard G-Mamma tried to keep it exciting and ready-for-action. Even the special entry hatch between their fireplaces had rusted shut.

Or at least, that was how it had been last time Janey had seen the Spylab. From the way G-Mamma had delivered her news the previous night with a sparkle in her eye, Janey sensed that there might have been a few changes.

'Come on, Blonde,' she muttered. 'Get on with it.'

Now she really *was* afraid – scared that it might all be a hoax.

It took all the self-possession she could garner to wait for the clock to tick past nine thirty, and then a wee bit more to dare to drop to her knees and shuffle over to the hearth. What if it didn't work? What if this wasn't all going to be as exciting as she hoped?

There was only one way to find out. Janey located the tiny button that used to release the sliding door, closed her eyes tight, and pressed.

Immediately, smoke billowed into the room, accompanied by a horrendous grinding sound like a car engine that wasn't in gear. Janey backed away quickly, coughing. It wasn't working. There must be a fire in the hearth next door, and now she'd created a hole for flames to waft through into her own bedroom. She could set the whole house alight!

Then suddenly, as she grappled through the fog to close the shutter, she spotted a familiar and much-loved sight through the murky cloud of fumes. A pair of luminescent green eyes were observing her carefully from the bottom of the fireplace.

'Trouble!' she called. She reached out a hand to the cat as the panel jerked upwards to reveal a pair of wobbly, dimpled knees in jeggings.

'Don't worry about the mess, Blonde.' G-Mamma's face appearing next to Trouble's. 'Just need to oil the machinery.'

Janey slithered under the creaking panel as G-Mamma applied the contents of a shiny oil can to its edges.

'Okey smokey, you're done,' carolled the SPI:KE, hauling Janey to her feet in one easy movement. The metal sheet between their homes slid noiselessly back into position.

Janey wanted to pinch herself. She was here again!

And so, she was astonished to see, was the Spylab. The entire room gleamed like a polished grand piano. It looked better than it ever had, even when Sol was heading up the organisation.

'Did you get a cleaner in?'

Both her mother and Rosie Biggenham had been professional cleaners for a while. Maybe she'd pulled in some favours – otherwise how could she have organised this so quickly?

G-Mamma rolled her eyes. 'Well, yes, but could a cleaner do THIS?'

She flung open a double-fronted, shiny white wardrobe that Janey had never seen before, and dragged its contents out onto one of the benches. 'Spysuit. Fleet-Feet. Aspic. Ultra-Gogs – new design with clever laser lighting and some other things I haven't had time to investigate yet. Girl Gauntlet for you, now in Invisibubble too so your whole arm can disappear. Bigger versions of all of them for me.'

Using the sparkling green acrylic nail encrusted with diamonds on her index finger, G-Mamma swirled the clothing into a tottering pile, then waltzed around the room yanking open the non-dusty cabinets. 'There's all sorts in here, Janey-Jane-Janey. Everything we ever tried and more. We're back! And we're better than ever.'

Janey followed G-Mamma around in a daze. G-Mamma was right. It was all here - everything she'd ever used in her fights against evil, along with heaps of articles she'd never seen before.

Hardly daring to breathe, she stepped in front of one of the massive fridges pulsing gently along the back wall and turned to G-Mamma. 'Is this what I really, really hope it is?'

'Open it and see,' said G-Mamma.

Moonlight-silver rays spilled out across Janey's face as she took a deep breath and levered the doors open. 'It is! It's a Wower!' she said, so filled with delight that it was all she could do not to race in there and let the magical robotic hands Spy her up right there and then.

But how? How was this all possible?

She closed the Wower doors firmly and leaned on them. 'What's going on, G-Mamma?'

'We seem to have a new investor, that's all. They started with developing the Vox-Pop, and then moved onto all of this.'

G-Mamma pointed furtively over Janey's shoulder at the Wower, and she turned slowly. Was the investor inside the shower cubicle?

Then her gaze dropped to the strangely shimmering surface of the Wower's door. Just about where the ice-dispenser would be if this was a normal fridge, something was forming.

Nostril. Lips. Teeth.

'G-Mamma, there's a mouth appearing on the Wower,' she hissed.

'I see it!' squeaked her SPI:KE. 'I *knew* someone was in there!'

'But there's nobody in the Wower; I just looked.'

Janey stepped back a little as the mouth swam out of focus for a second and then pinged back to life onto the silvery doors, stretching into a yawn as if someone was trying it for size.

And then, as the same deep chill that Janey had experienced the previous evening trickled down her spine, a tongue protruded slightly from between the teeth. It licked the thin lips back and forth, and suddenly the voice spoke.

'Thank you,' it said, 'for helping.'

Trouble spat venomously, leaping at the peculiar image before them, so Janey moved him carefully out of the way and looked round for a gadget that might record what was going on. Where was her LipSPIck when she needed it? Unable to find anything more technical, she reached into her pocket and took out her phone.

'Helping with what?' she said carefully, holding the phone close to her body so it couldn't be seen.

The mouth quivered momentarily, and then re-formed. In the same icy rasp as before, it continued:

'A story once told.
As an ancient boy turns gold,
The truth emerges.'

Janey stared at G-Mamma. 'Well, what kind of rhyme is that?' said G-Mamma rudely. 'That wouldn't make a decent rap at all.'

The lips pursed thoughtfully. 'Well, how about this?

'They took something precious.
And now I want it back.
The lodestone's there before us,
And you are right on track.'

'Better,' said G-Mamma. 'Could bust some moves to that one.'

Pins-and-needles flushed the length of Janey's body. That was quick-thinking on the voice's behalf, and G-Mamma was nodding approvingly. But the words seemed to indicate that the future involved them, and they hadn't agreed to anything yet.

The mouth elongated into a rather cynical smile that lasted only a moment. 'Then meet at the playground copse. Ten minutes.'

As quickly as it had appeared, the lips formed two thin parallel lines, merged immediately into one and then, like a zip folding in on itself, the mouth vanished completely.

Pressing replay on her phone, Janey scribbled down the words onto a pad.

'The truth emerges. Hmm. It's not a rhyme, exactly,' she said. 'I think it's a haiku. We just did them in poetry this afternoon.' Then something occurred to her. 'Have you seen that mouth before? You must have got news of our mission from somewhere.'

G-Mamma shook her head, her fluffy earmuffs sliding madly to one side. 'No, I just got a message via my Bigg Squid website. Look.'

Turning to one of the many devices lined up along one of the Spylab's benches, she swiped a fingertip along the screen and brought up her website. Sure enough, among the requests for birthday events and karaoke nights there was an email with no sender listed, entitled 'MISSION.'

The message was brief: Spylab Thurs evening 21.30, Gideon.'

'And just as I was thinking, "What Spylab?" this team turned up and began the upgrade.'

This was weird. 'So we have a new investor who just happens to have copies of all our SPI equipment?'

G-Mamma shrugged, just a tiny bit uncomfort-ably. 'Don't look a gift horse in the mouth, I say. Or rather, DO stare this one in the mouth. These are lips with tips. And watch my hips! Woah!'

Janey thought quickly as G-Mamma began to swing her body around in a manner that strongly suggested there might be a rap coming on at any second. The fact that someone had been keeping an eye on them and buying up their stuff like any old eBay trader was odd - and a little creepy.

But then, that was what spy organisations did, wasn't it? They sent in moles, or double-bluffed each other. And sometimes they merged and formed new, amazing, supersized set-ups.

'Do you think our new investor is a spy? They must have great equipment to do that mouth-message thing.'

'I'm not quite sure what they are,' said G-Mamma, trying a Boy Battler glove on for size and accidentally socking two ASPICs and a pair of rimless Ultra-Gogs across the room. 'Let's go and find out, shall we?'

Janey wanted to suggest they showed some caution, but this was beyond exciting. And it could be the perfect moment to try out one of the many forms of spy transport they'd used as spies: ESPIdrilles, SPIral staircase, Fleet Feet, even rockets and squirrel suits …

'How will we get to the playground in ten minutes?'

'I'll drive.'

There was only one thing she could be driving in. 'In the Bigg Squid van?'

'Too posh for my fancy schmancy van, are we, Blonde?' said Janey's SPI:KE with a sniff.

'No, it's just …'

It was just that Janey was older now. And they had cool stuff to hand. She really didn't want to turn up at their first mission in years in a hippy van decorated with sea creatures.

'It's fine,' she finished with a tiny sigh.

'I know it is. And as you said, we don't yet know if we can trust all these magic gadgets. Better stick with the tried and tested until we have more information.'

She had a point, boring though it was. Tucking Trouble under her arm, Janey followed G-Mamma down the SPIral staircase, past the cosy rooms the woman had furnished simply to try to convince the world she was the very ordinary Rosie Biggenham, and out of the front door.

From the house next door, Janey could hear her parents arguing over who'd given the right answer on QI, then falling apart with laughter at whatever it was Boz, her father, had said.

'The kids are playing nicely, Blonde,' whispered G-Mamma with a nod at the window. 'They'll manage without you.'

It was a very peculiar moment. Janey felt like she was the adult, going out and leaving the children in the house. Maybe she should have booked Alfie to babysit.

At the thought of her cousin, her brain gave a little twitch, and she caught hold of G-Mamma's arm. 'Is Alfie—'

'No,' said G-Mamma, very emphatically. 'Alfie is definitely not. It's time to leave the past behind, Girly Girl.'

Really? But this was Alfie … Possibly even her mum and dad. The odd moment stretched out a little longer as Janey listened to her former Superspy parents, Boz Brilliance Brown and Gina Bellarina, jeering at the TV and passionately debating Stephen Fry's cleverness, with not even a smidgeon of a suggestion about what a fabulous secret agent he'd have been.

Janey nodded slowly. 'You're right. Every-thing's changed. *I've* changed.'

G-Mamma snorted. 'No kidding. You've no idea how many of your clothes I had to nick to get the new size for your spysuit.'

'You've been stealing my ...' So that was what had happened to the jeans. Maybe she could have them back now that G-Mamma had taken her measurements. 'Never mind.'

Janey dropped down onto her haunches as the curtain twitched above her head. The last thing she needed right now was her parents stopping her before she'd even started.

'Let's go,' she mouthed, and they both crept from bush to bush until they reached the staggering creation that was G-Mamma's Bigg Squid transport, festooned with a giant plastic squid whose copper-coloured tentacles snaked across the roof and down the frames of the doors.

It was a relief that she was instructed to sit in the passenger seat with Trouble curled up in the foot-well. At least on the plush pink seat, rather than in the back of the van which was probably full of G-Mamma's costumes and portable karaoke machines, she felt a bit less as though she was in an episode of Scooby Doo.

G-Mamma started the engine. 'Lucky that I'm always going out at weird times to my gigs, so nobody suspects anything,' she declared. Then she eyeballed Janey. 'Or is it LUCK?'

'So all this time,' said Janey with a sudden flash of understanding, 'you've been inventing parties and appointments to go to as the Bigg Squid, just in case this moment ever arrived and you needed to dash out at a strange time of night.' Phew. What a relief! 'That's fantastic! All this time I thought you were actually inflicting your raps on paying customers.'

'Of course I don't rap to paying customers.' G-Mamma glanced at her sideways. 'I sing.'

So G-Mamma *had* actually been doing Bigg Squid-a-grams, singing at birthday parties. 'Good,' she said quickly as G-Mamma's face turned a little frosty. 'I bet your songs are great.'

'Want to hear one?' G-Mamma screeched around the corner, then suddenly veered off across a park towards the trees on the far side. 'Dagnannit, no time. We're here already.'

'Here? We're only just beyond the bottom of our street!'

'Another reason we didn't need spy-buys to get us here,' said G-Mamma darkly. 'Just the Octobus.'

'Octo-bus?'

G-Mamma sniffed. 'Okay. I'm just trying it out.'

While Janey was still figuring out a response, someone close by emitted a dark, musical shout of laughter that shot through her with the chill of the Vox-Pop. Trying not to shiver, she pushed open the passenger door and jumped down onto the grass.

Their visitor was already waiting for them in the dank shadows of a nearby oak.

'Daphne, I presume?' he said, his dark eyes flitting over the purple painted van. 'Velma and Fred already ran off, following a ghostly farmer into the forest.'

Janey lowered her voice. 'Oh, I know, it's embarrassing but …'

'No, the Octobus is amazing, actually,' said their visitor, changing his tone quickly as G-Mamma popped up beside Janey. 'I'm guessing you haven't seen inside it, yet?'

When the duo both looked blankly at the young man, he laughed. 'No time like the present, then,' he said.

He stood back politely as G-Mamma slid open the van door and stepped in cautiously, followed by a bemused Janey.

Only then did she discover what "amazing" really meant.

There wasn't a karaoke machine or stuffed fluffy octopus in sight. The back of the Bigg Squid-mobile was decked out like an FBI surveillance truck, with monitors and screens and flashing lights arranged along the length of each side, and a roof panel which bristled with satellite antenna, ready to flip over to the top of the van on command and take the place of the copper squid. Along the top of each bank of equipment was a narrow bunk, just wide enough for a travelling spy, and there was a slender, silver cabinet at one end which Janey just knew - judging by the glimmering rainbow droplets sprinkled at its door - must house a tiny, mobile Wowerette. Opposite sat an old fridge with a glass front, home to doughnuts, string cheese and fizzy drinks. It was the only part of the vehicle which looked like it had been there for ever.

'Vanderlicious,' whispered G-Mamma, immediately drawn towards the doughnuts. 'You must be Gideon. I'm G-Mamma, and this is Jane Blonde.'

'I guessed.'

Janey reached out a hand automatically, ready to greet their visitor, but the boy's hands were tucked firmly into his coat pockets. He was wearing a dark red suit with flared trousers, brown shoes with ten-centimetre platformed soles, and a cream and maroon patterned shirt with a collar that spread across his jacket like the wings of pterodactyl. Beneath his arm he clutched a … well, a baton for conducting an orchestra, Janey guessed, trying not to giggle. G-Mamma would probably want to work with him for his outfit alone.

'No hand-shakes, Jane Blonde,' said Gideon in a voice that clearly matched the laughter she'd heard from the back of the van. He extracted his hands from his pockets and waved them around. 'I have a condition which means I shouldn't touch people.'

'Ooo, is it leprosy?' said G-Mamma.

'No,' said Gideon abruptly. He sounded offended.

Janey elbowed her SPI:KE in the side and tried to sound business-like. 'That's fine. We've come across everything in our line of work. I mean it – everything.'

'Everything,' he repeated. He smiled, and Janey noticed that his dark eyes could convert from glacial to merry in a nano-second, and that his face, while thin and pale and youthful, sported a hint of a five-o'clock shadow. His mop of wavy black hair curled around his ears and onto his collar, highlighting the sharpness of his cheekbones. He certainly looked as if he could be ill – and he was older than he'd seemed at first. Definitely older than her. She guessed he might be sixteen or seventeen. 'That's good,' he said. 'That's exactly why I'm hiring you.'

At this, G-Mamma leapt around excitedly in a space that was much too small for G-Mamma-ish-ness. Janey wished she had a moment to disappear into the Wowerette to suit up properly. For a start, Gideon's outfit was making her feel very underdressed in her tracksuit bottoms and Baby Bear sweat shirt. For another, she wanted very much to impress him with their professionalism. This was their first mission in forever, and she didn't want to blow it.

Janey pointed to the small stools tucked under the surveillance banks. 'Let's sit down while you tell us what you need us to do.'

Gideon nodded briefly. 'You can sit. I prefer to stand. Achy joints – my condition,' he said, with a glance at G-Mamma that told them that it was all the explanation they were getting.

As Janey and G-Mamma squished themselves, side-by-side, onto the tiny stools, Gideon stretched his fingers out one by one as if they were stiff, unused, and then unfurled the baton. It was a roll of paper, on which he appeared to have written his notes.

'Right, well, I'm not sure how much Ms Biggenham has gleaned so far–'

'Very little, and please, as I told you, it's …' The SPI:KE practically sang her name, since she hadn't been able to use it in years. 'It's G-Mamma.'

'I can't call you G-Mamma,' said Gideon with a frown. 'That doesn't seem … respectful enough for a woman of your –' He paused, pondering. 'Your reputation. How about we call you "GM" in future?' he said smoothly, barely missing a beat.

Janey warmed to him instantly. Anyone who took G-Mamma seriously was pretty sensible, to her mind. As G-Mamma thought it through and then nodded, he smiled.

'I'll go over everything, then.'

He took a deep breath and stared at the back wall of the van. 'My name is Gideon Flynn. As I mentioned in the lab, I need to get something back that was stolen from me, and I need a team to do it. The team has to be some extraordinary individuals like you, Jane Blonde.'

Trying not to blush, Janey thought quickly. 'We know some really incredible people ...' she started to say.

Gideon Flynn interrupted her. 'Not just in-credible,' he said, his voice terse. 'Extraordinary. Superlative. I've already researched each of the team members. You're the first, Jane.'

He stared at her purposefully, and once again Janey shivered. It was the first time ever that she'd been called Jane by anyone other than her spy friends.

This was really happening. It was all she could do not to turn to G-Mamma – GM - and high-five her. Even start rapping ...

'Who are the others?' she asked quickly, when she realised he was still watching her.

Gideon returned to his roll of paper. 'One at a time, Jane, if that's okay. On a need-to-know basis.'

'Need-to-know?' blurted G-Mamma. 'Of course she needs to know. Janey is a super-spy, trained by the very best.' From the look on her face it was clear she'd only just stopped herself from adding, 'Me'.

'Exactly,' said Gideon. 'Jane has unique gifts and experiences, and so do each of the others. It's imperative that this team comes together in order. These people, and no others.'

Janey exchanged glances with G-Mamma. This guy meant business, but they'd only taken orders from super-spies before. This was going to take some getting used to.

Talking of business …

'So what exactly is it you want us to do?'

For a moment, Gideon seemed flustered, paler than ever beneath the dark curls falling into his eyes. He appeared to be struggling within himself, searching for the right words. Then all at once his head snapped up decisively, and he met their gaze.

'I want you to break into some people's homes and places of business,' he said steadily, 'and steal some of their stuff.'

He lowered his hands to watch their reaction, and as Janey got to her feet to protest that he'd got the wrong people, the top of the roll of paper drooped down towards the floor.

Upside-down, she could see a list of names of the four people who were meant to be in this 'team', though the text was too small to read them. If only she'd been able to Wow up, she thought again – her Gogs would have worked them out in an instant. Above the names, written very clearly in thick, inky letters, was the heading of the project.

SWAG

SWAG? That was what burglars – the ones in cartoons with stripy jumpers and eye masks - wrote on their bags of stolen goodies, wasn't it?

No way. He'd got them all wrong. And she'd done the same, it seemed, trying to be professional with someone who just didn't get them at all.

'We're not thieves,' said Janey stiffly, feeling disgusted. She threw open the van door and jumped down onto the grass. 'I'm sorry, but you'll have to find someone else to do your dirty work for you. That's not the kind of mission we're used to.'

'What she said!' cried G-Mamma as she stalked past Gideon Flynn, though Janey heard her pause and whisper, 'But we can keep the spy goods, right?'

Janey didn't want the goods. All the spy-buys and fancy vans in the world wouldn't be enough to turn her into a criminal.

The disappointment, though, was so raw that she almost – almost – wanted to cry. There was no mission. They'd made a mistake and it was over before it had begun. Not waiting for G-Mamma or even for her Fleet-Feet, Janey took off across the park towards home. It seemed she wasn't going to be a spy again, after all. Home was where she belonged, being ordinary. Ordinary, bored and dull. At least that was better than prison, though …

She could hear the vehicle starting up, so she increased her pace. Revving the Bigg Squid van's engine, G-Mamma caught up with her at the corner of the street.

Gideon Flynn was silhouetted in the open door.

'Come on, Blondette,' cried her SPI:KE. 'Back in the Octobus.'

'But you heard him, G-Mamma,' said Janey, not caring that Flynn could hear every word. 'He wants us to steal things for him. That's not spy work.' She kept walking, her breath puffing out little clouds of vapour in the cold night air.

'Depends on what you're stealing,' said Gideon softly.

Janey paused reluctantly. Then, suspecting she might well regret asking the question, she stopped short before they reached her house. 'What do you mean?'

'They were mine,' said Flynn. 'These items were stolen from me – well, my family – in the first place.'

'And now,' added G-Mamma, 'he has to get them back to sort out his leprosy.'

'Condition,' said Janey automatically.

'Right,' said Gideon. 'And you wouldn't want someone's leprosy-condition getting worse, would you?'

Janey tried not to laugh. 'No.'

G-Mamma opened the passenger door, and with Trouble yawning and stretching winsomely on the fluffy pink seat cover, Janey couldn't resist. She hauled herself back into the van as their investor jumped down onto the pavement.

'I'm sorry for blurting it out like that,' he said at the window. 'I'm not used to people, really. My social skills are somewhat rusty.'

G-Mamma blinked. 'I can't imagine that myself, of course, being the super-duper socialite that I am.'

But I can, thought Janey. She knew how it felt to be lost for words, or afraid to speak out in case she sounded stupid.

'Anyway, Janey So-Saney,' G-Mamma continued, 'apparently these people in this organisation called the Host stole these things, and he wants to get them back for his family's sake. And then he can be cured of his terrible disfiguring illness.' G-Mamma batted her eyes at Janey. 'You wouldn't want Gideon to be horribly disfigured, would you?'

Janey glared at her. She knew what her SPI:KE was up to – reminding her of all the reasons she loved being a spy in the first place, instead of an ordinary, skinny girl who was picked on for her dismal hair and knock-knees. 'I wouldn't want anyone to be horribly disfigured.'

Gideon's eyes bore into her, imploring her to take on his case. His face was quite nice, it was true, even if it was pale and a little sickly looking. It wouldn't do for bits of it to start dropping off …

And it was for his parents. She knew a thing or two about that, too.

'So we have to help you, then,' said Janey with a nod.

Gideon grinned, looking so overjoyed that Janey got a clear sense of just how much he needed their support.

'Thank you,' he said, stepping towards the trees. 'I must go now, but GM has your next instructions.'

Janey glanced at her SPI:KE who held up a piece of paper on which she'd scribbled some notes.

'You're welcome, but … oh,' she said.

He had already disappeared, lost in the darkness.

Chapter 3 – Helmet Head

Gideon says we'll have to find one of the boys on his list. We need his special talent to collect the first object.'

G-Mamma handed her a Google print-out, and Janey snapped back into the present.

It was a grainy photo of a strange-looking guitar, with an onion-like body and a fretboard that was almost as long as the man playing it. 'A sitar,' she read aloud. 'This is the object? It's huge. How on earth are we going to get that out from under anyone's nose?'

G-Mamma shook her head. 'Not the sitar. The ring that the sitar-player is wearing,' she said, just a little jealously. 'Some enormous stone from India. And it's more "under earth" than "on earth",' she said, keeping a wary eye on the lights now starting to shut off in Janey's house. 'Apparently it's in an underground bank vault.'

This was mad. Mad and dangerous and not at all the kind of mission that Janey was used to.

But she had to admit it: she was hooked.

'So which one of the team can help us with that?' she asked, and G-Mamma grinned triumphantly.

'Jack Bootle-Cadogan. I've got his address here.'

'You just wanted to keep the new spy stuff, didn't you?'

'No, no, of course not,' said G-Mamma, but she didn't see that Trouble was staring hypnotically at Janey, nodding his furry striped head.

Just then, the light in Janey's hallway dimmed – a sure sign that her parents were on their way upstairs.

'I left my lights on!' hissed Janey with a start. 'They'll think I'm still awake and check in on me.'

'Go, go, go!' howled G-Mamma. She leaned out of the window as Janey sprinted for her front door. 'Then come, come, come straight back!'

Janey gave her a thumbs up, shouldered G-Mamma's front door open and hurtled up the SPIral staircase. In milli-seconds she had flung herself feet first across the Spylab, grabbing the nearest object – a chocolate muffin - as she slithered along on her tracksuit bottoms. With long-forgotten precision, Janey wellied the muffin at the fireplace; at just the right moment, it hit the control button and the panel slid upwards. Janey slipped beneath it, slammed her hand on the button on her side of the fireplace to close it, and in the same smooth movement, flipped herself onto her bed.

She was just pulling up the duvet when her mother popped her head around the door. 'Night, darling. Shall I turn off your light?'

'Oh, yes please, Mum. I must have nodded off!' She grinned dozily, and blew her mum a kiss.

'Sleepyhead,' said her mother. 'It must be all that chemistry homework.'

'Yes, I worked really hard on it.' Wow. There she was, lying to her parents again, and hardly having to even think about it. Everything truly was turning *brilliantly* normal. 'Night, Mum.'

Moments later, she was back in the street where the van was idling. Through the windscreen, G-Mamma's face bore the vacant and slightly star-struck expression that betokened an upcoming rap – or maybe she'd switched to songs.

'Listen to this!' she barked as soon as Janey stepped back into the van.

Yep, it was song-time. Janey decided to head her off quickly. 'Are we going to find this Jack person now? It's nearly midnight.'

G-Mamma shone the torch-taser, now minus the Vox-pop, on the back of her hand. Instantly, invisible coordinates lit up in neon. 'It's a blacklight,' she explained, 'showing what looks like a Hampshire postcode in my Perfect Poppy red lip gloss. It shouldn't take us too long. Then a quick Wower afterwards and you'll be ready for brekkie and Alfie and schoolie in no time.'

Janey shrugged. 'I was just wondering if we should Fleet-Feet over there. Or use the SATISPI? It's been a long time, but I'm sure it won't mix our cells up too much.' Until they'd got used to it and it had some work done it, the SATISPI had created some very interesting people-mixtures as it flung their cells about the galaxy.

'Oh, that's my spy girl.' G-Mamma couldn't have been prouder if she'd been Janey's mother on the first day of school. 'Mad, bad and beautifully blonde.'

Janey ran her spare hand over her hair, still beige-with-yellow-bits. 'Not yet. We didn't Wow up.'

'Never mind. Let's see how the land lies when we get there. Like I said, Blonde, the other team members may not even be spies – if we turn up all suited and booted we might scare them off.'

Before Janey could argue that her spysuit made her feel powerful whether there were other spies around or not, G-Mamma put her foot down. 'Don't worry about speed cameras!' she cried as they accelerated to 150 miles per hour. 'Gideon's had an Invisibubble shield installed around the Octobus.'

'How has he done that? He barely looks old enough to buy a car, let alone bunches of spy-buys.'

G-Mamma shrugged happily. 'Maybe he's older than he looks. Maybe he's got wealthy parents. Maybe I just don't care!'

Janey grinned. It was hard to disagree with that when they were having the most fun they'd had for ages.

They rocketed for miles along the motorway and across a number of fields at warp speed, only slowing as a vast stone wall appeared in the distance. G-Mamma's eyes suddenly became very round, flicking desperately left and right to find a way through.

On an impulse, Janey climbed over the seat, wriggled her way into the back of the van, and quickly identified which of the instruments was a satellite-driven camera system with GPS.

'Errr, satellite!' she shouted optimistically.

It was enough; the panel above her head swivelled instantly, switching the majority of the squid onto the ceiling so that the antenna stood upright on the van's roof, sandwiched between the remaining ends of two coppery tentacles. Immediately a picture of the area before them fizzed onto the screen.

'Left, G-Mamma,' she shouted. 'There's a break in the wall where a stream runs through it. I'm guessing the Octobus is amphibian?'

'You guessed right, Blondette,' yelled G-Mamma, a cry which was quickly followed by 'Yeeeeehaaah!' as the van careered right, dropped vertically almost onto its headlights, then sloughed along a brook through a small gap in the wall.

They skidded to a halt on a lawned area just behind a fountain. Janey clambered back into the cabin and opened the door, carefully hooking a finger though Trouble's collar. With this much water around, there was no guaranteeing his behaviour. Unusually for a cat, he was incredibly fond of water.

Sure enough, as soon as Trouble felt a splash from the fountain's pool on his nose, he struggled to escape her hold and launch himself into the water, but Janey hung on tight.

'Not now, Twubs. We're on a deadline.'

G-Mamma glanced at the fountain. 'Is it a water park?'

'I don't think so. Look at this.'

Stepping out from behind the stone fountain, Janey pointed up the grassy hill. It was a neatly mown grassy hill that stretched on for miles, suggesting that this *could* be some kind of park with keepers and ride-on mowers. Peeking over the crest of the hill in the murky darkness was a series of turrets. 'Maybe it's Disneyland,' she whispered.

The trio made their way up the slope, checking for onlookers, and stopped once they reached the top.

'Oh my starry eyes,' bleated G-Mamma. 'It's not Disney. It's Downton.'

It certainly was - exactly like Downton Abbey, from the crenelated roofline to the scrunchy gravel drive that led to its immense doors and then circled the grand building.

'Have we gone back in time too?' said G-Mamma hopefully.

'I don't think so. Those are satellite dishes on the roof. But there's only one way to find out for sure.' Breaking into a trot, Janey headed for the massive front door.

'What are you doing?'

'Surprising them by doing the obvious,' said Janey. 'Just like you taught me.'

'Yes!' G-Mamma hurried after her protégée. 'I *did* teach you that. I'm *brill*iant!'

The great house was gloomily dark. Even though it was night-time, Janey would have expected there to be some activity in a building this size, but there was very little light, and the only sound she could hear was a strange hissing noise that seemed to be coming from her chest. When she looked down, she discovered that it was Trouble, his back arched almost to her chin as a horrified yowl rattled in his throat.

She stroked his head as she ploughed on towards the doors, the stone chips of the driveway crunching beneath her Nikes. 'Trouble, it's okay. You're just out of practice with spy missions. Actually, we're all a bit out of practice.'

The cat wasn't having any of it, however. Just as she loosened her grip to rap on the door before her, Trouble wriggled out of her grasp and shot off around the corner, back towards the fountain with his fabulous tail bolt upright in 'offended and offensive' position. Luckily, Trouble could handle himself if the estate was home to any larger cats, so Janey just watched him go, then inspected the front door as she waited for her mentor.

G-Mamma caught up with her, puffing slightly. 'Anyone home?'

'I don't know. It's really quiet.'

She lifted a hand to knock again, but pulled it back in surprise as a male voice called out.

'Who's there?'

Janey turned to G-Mamma. 'What do we say?' she whispered.

G-Mamma thought about it for a split second, then said loudly, 'It's Biggenham and Blonde – I mean, Brown – from … SWAG.' So she'd seen the name on Flynn's list too. 'We'd like to talk to you, sir.'

'Did you have to say SWAG?' hissed Janey. 'We sound like burglars. And by the way, I don't think it's a sir kind of person. This guy could be Alfie's age.'

'Like I said, we don't know who we're dealing with,' said G-Mamma. She reached into a pocket in her flowing coat and pulled out the Taser-Torch. 'Just in case,' she added.

'I … Is SWAG a paper or a magazine or something?' said the voice, sounding nervous. And posh. Definitely the kind of voice that belonged with a mighty mansion of a house. 'Only I don't want to give any more interviews. I've taken over here and that's that. Now please leave me alone.'

Cursing herself once more for not even putting on her Ultra-Gogs so she could X-ray the door and see who was on the other side of it, Janey interpreted what she'd heard. A male voice, someone not much older than her. Something had happened recently, and the press had been involved. Whatever it was, the event had left the person feeling vulnerable, as well as something else that Janey recognised …

Lonely.

The person on the other side of the door was feeling very alone.

Suddenly she knew how to deal with it.

'Sorry,' she said calmly. 'We didn't mean to bother you after everything that's happened. But we're not from the press or anything. No, SWAG is a … social club.' Okay, so she was making it up as she went along, but it felt right. And true, somehow. 'A special one, for people just like you.'

There was a pause, followed by a deep, deep sigh. 'There's nobody just like me.'

'I bet there is. Me, for instance. I've known adventures – situations, even - like you wouldn't believe. Except I imagine, somehow, that you would believe them.'

There was another long pause, which was a good sign. At least he hadn't wandered off in boredom, or perhaps even scampered away to find a baseball bat or something to hit them with.

Finally, as Janey and G-Mamma stared at each other anxiously, there was another sigh. 'Just give me a minute.'

They pressed their ears to the door, once again regretting how quickly they'd headed out of the Octobus without first going through the Wower. They definitely needed some catch-up training …

Beyond the half-a-forest that made up the oak barrier between them and the boy, they could hear faint shuffling and then a clanking sound. It clanked towards them.

Clank. Clank.

'Robot?' suggested Janey as the metallic thudding came closer.

G-Mamma shrugged, then slipped behind the archway and trained the Taser on the opening door, ready to cover Janey who stood her ground as the massive door creaked open.

It wasn't a robot, though. It was a tall, gangly teenager dressed in jeans and a grey hoodie. The clanky noises were coming from the knight's helmet wedged on his head. Behind him, Janey could see a headless suit of armour.

The helmet moved up and down as their host took in their appearance, first Janey and then G-Mamma, who tucked the Taser into the top of her boots and smiled in a way she must have thought was beguiling but was actually terrifying.

'Hello. I'm sort of the leader of the sort of club that is SWAG,' she purred. 'Rosie Biggenham. Call me the Big G. I mean, GM.'

There was a snuffling noise inside the metal, and then the helmet creaked around towards Janey. 'And you?'

'Janey Brown.' There was something about him. Something quiet and dark but weirdly comforting. This was someone she could trust, she just knew it. 'Also known as ... Jane Blonde,' she added softly.

The guy just stood there, hands resting softly on his pockets, legs long and lean and ready to run if needs be, and the helmeted head swaying left and right, left and right as he weighed them both up.

Then at last, he opened the door wide. 'I'm Jack Bootle-Cadogan,' he said. 'Also known as Lord BC of Lowmount. You'd better come in.'

As they stepped through the brooding doorway, a sharp chill wrapped itself around Janey's bare arms, so cold it felt like needles prickling her flesh. It was the same sensation she'd had in her room the previous night.

Then the door swung shut behind them.

What craziness had she let herself in for this time?

Chapter 4 – Dog Fights & Cat Cries

Janey and G-Mamma trekked after the guy in the knight's helmet down the long, echoing corridors. He paused at a plain wooden door painted in simple white gloss - the simplest of the many they had passed - and cocked his head towards it. Appearing to hear nothing untoward, he waved them on.

'My mother's rooms,' he whispered, although the sound of his voice was weirdly amplified by the metal headgear that it boomed slightly in Janey's ear. 'I think she's asleep. She does that a lot these days.'

Janey hurried after him to catch up with his long, loping stride. 'What happened, Jack? Why are the newspapers after you?' She wondered if it was because he walked around in a suit of armour, but decided not to say anything.

'My father died recently,' Jack said, reaching a T-junction in the corridors and checking both ways before choosing a direction and lolloping towards a distant aroma of burning. 'Mum's taken to her bed.'

G-Mamma knocked on his helmet to get his attention. 'And you became Lord of Lowmount?' she bellowed. 'Lucky you! Is that why you wear that helmet? Because you're sort of royal? I've heard that you blue bloods are all eccentric.'

'Right. *We're* eccentric,' said Jack with a heavy irony that would have made Alfie faint with jealousy, as his head angled towards G-Mamma.

He had a point. G-Mamma was dressed in an enormous fluffy white onesie that was obviously her pyjamas, all topped off with pink ear muffs which she'd slipped onto the top of her head so she could hear properly. She looked like the Easter bunny – and Janey was so used to the way she dressed that she hadn't even noticed.

The Lord of Lowmount stopped suddenly. 'I'm very sorry, Ms Biggenham. GM. That was uncalled for. But it's not my *blue* blood you need to worry about.'

He let out a joyless bark of laughter that sounded so sad and hollow that Janey wanted to kick her SPI:KE in the shins. Sensitivity had never been G-Mamma's strong point, but this was unforgiveable. It didn't sound at all as though Jack was glad to be a lord, and as for the reason he wore the helmet – well, maybe he was deformed. Horribly disfigured. Perhaps he had the same disease as Gideon Flynn! That would make sense. Or he could have been viciously scarred in a fire. There was obviously something burning further along the corridor, so perhaps it had happened before. Putting a finger to her lips, she frowned at G-Mamma and turned down the corridor behind Jack.

After a few minutes trudging along the dusty parquet flooring, the wooden tiles gave way to terracotta stone. They were heading into a kitchen, which explained the stench of blackened food.

It was very large with cupboards all around the outside, a cavernous cream-coloured Aga across one end and a vast scrubbed pine table positioned in the centre. It was spacious – with school hall levels of spaciousness - but not especially luxurious. In fact, when Janey peered more closely she could see that the cabinets were ancient, and a lick of paint was well overdue. It reminded her of the Spylab before its most recent transformation.

'This room needs a Wower,' said G-Mamma, reading Janey's mind.

'Who's Awower?'

Thankfully, Jack didn't wait for an answer as the reek of cindered vegetables overcame them all. Pushing a couple of chairs away from the table for them, Jack folded his lanky body into the seat nearest the oven, then reached out and opened the stove door. Poisonous black fumes curled out into the kitchen. Jack sighed, closed the door again and turned the oven off. 'I'm trying to learn how to cook,' he said.

Janey smiled. 'Not working?'

Jack shook his head sadly.

'Don't you have chefs? A fine house like this.' G-Mamma wafted smoke out of her face. 'They have them in Downton Abbey – dozens of them.'

From inside the helmet, Jack's laughter had a metallic ring. 'No money for chefs.'

'A microwave?' Janey suggested.

'No money for microwaves.'

'Where's the nearest takeaway?' asked G-Mamma.

'No money for takeaways.'

'I'm sensing a theme here,' G-Mamma said. 'Big house. New lord. No staff and no money.'

'That's about it,' said Jack.

Janey felt a surge of sympathy for him. Fancy being all alone, responsible for this great big castle of a place with no means of doing anything to it, and nobody to look after his mother for him while she mourned the loss of her husband.

She walked over to the fridge and peered inside. 'G-Mamma, you like cooking. Could you make us bacon and eggs while I talk to Jack?'

G-Mamma's eyes had glazed over into an "incoming rap" expression, and she was muttering to herself: 'Big house, new lord, no staff and no money. On your own in the Abbey; well, it just ain't funny.'

'G-Mamma,' repeated Janey. 'Could you cook?'

The SPI:KE huffed as if she was about to object, as Jack leaned forward. 'What did you call her? I thought she said her name was Rosie Big Enough or something. Who … who are you guys?'

Here we go again, thought Janey. Still, it was a long time since she'd had anything to tell people other than 'Yes, I'm doing French and Russian GCSE,' and it was fairly obvious already that Jack was going to be a kindred spirit.

'Have you heard of someone called Gideon Flynn?'

The helmet clanked from left to right. No. 'Would I know him from Eton?'

Eton was a posh school, as far as Janey knew. It made sense that it would be the kind of place that Jack studied. 'I don't know. He might have left school; he looks about seventeen.'

'Sorry. No, I don't know him.'

Janey pondered where to start, and decided to dive right in. 'Flynn is gathering a team together, starting with us. G-Mamma – that's Rosie Biggenham's spy name, like Jane Blonde is my spy name. That's right,' she said when Jack's shoulders tensed, 'we're spies.'

To her astonishment, Jack simply sat very still for a few moments, then nodded for her to continue. This was definitely someone unusual.

'The team's job is to take back some items that were stolen from Gideon Flynn and his family. He needs them to create a cure because he has this condition where he can't touch anyone, sit down or use his hands properly.'

He was so silent, it was unnerving. Then the metal helmet moved up and down. 'Okay. Honestly, I've seen many things that are way, way weirder than that.'

So far so good, then.

'I'm the first one he found,' said Janey. 'He's paid to have all our spy gear updated, and we just met with him earlier to find out what he wants. Which, basically, is you.'

'Me?'

'And two other people. But you're the one for this first job of breaking into a bank vault. We need to find a stolen Indian ring that was worn by someone playing a guitar.'

'Sitar,' corrected G-Mamma from the stove top, busily sizzling bacon on the ancient range that she'd somehow managed to ignite. Lured by the smell of food, Trouble appeared at the window, eyes focussing instantly on the goodies. Janey spotted him and flicked open a window to let him in.

'Why me? I'm not very musical,' declared Jack through his visor. 'I'm not very anything, really. Not usually.'

Not usually, huh?

'What are you when you're not … usual?' said Janey carefully, picking Trouble up and carrying him across to the table.

Jack emitted that same hollow laugh. 'Oh, I'm … ah,' he said, catching sight of Trouble. He reached a hand across towards the cat; Trouble retaliated instantly by lashing out with a sharp claw. It was a good job he hadn't Wowed, or it would have been as sharp and deadly as a pirate's cutlass. As it was, he managed to slash through Jack's finger, and the boy quickly withdrew his hand.

'Trouble! Bad cat.' What was wrong with him? Trouble was so easy-going these days that he hardly got up off his mat, even to chase frogs. 'I'm so sorry, Jack.'

'It's me,' Jack said. 'Cats don't like me. Well, not all cats – certain Egyptian ones practically … ahem … worship me. But ordinary domestic cats pretty much hate me.'

Weirder and weirder. Trouble vacated the room with a flick of his enormous tail, resenting the insult of being called an ordinary domestic cat, as Janey sat down again.

'Jack, do you … would you mind taking off your helmet? It's a bit hard to talk to someone when you can't see their face.'

'That'll be the spy in you, reading facial expressions,' Jack replied. 'I go by other senses, mainly.'

He was playing for time. 'Please, Jack?'

G-Mamma arrived at her side with two overloaded plates of fried eggs and streaky bacon. 'You can have your food when you take your helmet off.'

Under one plate, G-Mamma held the Taser gun. She dropped it into Janey's lap and an unspoken agreement passed between them: if this turns nasty, stun him. A tiny bit unwillingly, as Jack seemed genuinely nice, Janey trained the stun gun on his midriff, below the table.

Jack's head was leaning visibly towards the food. He was making some very odd snorting sounds. It must have been a really long time since he ate.

'Not fair,' he said. 'I can't resist food, but you really won't like it. I scare people.'

'We're not people,' said Jane, sliding back the safety catch. 'We're spies.'

'Yeah, but you're still human.'

Still human? Of course they were. What did he mean?

'Aren't you? Human, I mean?'

Dropping his head into his hand, Jack sat opposite them for a long moment, clearly undecided how to answer. Then G-Mamma wafted the bacon closer to his face and his resolve disappeared.

'I'm a bit human. And a bit not,' he said simply, and then he pulled off his headgear.

Dropping the plates with a crash, G-Mamma body-rolled under the table. 'Shoot it, Blonde girl. Shoot!'

But Janey didn't. Couldn't. She simply sat wordlessly and took in the sight that had appeared before them.

Jack Bootle-Cadogan had the body, mind and mannerisms of a teenage boy … and the head, neck and collar bones of an enormous black dog. Its liquid black eyes were gazing at her, not threatening in any way, but in fear. He looked as if he was most worried that she'd be scared of him- when only a few hours ago she'd been afraid of never being afraid again.

And she wasn't afraid of him. She just knew instinctively that there wasn't a bad bone in Jack's body, and that he'd never harm anyone or anything if he had a choice about it.

Finally, she forced herself to speak. 'So Trouble doesn't like you because you're a dog.'

Jack nodded miserably. 'I'm only a dog some of the time, and only the head. Plus some of the instincts. I'm usually better at controlling it but these last few weeks have been rather emotional and … well, I've been finding it hard. Everything,' he added simply.

Poor Jack. He needed them as much as they – apparently – needed him. Though how he was going to help them break into an underground bank vault with his canine senses, she wasn't quite sure. Maybe he could sniff it out, or something.

He seemed to be remembering why they were there at the same moment. 'So, this Gideon Flynn. You said he's paying?'

'Wh … what?' said Janey.

'Is he hiring us with actual money to do this bank vault heist thingummy?' Jack pointed to the dilapidated walls. 'Only I've got a castle to maintain, and I'm thinking of setting up a school.'

'I don't know,' said Janey. 'I never thought to ask. But he's sorted out all our spy gear, so I expect so.'

'There was even a mention of gold in that bad poem he wrote, remember?' said G-Mamma.

That decided matters for Jack. 'Then I'm in.'

Jack loped around the table and pumped Janey's hand up and down. Her own fingers felt tiny in the grip of his enormous fist, and she wondered if he also became bigger when he was in dog form.

'Great,' she said. 'We'll get some more instructions about the ring, and then I'll message you.'

'Please do. Please, please do,' he said, writing his number down for her on a frayed linen napkin. Jack sounded wistful, and once again Janey could sense how lonely and out-of-touch he'd become.

But with business completed, it was time to leave. They still had a couple of hours to power-drive back home, and perhaps Wow up so that Janey could get through school after a night of no sleep.

Handing over the napkin, Jack accompanied them to the kitchen door through a damp cloakroom full of muddy boots and dogs' beds. 'Not mine,' he pointed out quickly. 'It was Roger's, our gun dog. He died too.'

'Oh, Jack.' She felt like giving him a hug, but Janey suspected it was too soon for that. She patted his arm instead, hoping he didn't mistake it for dog-like affection. 'You've been having a really tough time, haven't you?'

He laughed. 'That's okay. I can cope with death. It's the living I find a tad difficult.' Lifting his head, Jack pointed to a rustling bush halfway across the tangled kitchen gardens. 'That's your cat in the raspberries. Trouble!' he called hopefully.

But as soon as Trouble saw Jack he scarpered, haring through the gardens and out beyond the low hedges surrounding them.

'He's heading for the maze!' shouted Jack. 'Don't let him go in there, or you'll never get him back.'

'Trouble!' shouted Janey and G-Mamma at the same time, but it was too late.

It took forty-five minutes, Jack's deliberate absence and several packs of fried bacon to lure Trouble out of the maze, which left them only one hour to get home. They wished Jack good night again as he wiped bacon juices from his muzzle, and the spy trio raced back to the Octobus.

Only it wasn't there.

'I'm going to be so late. Maybe Jack will know where it is – and a short cut,' said Janey, texting Jack as she spoke.

Van gone. Ideas?

Where are you? he texted back.

She looked around for a landmark. **Fountain with 4 dolphins.**

To her astonishment, she was still only putting her phone back in her pocket when Jack appeared at her shoulder.

'You must have been close by. Were you following us?'

'Not really.' Jack was now wearing a balaclava and there was no sign of the clanking helmet, so he must have gone back to the house. 'And so sorry about the van. I've got the local police doing patrols because of all the press people hanging around. They must have taken it to the pound.'

'No! Do you have a car? I've got to get back home in less than an hour or my folks will have heart attacks. Sorry,' she added, just in case that was what had happened to his father.

Jack winced. 'Well, yes, there's the Daimler, but I can't drive it, and my driver ...'

'Let me guess,' said Janey. 'He died?'

'Yes and no, no and yes,' said Jack vaguely.

This was all getting a little worrisome. Had he murdered all these people? Maybe they should have stunned him. G-Mamma was clearly having the same thoughts and was backing away from Jack as she rummaged in her bag for the Taser.

Then it all became even stranger.

'Do you trust me?' said Jack suddenly. 'I can get you home in time, but you have to *really* trust me.'

G-Mamma was still fumbling in her bag, but Janey put a hand on her arm. 'We don't have a choice, G-Mamma. And anyway, I do trust him.'

The SPI:KE stared at her, then nodded as she saw the determination on Janey's face. 'Okay, Blonde. Your instincts have never let us down in the past.'

Janey turned to her new friend. 'We trust you, Jack.'

'Good. Because what I didn't mention when I fessed up about the dog thing is *why* Egyptian cats worship me.' Jack shrugged modestly. 'I'm also ... well, a god.'

'A god?'

Jack nodded. 'Yes. Anubis, Egyptian god.'

'Of ... death?'

'Correct. Not that I kill people. Just process them.'

'I don't even want to know what that means,' said Janey.

'And I hope you never have to find out,' Jack replied softly.

Janey stared at him. If what he was saying was true, it would explain why he hadn't been too worried about letting them in. 'Are you immortal?'

'Pretty much.'

He gave his modest little shrug again, then, 'Grab your cat,' he announced, 'and show me a picture of home.'

He glanced briefly at the street view of Janey's house and the Spylab next door on Janey's phone and closed his eyes.

Placing an enormous hand on each of their shoulders, Jack took in a deep breath. 'Hold Trouble very tight,' he said in a voice which was suddenly extremely deep, 'and I apologise in advance for how hard my grip has to be. Three, two, half …'

Before Janey had time to shout or even think, Jack's powers took over. It suddenly became abundantly clear why he was going to be extremely useful in plundering a sunken bank vault.

Because nothing – absolutely nothing – got in his way.

Gideon was so tired of following, always following. Always in the shadows and the half-light. His condition made it necessary, but with every single atom of his being, he wanted it to be different.

That was why he'd hidden in the Octobus when Jane Blonde and her strangely energetic mentor had leapt into it to track down the next member of the team – Jack Bootle-Cadogan. Doghead. He'd only wanted to be sure that the meeting would go well. Jack BC had to be on board, or there was no hope. They hadn't detected Gideon's presence as they ploughed up fields on the way to Lowmount, and he hoped that nobody had detected theirs either with the Invisibubble shield across the van.

The changes in the spies' circumstances hadn't, however, gone un-noticed. It was probably the money disappearing from his account. The recent expenditure must have alerted the others to the team he was pulling together – or at least to the meeting with Jane Blonde – and so they were watching every move the spies made.

Now some of their henchmen were here, prowling around the van, sweeping their sensors across it to work out what equipment was contained within. Soon they'd open the door, and see exactly how far they'd already gone.

He had to get the Octobus out from under their noses. But how? He could hardly touch anything as it was. Then he remembered the slender silver cabinet in the corner. The ... Wower, he believed it to be called. The previous day, it had given him some relief from the horrors of his condition so that he'd at least been able to meet with Blonde and GM. Unrolling that scroll had been the most tactile thing he'd been able to do in ages, even if it was all for effect. Without the Wower's powerful intervention, even that would have been impossible.

Perhaps, now, it could help him again.

The tapping and quiet discussions beyond the metal walls of the van were approaching the door. There wasn't much time if he was going to stop them uncovering the equipment ... stop them ending the game before it had even begun.

Gideon eased silently into the cabinet and whispered, 'Wower, do your thing. Please!'

Instantly, the top of the cabinet above him slid back to reveal an enormous showerhead the size of a sunflower. Multi-coloured sparkles with the lightness of dandelion clocks cascaded from the sunflower as if it were shedding its seeds over him, and Gideon felt his skin tingle. It was such a miraculous sensation that he only just managed to prevent himself from gasping aloud. The tingle descended *across his whole body, past his elbows, his fingertips, his knees and the tops of his feet, and then a warm breath of air parted his flowing hair and enveloped him like a tropical sea breeze. It felt as though the Wower was blow-drying him. Blowing the paint dry.*

Gideon held up his right hand. It was perfect. Whole and pink and knobbly in the right places, where his knuckles punctuated his slender fingers. Hardly daring to look, he pulled his other hand into sight, and that was the same.

'Thank you,' he murmured to the Wower, although he knew that it was really the people who'd invented it – the people whose blueprints he'd followed and even improved upon - that he needed to thank.

And one day, he would. But right now, there was something he needed to do.

His enemies were about to infiltrate the Octobus. Gideon could hear their voices as they reached the door.

'... operate from the inside or remotely?' said one of them. The voice was young and light; its owner didn't sound threatening, but then, voices often played tricks on people. Gideon knew that better than anyone.

He had to go. Hardly able to tear his eyes from the glory of a pair of normal, teenaged hands poking out beneath the turned-back cuffs of his shirt, Gideon pushed open the Wower door. He could touch it, effortlessly.

Amazing! And if he could touch that, he could also handle a steering wheel.

'Now or never,' he told himself, before running up the narrow aisle between the banks of technological devices and sliding through the curtains that separated the equipment from the van's cabin.

Behind him, he could hear a knife scraping down the edges of the back door. The men from the company he thought of as 'the Org'- he couldn't bring himself to use its proper name - were prising it open.

The key to the van was a button on the dash-board. Amazed that he could press down on it just as hard as he liked, Gideon Flynn sparked the engine just as the Org guys slid open the back door and stepped into the van.

Then his foot – his miraculous right foot that felt normal and functional again thanks to the Wower – slammed down on the accelerator, and the Octobus took off, slamming through a fence and ousting the Org guys one after the other as Gideon threw the van around the grounds, rattling them out of the open door like dice from a cup.

They hadn't seen him. Of that he was pretty sure.

And they weren't going to see him, either. That was definite.

As shouting and the revving of a car engine rang out from the field behind him, Gideon Flynn flicked the Invisibubble switch and made for the M3 motorway.

'Sorry, Blonde,' he muttered.

Not only had he made off with the most exciting bit of kit they'd had in many a year - he'd actually stolen their ride home. Jane Blonde would have to find another way to get back.

It was very, very lucky that the people he'd selected for SWAG were unusually resourceful.

He relished every second of the journey until the Wower power began to wear off. It didn't take long for that to happen in his state. His extremities numbed, first the tips and then the rest of his fingers, and he realised he would soon lose control. Panicking, he pressed the brakes as hard as he dared before his feet gave out too. The van slewed around, flinging him against the window and then the dashboard as it collided with a lamppost. At least it was in the right street, he thought as he stumbled from the cab and made for the trees – and still mostly invisible. The repairs could be paid for and organised in a jiffy.

As for the repairs to his own body – well, they'd been less successful. Clutching his burning fingers, he hid among the shadows to check for the safe return of the spies.

Deep in the shadowy blackness.
Back where he belonged.

'So what exactly are you planning?' Janey had cried to Jack Bootle-Cadogan as he seized each of their shoulders.

'Not a lot of planning goes on, to be honest.' Jack tightened his grip so much that G-Mamma squealed, causing Trouble to hiss violently in Janey's arms. 'It's more instinct.'

'What is?' she said, even though she already knew what he meant. Instinct was what guided her spy work a lot of the time – that bubbling feeling in her gut that told her she was onto something, and she simply had to … trust, like Jack had said.

Jack's fur-covered face wrinkled up with concern. 'I don't know how to explain it.'

But Janey understood now. It didn't matter what it was. It was something that had worked for him before, and they all had to believe in his ability to follow his shiny, wet nose if they were going to get anywhere.

She patted the massive hand that was gripping her shoulder and took a tighter hold of Trouble. 'It's all right,' she told him. 'Just do it.'

Complete with her fake yellow eyelashes, G-Mamma's eyes goggled like snooker balls. 'Thanks for asking me, Blondette! What if I –'

But whatever G-Mamma might have been about to say was lost to the wind as Jack curled his fists over their shoulders and … tobogganed.

That was the only word Janey could think of to describe the sensation of what Jack was able to do. It felt as though they were in an Olympic bobsleigh, rocketing along an ice tunnel with sides so smooth that there was no resistance to their supersonic speed, and so clear that she was able to see the world rush by on either side of them … and below their feet … and above their heads. Her insides twisted with nausea, in the same way as they had whenever she SatiSPIed up to the satellite in the sky before bouncing down to earth in some other spot, but this was a little easier. More comfortable. It felt grounded, somehow, being able to identify trees and cars and trucks and buildings as they ploughed headlong through them, stopping for nothing, slicing through brick and concrete, wood and earth, metal and plastic and upholstery as if it were oxygen.

She risked a glance behind them as they passed effortlessly along the exact centre of a family car – across the boot, zipping through the back seat in the armrest between two child-seats, each containing a child who seemed to feel but not see them, and then along the handbrake between the parents and on through the dashboard, the bonnet, the engine and out through the front registration plate. Nobody in the car seemed to have much idea that three people (mostly) and a cat (again, mostly) had just whipped through the entire car. Furthermore, the car was perfect. There was no sign that anything at all had just happened.

And why would they have noticed anyway? It had all taken less than quarter of a second; Janey was sure of it. It was so fast that the car with the family in it had already fallen way out of sight, and they were zinging through fields and office blocks and libraries and stations, then gardens and conservatories and kitchens with dressing-gowned adults making early morning cups of tea – until Janey realised with a lurch of her heart that the adults she'd just seen as she slid by were her actual parents, her own Boz and Gina, making early morning cups of tea - one of which they'd be delivering to her at any second.

How did she stop the Jack-train? She'd trusted him to set off, but she hadn't told him where to go other than by showing him a picture, and he certainly wouldn't know when to slow down. If he carried on at this speed they'd be on the way to the English Channel before they knew it.

She was just about to attempt to snap one of his fingers off her shoulder when Jack let go anyway. Passing together through the wall of the living room, G-Mamma, Janey and Trouble slammed into the hedge between her own house and the SPI:KE's, trying not to screech as twigs poked into their eyes and ears and lacerated their limbs.

'Sorry,' said Jack, hardly even breathing heavily. 'Haven't tried braking with a couple of hitchhikers before.'

Trouble yowled nastily.

'And a cat. Sorry.'

Janey leapt to her feet. 'My parents …' she squeaked by way of explanation.

'Oh, right!' Jack cottoned on quickly. 'Hold on a moment.'

He unfurled his gigantic hand as if he was rolling out a carpet, his round, black eyes glinting in the weak dawn sunlight. Janey grabbed it, and instantly they bob-sleighed through her front door, up the stairs and into her room. As he let go and they separated, Janey landed on her bed with a bump.

'Don't say sorry!' she said quickly.

Jack's canine face grinned back at her. 'Okay. It's annoying, I know.'

'No,' said Janey, although it was a bit annoying. 'It's just that you have nothing to apologise for. I'm back in my room before my parents arrive.'

Jack's left ear pricked up and changed position like one of the satellite dishes in the Octobus. 'Your dad, by the sound of it.'

He sounded glum.

'Sorry,' said Janey.

'Don't say sorry!' he shot back easily. 'Not your fault.' He pointed to the window. 'Do I go this way? I can't use the stairs at the moment unless you want me to zip through your father.'

'Eugh! No, go through to G-Mamma's Spylab. I'm sure she'll want to de-brief anyway, and line things up for our first mission.' She stood up, about to press the button on the fireplace.

'Oh, don't worry, I'll just …' and Jack mimed sliding through the wall.

'Right! Of course.'

He was half-way through the chimney breast when Janey thought of something. 'Jack!'

He turned around, half of his body blending with bricks.

'How did you know where we live with just a picture? We didn't give you an address or anything. Was that instinct too?'

Jack shifted a little, embarrassed, then pointed to his vast snout. 'Dog skills,' he said simply.

'You … you smelt us home?'

'Yeah.' The boy – albeit a boy as big as a wardrobe with the head of a dog – held up his hands. 'It's very unpleasant. Lots of what I do and am is very, very unpleasant. Gross, really. Sorry.'

She let that one go. He just did what he had to do, using the gifts he'd been given. How many times had she done that too, using her instincts or her gadgets?

'It's fine. See you later, Jack.'

He looked incredibly pleased about that as he disappeared through the wall into the Spy-lab. It was probably a long time since he'd had anything fun to do later, or anytime at all.

Deep within her, Janey's spy senses whirred into sharper perspective. It was the same for her. Exactly the same for her.

And now she was ready for action.

Chapter 6 – X Marks the Spot

'The Octobus is back,' announced G-Mamma gleefully as Janey checked in with her after a long and agonising day at school. Much as she enjoyed them, no amount of quadratic equations and scientific formulae was ever going to compete with the prospect of a new mission with her old SPI:KE, and a new team member with ears like a border collie.

Janey stared out of the spy-lab window, which were carefully disguised so that nobody could look in but any spies inside the lab could gaze out, unseen. 'Where is it?'

'Right there.' G-Mamma pranced over to her side and stabbed a bejazzled finger towards the front garden. 'It's been Invisibubbled and disguised all over, and so have its spy-buys. Even if someone does spot it and get inside, they'll still think it's a camper van. Just two bunks, a teeny-weeny sink and kettle.'

'When really it's two bunks and a teeny-weeny Spy-lab,' said Janey, shivering with anticipation, or was it something else, like … anxiety? 'Gideon Flynn seems to really know what he's doing.'

'And apparently he has endless funds to do it with!'

'True,' said Janey with a frown. 'Which makes me wonder why he needs this stuff back to start with, and why he can't pay to get whatever it is he needs to cure his condition.'

G-Mamma scratched the dazzling nail down the window, creating a horrible screech as if she'd done it on a blackboard. Dragging her finger round in a circle, she drew a ring about the size of an egg cup and then tapped it lightly. A disc of glass pinged out of the pane and dropped onto the lawn outside, much to the surprise of Trouble who was sitting on the grass licking his paws like any normal cat. Without further ado, however, he fluffed out his tail and laid it over the glass circle so that no passers-by would see it, then continued with his paw-licking.

Inspecting her finger, G-Mamma turned to Janey. 'And that's without a Girl Gauntlet. Imagine what that poor young man must go through every day if he can't use his hands properly. I lerrrrv my andy-pandies.'

Janey grinned. 'I see what you mean. But you've just drilled a hole in the Spy-lab window.'

'Darn and dash it all,' said G-Mamma, glaring at the hole as if it had put itself there. 'Now I'll have to explain it to Gideon Flynn and get it replaced. Oh! Hang on.' She rummaged around in one of the Spy-lab drawers. 'There.'

She'd stuffed a purple eyeshadow into the space; now it winked, the light streaming through it like a stained-glass window.

It looked very much as if she was up to something.

Janey watched her for a while with narrowed eyes, hoping to work it out for herself, before her curiosity got the better of her.

'Okay. What's going on?'

'Yee-hah, Janey Zaney! Got you there eventually. As if I'd deliberately destroy Spy-buys!'

Actually, she'd destroyed plenty accidentally and then quaked at the thought of how much trouble she'd be in for wasting money and ruining gadgets, but Janey thought maybe this wasn't the moment to remind her of that. Anyway, this time, it appeared, she'd sliced through the spy glass on purpose.

But why? Janey followed the shaft of pale purple light that slanted across the laboratory to the bench in the middle of the room. It was the most unremarkable of all the tables in there, mostly used by G-Mamma to lie on while she was getting pedicures.

Right now, though, there was something lying on it.

A newspaper.

'Is that our mission?' said Janey, feeling a little breathless.

'I do believe so, Super-Blonde. It arrived while you were out, and I've been trying to de-code it all this time.'

Janey raced over to the bench and picked up the paper with a finger and thumb, holding it carefully across the corner so as not to smudge or obscure any clues. This was almost her favourite thing about spying – apart from the gadgets and the space travel and the massive adventures, of course. Puzzles, dingbats and crosswords had formed her introduction to the world of spying, and she loved nothing better than trying to piece together some odd or innocent-looking piece of information in a logical and precise way, and make some sense of it somehow.

Spy sense.

Poring over the headlines, she read aloud to help herself think more clearly. She often spotted tiny typos and errors by voicing the words, and had discovered more than once that sometimes those little slips were not accidental.

'World Community Games countdown,' she said, scanning the main headline.

'Only three days to go until the inaugural session of the World Community Games takes place - with plans to incorporate the Olympics and Commonwealth Games, both winter and summer, into one united event in the future, if it proves to be as successful as the sponsoring company hopes.

Oscar Sullivan, CEO of the philanthropic HOST organisation (Helping Others Save Time), commented: "The Board very much sees the World Community Games as a way to bring all the nations of the world together for fun, recreation and competition, while also minimising financial and time constraints and concerns for all. Wherever you are in the world, it's daytime or winter somewhere, and we're going to capitalise on that to the advantage of all."

Leading edge technology will be used to live-stream all key events simultaneously using special (and secret) virtual locations and web-platformed, forum-led fan gatherings.

Sullivan declined to comment further on recent allegations that veteran high-jumper, Vance Kettering, is suing the HOST organisation, after their claims that he was too old for the digital generation caused him to withdraw from the Games. 'Vance's issues are to do with his age, not with HOST. Regretfully, his career was already over. These Games are what the current generation have been waiting for.'

Concerns that the games would be postponed in light of the recent death of HOST co-founder, Trent Varley, were cast aside by Wentworth and by Varley's wife, Simone. "Trent wanted more than anyone for this new community to come together. We'll be pressing on, knowing that this was his wish."

Janey paused for a moment, letting this sink in. 'So they're going to have athletics competitions happening all over the place and at different times, all brought together by technology so nobody but the athletes need to travel. Is that what this is about?'

'Maybe.' G-Mamma gazed at her and then looked innocently around the room, so Janey knew there was more.

She skimmed through the other articles on the page. There was more about the new games, and a piece on the death of Trent Varley accompanied by a photo of his weeping widow. Another column was discussing the US economy, with so many words that Janey didn't understand that she switched off almost immediately.

Finally, tucked away at the bottom, there was a small and insignificant-looking snippet about a theft in a museum in Venice. Feeling G-Mamma's eyes boring into her, Janey read the headline aloud.

'Guard Apprehends Relic Burglar One-handedly. Yesterday, a museum curator in Venice's Cantalo Museum prevented the theft of an ancient toy which is believed to come from a Roman villa in Cirencester, England. While having no intrinsic value, the relic is part of a collection bequeathed by a famous benefactor in the 1960s, possibly one of the Beatles, and the museum was very glad to retain it. The guard has been commended for his observational skills and timely actions.'

Janey read it again, just to get the feel of it. Her instincts were buzzing, and without knowing quite why, she understood that this was the article to concentrate on.

'It's weird,' she muttered. 'It's a very tiny article about a theft that's not very important, and it … it has no real facts in it! Nothing about what the relic or the object actually was, or how the guard stopped the burglar, and who the benefactor was, and …' Her eyes swept across the headline again. 'And that headline is the most peculiar thing. For a start, don't burglars go into houses? We'd call someone a thief if they stole from a museum, wouldn't we?'

'We probably would, Girly-Girl,' agreed G-Mamma, tapping out a rhythm with her fingernails. 'What else?'

'Well, ancient toy sounds a bit like ancient boy, as in Gideon's haiku. And then … that headline. I can't quite put my finger on it, but it's not just the burglar bit, it's … I know! One-handedly! We would say single-handedly, wouldn't we? So either it's been poorly translated from the Italian version, or …'

G-Mamma squeaked, no longer able to contain herself.

'Or it's deliberate! Deliberate misinformation.'

'Misinformation?'

'Something that's designed to be misleading and send people down the wrong path. The world's most brilliant double-agent was a master at it, and do you know what you just helped me to work out? His name is in the title.'

Janey stared at the headline. 'Oh! Was he called Burglar? Or … wait a minute …'

Then she saw it, shining up at her from the strange wording of the header.

'Guard Apprehends Relic Burglar One-Handedly. That's really clumsy phrasing, and the words all start with capital letters. So … G, A, R, B and O. Was the double agent called Garbo?'

G-Mamma punched the air. 'Yesss! Well, that was one of his names; he had many, being a brilliant double agent with a whole network of made-up spies. Your uncles were definitely inspired by him when the news came out about him in 1972.'

'What news?'

'During the Second World War,' said G-Mamma in an undertone, speaking in such a reverential whisper that Janey knew he must be one of the SPI:KE's heroes, 'Garbo sent so much misinformation to the Germans that they sent troops to the wrong places, away from where the allies were actually landing. Eventually, Garbo's work made the Nazis lose the war. And he always did it the same way: he'd send a letter that looked normal, and then in the spaces between the lines he'd write a message in invisible ink.'

And suddenly the eyeshadow in the window pane made sense. 'Which could be read--with—' She checked the name on the eye shadow. '- Ultra Violet light?'

'Exactly, Blondelicious!'

Excited, the two of them angled the newspaper up towards the lilac beam. Immediately a section of the secret message blinked into view as the light shaft fell across it, inked cleanly between the lines of the Venice Museum story. Between them, they wrangled the paper into a better position across G-Mamma's lurex-covered arm, and Janey noted down the details.

'It's an address,' she said at length, after she'd copied everything down onto a blank Post-It note, specially made from edible rice paper so that she could eat the evidence if necessary. 'In Holland Park, London.'

'Just the kind of place to have a bank vault under it,' said G-Mamma with a nod. 'What time?'

Janey paused, puzzled. There was no sign of a time to meet on the message. The date was easy enough to work out as it would be the same date as the newspaper – it would have to be today - but there was no time stated. Unless ...

'G-Mamma, was Garbo represented by any kind of symbol that might relate to a time? An Italian sign, perhaps, as his name sounds Italian. Maybe something to do with Venice? Or maybe the Romans. Yes! Did he have roman numerals associated with his name?'

'Not as far as I know ... but maybe ...' The SPI:KE strolled around the bench, half-dancing, mesmerising herself into a trance so she could think straight. 'That's it! The Twenties.'

Crossing over to where Janey had noted down the address, G-Mamma penned a simple symbol underneath:

XX

'All the double agents around at the time were known as the Twenties, because their sign represented a double-cross. Get it? They were double-crossers. And the sign in Roman numerals means twenty, and that's where the whole club got its name from.'

Janey traced the numbers. X and X. Not twenty, because that wouldn't mean anything on its own, but—

'Ten Ten!' she cried. 'It's at ten past ten tonight, at the address in Holland Park.'

'Bingo!' G-Mamma's dancing hips burst back into life. 'It's ten past ten, in the London den; in the Holland Park, where it's very very dark. Oh! Should we take the Octobus?'

It was tempting, but from what she knew about central London, it might be quite hard to park an enormous van topped by a giant squid, even it was invisible.

'I think we'll get a lift,' she said.

And she texted Jack. 'Mine at 8. Don't be l8!'

He got back to her immediately. 'R U kidding? Can't w8!'

Truth be told, neither could she. The mission was on again.

And this time, it was bigger than ever.

True to his word, Jack Bootle-Cadogan slipped straight through G-Mamma's front door and up into the Spy-Lab at one minute to eight, carrying a suitcase.

G-Mamma snorted. 'Good Gawdy-Lordy, are you planning a holiday? I don't think you understand how our missions work, young dog… young man.'

Jack's canine face crumpled self-consciously. 'It's just that I didn't know where we were going or what I should wear, so I've brought a few options with me.' He opened the case with a flourish. 'There's my helmet for if my dog head doesn't disappear. It normally does when I relax, but I don't imagine that breaking into a bank vault will be exactly peaceful. I brought normal boy clothes for if we're meant to be just mingling in like ordinary teenagers, and I've got black tie in case we're mingling like not-so-ordinary teenagers.'

'Just a black tie?' said Janey. 'I don't think that will go with your hoodie.' He'd brought jeans and tee-shirts for his teenager outfit, to be topped with a soft, burnt orange hoodie that looked about ten sizes too small.

'No, black tie the outfit. Formal dress. For dinner. With a dickie bow?' he explained as Janey became increasingly confused. 'You know, like James Bond would wear. I thought … you know … seeing as you're spies …'

'Oh! Right.' Janey chewed her lip, wondering what to tell him. 'The thing is, Jack, I don't really think it matters what you wear if you've still in your dog get-up. It's going to be quite hard to hide you if you're clanking around in half a suit-of-armour.'

'It's only the top bit,' said Jack in a small voice. Then he sighed, deeply disappointed, and Janey could hear the old sad Jack from Lowmount re-appearing.

'G-Mamma, what if Jack Wowed?'

'What if I what?'

G-Mamma circled Jack with a finger on her lime-green lips. 'The Wower does bring out the best in everyone. Shows them their finest version. Are you up for it, Jack? You might discover your finest version is – I don't know … maybe a Yorkshire Terrier?'

'Oh. I'm not sure.' Jack looked from Janey to G-Mamma and back again. 'What happens to you if you get Wowed?'

G-Mamma rolled her eyes. 'I'm always in my best version, Jack the Lad! I Wowed before you arrived.' She was wearing builder's overalls spattered with paint and make-up of every hue to match. 'If we get caught, I'll just say I'm the decorator. I'll blend.'

It was highly unlikely that G-Mamma would blend anywhere but a paint factory, but by now Jack was looking so miserable that Janey decided it was time to help him out.

Besides, she was absolutely desperate to get inside that Wower!

'I'll go first, Jack,' she told him. 'You can see what it does to me and decide for yourself if you want to try it. You can always de-Wow if you don't like the result.'

'Back to this?' Jack pointed to his furry face. 'Yay.'

There was no answer to that, really, so Janey just gave him a small smile, trotted across the lab and opened the doors of what appeared to be the large American-style fridge.

As she stepped in she breathed deeply. Heaven! The scent was just as she'd remembered: faintly medical with a hint of vanilla and chocolate, and a beautiful earthy warmth that reminded her of beaches and sandcastles.

'Wow me,' she told the machine, and it began instantly – the robotic hands massaging her head into a pony-tail that would be part-fashion and part-weapon; the gossamer threads of silver encasing her in a fluid but hard-as-nails lycra body-suit, and gold and multi-coloured laser beams that layered sparkles through her hair, wrapped her hands and feet in state-of-the-art gadgetry and, last of all, placed a new pair of Ultra-Gogs on the bridge of her nose.

'Oh! That's different!' she exclaimed, as a dropper appeared from the wall of the Wower and inserted latex into her ear. Suddenly she could hear everything clearly:

the conversation G-Mamma and Jack were having outside the door; even the low buzz from the radio next door where her parents were listening to a quiz, believing her to be safely in her bedroom.

'So will I still recognise her?' Jack was saying as she stepped out of the cabinet. His canine jaw dropped open. 'Wow.'

If there wasn't so much spy-power coursing through her, Janey was quite sure she would have giggled nervously at his reaction. But with the combination of spy-suit, spy-buys and spy senses, Janey felt incredibly grown-up and pretty much invincible. It was an amazing sensation, and suddenly she realised just how much she'd missed it.

'Wow indeed, Blonde girl,' echoed G-Mamma. 'The new improved Jane Blonde. Jane Blonder – that's what we might have to call you.'

As she turned to the mirrored surface of the fridge door, Janey almost laughed aloud. It was the same as she used to be, but better, as G-Mamma had said. The Lycra outfit was not so much silver as a pearly white, which suited her better now that she was older. Light armoured padding ran down each of her limbs and across her ribs. Her hair, too, was paler than before, and instead of springing out sharply from the crown of her head, her ponytail lay in a silky rivulet across one shoulder and down her front. It might not be a dagger any longer, but it was long enough to be a lasso or something. The Ultra-Gogs, meanwhile, had all but disappeared since they were constructed from some material that weighed nothing, on super-light, almost invisible frames. From behind lenses which were almost impossible to see, her grey eyes flashed with excitement.

Jack's doggy eyes were still staring at her, and now it was getting embarrassing, so she spun back around to him quickly.

'Yes, Wow,' she said. 'That's what the machine does. So that's what it will do to you too, if you want. Not the spysuit and everything – that's just for me – but whatever's right for you. Just close the doors and say, "Wow me", and it does the rest. Don't worry; it's straightforward.'

'I'm not worried,' said Jack. 'That's all very low-key compared with some of the transformations I've witnessed. Although still …' He gave her a double thumbs-up as he backed into the cabinet. 'Wow.'

The two spies waited until they heard Jack utter the magic words so that the Wower sprang into life. He was sweet, Janey realised, and she hoped above all else that the Wower would capture that and set him free from his Doghead alter-ego, at least for a while.

She was about to say this to G-Mamma when she noticed that her SPI:KE was close to tears. 'G-Mamma, what?'

'Oh, it's youuuuuuu!' bleated the woman, fishing for a paint-spattered cloth in the enormous bib pocket of her dungarees. 'My blonde girl! Spylets really are forever. But you look so … so different, Janey Zaney Blonde and Brainy. My little spylet's all grown up!'

And then she crushed Janey to that same bib pocket across her voluble bosom so that her Ultra-Gogs ground into her nose and her waterfall of a pony tail got caught in G-Mamma's braces. 'Owww,' she said plaintively.

'Sorry.' G-Mamma pushed Janey away and blew her nose on the painting cloth. 'Got carried away.'

'You smudged your make-up,' Janey pointed out.

'Doesn't matter,' sniffed G-Mamma. 'It goes with the overall look. Oh! Ha. The Overall Look! See what I did there?'

Some GM self-congratulation and possibly a rap about overalls were about to start up, so Janey held up a hand and pretended to be listening to the Wower. Actually, she didn't need to pretend. She could hear quite clearly that, deep within the cabinet, Jack was actually singing.

'Are you getting that?' she asked. 'I've got new plugs in my ears or something. I can hear loads more than usual!'

G-Mamma tried to shake her head and nod at the same time; it came out in a weird spasm, so the effect was like an earthquake in denim. 'I can't hear it, but I thought you could hear something, and no, I don't know what

you're hearing, but oh! You must have been given BATS –
Bionic Audio Transmission Selectors. You can tune in to
the good stuff and tune out the bad. Oh, Blonde! You'll be
able to tune in to my rapping from your bedroom! Or even
further away!'

Luckily, Janey was saved from having to respond by
the appearance of Jack Bootle-Cadogan. Without the dog
head.

'Wow to you too,' she said with a grin, as she took in
his normal boy appearance.

She turned him around by the shoulders – which she
could now reach – and showed Jack his reflection in the
mirror. He was tall but not gigantic, with a kind, thoughtful
face and a thatch of fair hair that she somehow hadn't
expected, since it was in stark contrast with the ebony fur
of his canine head. He was dressed in pretty much an
identical outfit to the 'ordinary teenager' one that he'd
brought with him, apart from this one looked like it had
been ironed. He touched his ears self-consciously and
Janey noticed that his lobes were a tiny bit bigger than
usual, but his limbs, while long enough to make him tall,
were all in proportion so that he seemed very …
connected, somehow, and not at all gangly and awkward
like Alfie. More like Gideon Flynn, she thought suddenly,
startled to find her cheeks growing hot.

'Yes, that's me,' said Jack after a moment of looking himself up and down. Janey was only glad that he hadn't been watching her at all in the last few minutes.

'Aren't you different to normal?' she said, clearing her throat. 'That's what the Wower usually does.'

Jack stared a little more, then shook his head. 'No, exactly like I am normally, apart from when I'm chewing on bones and chasing sticks.'

'Well, you must just be perfect all the time then,' she said with a smile. Which had to be true, basically. 'You must always be the best version of yourself.'

'Perhaps.' Jack shrugged and held up his nicely normal-sized hands. 'Or maybe I don't have a best version. Maybe there's only this and the dog. How about that?'

'I don't think so …' started Janey.

But the truth was, she didn't know. The Wower seemed to work it out, somehow, but it was a machine, after all, and it must have been programmed somehow – by Gideon Flynn and his team, to some specifications that hadn't been shared with the spies.

It was almost a relief to remember they had a mission to complete.

Janey led Jack across the newspaper on the bench and explained what they'd discovered. 'I didn't put it into the text in case someone's tailing you.'

'Tailing me! That's funny.'

'No, not because you're a dog, but because you're in this team – this SWAG set-up.'

Jack screwed up his nose. 'Yes, I wonder what that's all about? And where is our esteemed leader, the mysterious Gideon Flynn? I'd like to give him my bank account details, for a start.'

He was mysterious, she had to admit. They knew virtually nothing about Gideon Flynn. He'd paid for their spy-buys make-over, told them who to contact, named the team of which they were now a part without any explanation, sent them off on a dangerous mission, and completely failed to show up for anything other than the first meeting.

'G-Mamma, that's true. Where is—'

'He's meeting us there,' said the SPI:KE, tilting one of the screens in their direction.

There was an email entitled: Dog-walking.

Janey winced, wondering what Jack would think of that, but he simply read it through with interest.

Give me a ring when you're through, said the email, and I'll meet you with treats. Can't wait to pat the doggy. It was signed off by someone called Greta.

'Greta Garbo, like that double agent's name,' said Jack with a nod. 'One of my grandfather's favourite actresses.'

'Greta Garbo was also a spy herself,' added G-Mamma.

Janey could hardly believe they were discussing spy names when Gideon had been so rude. 'Pat the doggy? Meet you with treats? Who does he think he is?'

'Don't you think it's clever?' said Jack evenly. 'Give me a ring reads as though it's just giving him a call, but he actually means, you know, give me the ring! And then we'll get our rewards. And if he's going to pat me then it must mean that the ring really does help his condition. Or maybe he thinks his leprosy won't affect me because I'm … you know.'

'A dog,' G-Mamma reminded him.

'A god,' said Janey sternly.

Jack obviously needed reminding how special he was. As this was something that she

used to require in order to believe in herself, she was well cut-out for the job.

Jack, however, didn't seem to be bothered by it. 'Well, it's after nine,' he said, rubbing his own hands together. 'Are we going to do this thing? I'd really love some treats – I mean, money.'

He took careful note of the address, the picture of the house and the image of the Indian ring, and without even thinking about how long it had just taken him to get rid of it, he snuffled for a second and grew instantly into his dog-headed self. Then he grabbed each of their shoulders, bob-sleighed down - or rather through - the SPIral staircase, and blasted off towards London.

What nobody had considered was that the house would be full of people. And that it would be an enormous great house, one of several on a wide, tree-lined avenue. The houses were like small palaces – white and opulent, with grand staircases leading up to the massive doors in the middle, and symmetrical ranks of gleaming windows reaching up for three, four, even five storeys.

Janey peeked at the house next-door from their reconnaissance position beneath one of the horse chestnut trees. 'Zoom,' she said to her Ultra-Gogs, and instantly they focussed in on the doorway.

There were eight different doorbells lined up on a pewter plate to the left-hand side of the immense doorway. So that house had been divided into flats – eight different flats each with four to eight rooms per flat. The one that they were about to infiltrate was a single house with what appeared to be about fifty rooms – and a large basement harbouring a bank vault.

She trained her Gogs on the lower floors of the beautiful mansion until images of the basement pinged up onto her lenses. At first she couldn't see the vault. The lowest level of the house seemed only to house odds and ends: a massive wine cellar, some small utility spaces containing washing machines and ironing boards, and – to her surprise – a darkened room that resembled the inside of the Octobus. On every wall was a bank of screens, all flashing grey and white. Two foreboding guards, each dressed from head to toe in dark khaki uniforms, were both concentrating hard on separate screens. Janey could see they were watching something going on inside the house, although she couldn't work out the details.

Then she saw it.

'Okay, I've found the vault,' she said. 'It's in the very centre of the basement, right behind the room where the security guys are keeping tabs on what's going on in the house.'

'Well, that makes sense,' said Jack, unperturbed.

'Spies alive, what IS going on in that house?' said G-Mamma. 'Is it a party?'

'Looks like it,' said Janey, watching the lines of guests approaching yet another be-suited security guard at the top of the steps before being let through into the rooms beyond. Janey could just see a waiter handing out glasses of champagne as the visitors where ushered inside. She was reminded of another time when she found herself at a ball, having to dress hurriedly in her spy-suit and a shower curtain to gain admittance. That had been a few years ago. Now she doubted whether she'd get away with a home-made dress made of sparkly plastic – and anyway, this time they weren't going to go into the party itself.

This time, they were only there to plunder the vault.

'See? I knew I should have worn black tie,' said Jack, gazing down at his neatly pressed jeans. 'I'd have fitted in perfectly.'

'The only thing you have to fit into is that bank vault with your enormous doggy noggin,' snapped G-Mamma. 'And then maybe after you've done that we'll head to the kitchens and get some food.'

Ah. She was hungry. There was nothing worse than a hungry G-Mamma.

But Jack didn't know this yet, and his eyebrows shot up in surprise. Ever polite, though, he soon recovered and said amiably: 'Good plan. I like food.'

'We noticed,' said G-Mamma, but then, she was hardly one to talk. 'And I … quite like it too,' she said after a moment. 'And I might just be a little peckish which is why I'm a smidgeon on the irritable side. So let's get this heist underway and then on to the important business.'

'Very, very good plan,' said Jack with a smile, so charming and sweet that even G-Mamma couldn't stay mad at him.

Waiting for the right moment to enter, Janey observed quietly as a black car decorated with flags pulled up near the house, followed by another. In fact, when she looked up along the street, a whole cavalcade of limousines was appearing, each one disgorging important-looking guests in evening dress who were all being funnelled through the vast front door into the party beyond.

'Who are all these people?' She zoomed in on a flag; obediently, the Gogs popped up a description of the country it belonged to. 'They're from Ecuador,' she informed the others. 'The second one is … Cayman Islands … and the one behind it is Brazil. Why are they all from other countries?'

'I might happen to know that,' said Jack. 'My father told me about it. This area is embassy land.' He pointed to the houses on the other side of the street, all enormous, and several with security guards talking into the cuffs of their jackets. 'This single street probably represents twenty different countries.'

'And they're all going to this party.' Janey checked her Ultra-Gogs again. 'What's the time?'

Actually, she didn't need to ask, because just at that moment a bell rang out across the city from a nearby church, chiming ten times.

'Ten o'clock,' they said together.

'Something must be timed for ten so that the rooms all empty,' said Janey, training her night-vision glasses on the security room in the basement once more. 'Or everyone's in one place. That way the coast will be clear to get into the vault.'

As if they'd heard her words, the security guards in the cellar suddenly glanced up and nodded to each other. If only she could work out what they were saying! Then it occurred to her: she had new BATS hearing. She cocked one ear towards the distant house and closed her eyes so that she could concentrate.

'... one for each country,' the smaller guard was saying. She could hear the sound of keys jangling on a fob, then the solid thunk of a single key sliding into a lock and turning. 'You take that tray up to Wentworth, and I'll bring the other one.'

Janey opened her eyes quickly, but it was too late to see what the guards were taking upstairs. Already, she could spot their outlines heading up the cellar steps, ghostly shapes marked out by the heat sensors in her Gogs. All her equipment really had been upgraded.

G-Mamma gave her a nudge. 'Action stations, Blonde?'

'Yes. We've got about ten minutes, I reckon, although I doubt we'll need that long. Jack, you'd better stand right behind this tree so nobody sees you change.'

'Right you are,' said Jack.

It was a good job they'd already experienced what Jack looked like in his dog-god form, or they'd have completely given away their location by screaming. It was still quite unnerving to watch Jack change from the easy-going teenager he'd transformed into when they arrived at their target destination to an intimidating, canine-headed bruiser – but it did at least mean that, this time, they wouldn't have to face any other intimidating bruisers like the many security guards in the vicinity.

'Oh! Here,' said Janey, whipping off her Ultra-Gogs and planting them on Jack's long furry snout. 'That's the room you're looking for.'

'Great,' replied Jack in his slightly deeper voice with was just a shade growlier, after squinting at the mini screens for a moment. 'Would you mind taking the glasses off now? With my canine vision they make me a bit dizzy.'

'Of course. I'd rather have them myself anyway.' Janey parked her glasses back in place. 'Ready?'

Jack nodded. Now that they'd done this a couple of times, he no longer needed to clap his massive hands onto their shoulders. This time they simply stood side-by-side in front of Jack and waited for him to wrap his arms around them, and then the miraculous sliding began: straight through a limousine where the snoozing driver didn't even stir; along the wall to the side passage where they passed through a padlocked iron gate as if it were air, then through brick walls, washing machines, racks of wine with not so much as a drop spilled, and suddenly into the security room. The faintest tingle of electricity simmered in Janey's chest as they oozed through the computers, until a heartbeat later, they found themselves in the vault at the very centre of the basement.

Jack let go of them, wrenching his feet out of the floor into which they'd accidentally become embedded. Then he closed his eyes for a moment and, with a sigh of relief, changed back into Boy Jack.

'I must be relaxing more to be able to that. Oh, look at this! Well, that's not what I expected,' he whispered. 'Our vault's full of old portraits and dusty artefacts. This is sharp!'

'You have a vault?' said Janey with a laugh.

Jack gave his little embarrassed shrug. 'Yeah, well, we're kind of posh. But it's not like this. More of a museum, really.'

They looked around them. It was, as Jack had stated, very sharp. There was nothing visible to the eye to begin with; it was as if they were standing inside a black cube of marble. Then, as they adjusted to the light, the walls became marked with fine grey lines and a grid of hundreds of rectangles appeared on each surface, including the floor and the ceiling.

Janey peered closely at one of the rectangles.

'They're boxes,' she said. 'Each one is a separate box with something in it. I can see money in this one – piles of cash, in fact – and some … well, trainers, I think …'

'Time's a-ticking, boys and girls,' said G-Mamma. 'It's nearly ten past ten. Which one has the goodies in it?'

Fishing in the bib on the front of her decorator's overalls, G-Mamma pulled out the blurred photograph of the sitar player wearing the ruby ring.

Janey swallowed hard. 'G-Mamma, there are hundreds of boxes in here. Even with the Ultra-Gogs, I won't be able to locate one tiny ring in just a few minutes.'

'How about you take two walls and I take the other two?' said Jack, scrunching his eyes up until his ears turned black and furry and his alter-ego appeared. 'I'll just go in and have a rummage.' And with that he stepped through the surface of the wall and disappeared inside the marble.

'That might have triggered an alarm,' cried G-Mamma. 'They'll be on us in seconds!'

From the security room next door they could hear a distinct intermittent bleep that hadn't been there before, and although the guards weren't there at that moment, there was no doubt they'd be back very soon.

'Hurry,' said Janey. 'You take the ceiling and floor. You've got Ultra-Gogs?'

'Contact lenses. Better with my make-up.' Her mentor blinked her painted eyelids a couple of times to activate the lenses, then dropped effortlessly to all fours like a ragdoll, scanning the boxes with occasional squeals. 'Oo, Monroe memorabilia! Hey, your uncle had a watch just like that when he was a kid. Oh, nice!'

Tuning her out, Janey concentrated on her own element of the mission. She peered into box after box but found nothing that looked like jewellery, especially a ring.

Frustration rising, she rushed along the wall, unable to see anything that fitted the picture they'd been given.

To her surprise, however, in the corner of the room it appeared that many of the boxes had been knocked together to create a wardrobe-sized space. In it was the sitar, all glowing wood with a great onion bulb at its base and a fretboard that was almost as long as Janey was tall.

'The instrument's in here,' she said to G-Mamma. 'Maybe the ring's inside it.'

G-Mamma leapt to her feet. 'Only one way to find out.

She lifted Janey's hand, complete with her spy Gauntlet, and squirted the index finger in the sitar's direction. Smoky white gas poured out of the glove, settling over the black surface in a mist.

'Punch it,' said G-Mamma, so Janey balled her fist and slammed it into the box.

It shattered like crystal.

'Liquid nitrogen,' explained the SPI:KE. 'Liquid while in the Gauntlet, gas once it's outside it, rapid freezing of whatever it lands on – so don't split your glove, Blonde!'

'I'll try not to,' said Janey, pulling out the Sitar and scouring it for signs of the ring. She shook it to see if it rattled; it simply vibrated gently in the vault, sending soothing guitar sounds around the room.

Unfortunately, they weren't the only sounds it created. Suddenly the beeping from next door elongated into one long blast of a horn before increasingly hideously into the siren scream of a fire-engine. Above and around them, the footsteps of several meaty security guards rained down on them.

'We're too late!' hissed Janey. 'The ring isn't in the sitar, and we don't have time to keep looking.'

It was a terrible realisation. Her first mission in months, maybe even years, and she'd failed.

'We have to go!' She smacked on the wall where Jack had disappeared. 'Jack, we have to—'

At that exact moment, he emerged from the wall, brandishing a small velvet box.

'I've got something! It was the only jewellery box in the whole place – all the rest of it was either porcelain objects like little statuettes and stuff, or necklaces laid out on pads. I haven't looked in it yet, but—'

'No time, Jack. The guards are coming.'

It was worse than that, actually. The guards were all around them. They'd imagined that the only entrance was the one through the back of the security room, but what if it wasn't? Shouts and the stamping heels of hard-soled boots were ringing out from behind each of the walls. She checked with her Gogs, and sure enough, the outlines of a dozen or more burly men radiated onto her mini screens. They were surrounded.

'The only way is up,' she said briskly, turning G-Mamma around so they stood shoulder-to-shoulder, ready for Jack to transport them.

G-Mamma grabbed the sitar grimly.

'I can't do up.' Jack sounded pretty bleak. 'Only on stairs.'

But luckily, Janey had thought of that already. 'Okay. You do through, and I'll do the up part.'

'I beg your pardon?' Jack started to say. A crack of light from the nearby utility room was beginning to appear as the door opened from the outside.

'Just be ready!'

As Jack's mighty hands curled around their upper arms, Janey leaned backwards against him, drew her knees up to her chest and – hoping desperately that her spy-buys all still worked in pretty much the same way as they used to – she slammed her feet down as hard as she could against the marble floor.

As more light spilled out across the gloom of the vault, Jane Blonde's Fleet-Feet burst into action with a bang like cannon-fire. She shot into the air with her SPI:KE at her side and her new ally behind her, and the three of them touched the ceiling, melted it, then vaporised the roof, insulation and floor above so that it closed seamlessly in their wake. In moments they were all tottering unsteadily in the downstairs bathroom of the enormous meringue of a house.

Jack was staring at her, eyes wide. 'That was …
outstanding!' he said with a wolfish grin.

'Great teamwork,' replied Janey, as pleased as he was
at what they'd accomplished together. 'Now let's see if we
got what we needed.'

They all gazed at the neat leather box on Jack's palm,
and Janey held her breath as she opened it, awaiting the
lustrous glint of ruby …

But the box was empty.

Their mission had bombed.

Chapter 8 – A Ring of Truth

Janey felt doubly despondent. First of all, they'd had one simple thing to achieve, and they hadn't managed to do it. Secondly, Gideon Flynn was going to turn up expecting them to have the ring and help him with this condition, and they were going to let him down. For some reason, the second thing felt even worse than the failure to complete the mission…

All at once, though, as Jack and G-Mamma discussed the issues of Jack-Training through a toilet and she realised they were planning to leave, Janey's own spy instincts kicked in.

'We're not going yet,' she said firmly. 'We've got a mission to finish, and anyway, Jack won't get the money to maintain his castle if we don't provide the ring for Gideon Flynn.'

Jack grinned. 'True! No treats for Jacky-Boy without the ring, apparently.'

'Besides,' Janey said, picking up the ring box, 'it doesn't make sense. Why keep an empty ring box in a vault? The ring must usually be in it, and at the moment …'

'Someone's wearing it!' Holding up her own hands which, despite the decorator's outfit, were laden with outrageous jewellery, G-Mamma whooped. 'Someone who likes to bling it up for a party! Brilliant, Blonde. We just have to mingle with the blingle until we spot it.'

Janey laughed. 'How? I'm in a spy-suit, Jack's about a quarter dog, and you're dressed in dungarees. It's a very smart party! It's not even as if there's a shower curtain to disguise myself in.' She knew this because she'd already looked, and while there was a shower in here it was built-in, with a glass screen.

'All righty, Blondette. But you're a spy, and sometimes spies have to do the obvious. You could hide in plain sight.' G-Mamma looked her up and down, nodding. 'Yep. If Jacky-Boy puts his floppy fair head back on, and you just waltz out of here, I don't reckon anyone would know you weren't the son and daughter of a diplomat. And who knows how they dress in say … Greenland?'

'Oh! That's brilliant!' said Janey, although the thought of just marching out of the downstairs loo in her spy-suit caused her stomach to clench.

'But what if somebody recognises you as a famous spy?' Jack pointed to her outfit. 'Or me, as Lord Bootle-Cadogan?'

G-Mamma leapt up so quickly that her contact lens fell out. 'Even more brilliant, Jack! You could just introduce yourself as Lord Booty-Delicious, and Janey as your cousin or your plus one, and even if they check they won't find anything suspicious because you're telling the truth.' She goggled at them as if nobody had ever thought of telling the truth before.

'What's a plus one?' Janey had a horrible feeling she knew the answer, but held her breath anyway.

'A date for a posh party,' said G-Mamma.

Jack checked his hairy face in bathroom cabinet, watching Janey over his shoulder. 'It sounds like the easiest solution, and of course we'll have to shake everyone's hand so we can check for the ring.'

And so it was decided, though suddenly Janey wished she'd just insisted that they go home. As Jack concentrated on transforming into Lord BC of Lowmount, she stared in the mirror and tried to do something different with her hair. It was no use – whatever magic the Wower had wrought meant her ponytail insisted on staying in a long wavy side-pony that trailed almost to her waist at the front.

'I look ridiculous,' she muttered.

'You're perfect,' Jack said with his normal teenager mouth as he pulled her hand through his arm. 'Ready, Plus One?'

She wasn't really, but on the other hand, it would be interesting to see just what kind of party this was. There was no danger of anyone recognising her, as she was sure she'd de-spied everyone in the spy world apart from G-

Mamma. She could do this as her new self – Jane Blonder - for her new client, Mr Flynn.

Taking a deep breath, she checked through her Gogs for by-standers on the other side of the cloakroom door, confirmed there weren't any, then pushed it open. She and Jack moved along the corridor, grabbed some empty glasses from a nearby table, and stepped into the throng. What G-Mamma was going to do, she wasn't sure – but then she turned around to see her SPI:KE sticking up a 'WET PAINT' sign at the cloakroom door, and standing before it in her painting gear in case anyone didn't quite believe it.

Through the arm he'd clutched with his own, Janey could feel that Jack's heart was pounding practically out of his chest. 'Always hated this fancy stuff,' he moaned out of the corner of his mouth. 'Wish I was in black tie.'

'You look fine. Think how Prince Harry dresses. He's not in a suit all the time.'

'True. And I know him and William, sort of, so … well, here goes.'

And with that, Jack tightened his grip on her arm and steered her towards the nearest group of dignitaries.

'Evening,' he said smoothly, pumping the hand of a gentleman that Janey recognised as the man from the Ecuadorian limousine. 'Lord Bootle-Cadogan. This is my friend, Jane Blon … Brown.'

The man positively simpered. 'Lord Bootle-Cadogan; I knew your father. Kept very fine horses. So sorry to hear of your loss.'

Jack gulped ominously. 'You're most kind.'

'Do send my condolences to your mother. From Carlos Litardo - we were at Oxford together.'

'I will, Senor Litardo. Thank you.'

Jack made to move away as they'd already had time to check that nobody nearby was wearing an ostentatious ruby ring, but Senor Litardo grabbed Janey by her free hand.

'And Miss Blon-Brown, are your family into polo too?' His smile was like an oil slick spreading across his face. 'We have fabulous horses in Ecuador – as you shall see in the World Community Games!'

Janey shook her head, playing for time, and feeling completely out of her depth. Were her family, the Blon-Browns, into horses? She had no idea!

'Jane's family prefers smaller pets,' Jack said with a smile.

Phew, thought Janey; thanks, Jack. She nodded. 'Yes. We're cat people,' she said, trying to match Jack's easy charm.

Close behind her, someone suddenly erupted with laughter. Janey turned quickly. Nobody appeared to be paying her any attention. She hoped she'd imagined it, but it sounded very much as though someone had sniggered at what she'd said.

She tugged Jack's arm gently, and he took the hint. 'You must come and try our stables, your honour,' he told the Ecuadorian minister, adding 'I'll be in touch just as soon as the mourning period is over.' He pulled a sad face. 'That'll put him off,' he murmured to Janey.

The man stuttered his farewells as Jack waved airily and moved on to the next group. 'Good evening. Jack – sorry, Lord Bootle-Cadogan. Yes, the Lowmount Bootle-Cadogans. Oh, thank you. Yes, we miss him sorely, of course.' Shake, shake, shake, on he went, holding out people's hands and inviting Janey to inspect them under cover of a greeting. Some wore many rings and absolutely dripped with jewellery, but nothing as flamboyant as the piece they sought. They all sported the official orange security tag, of course, hanging from jaunty multi-coloured lanyards around their necks, but apart from the tiny sparkle of red that shone from the centre of the letter 'O' in the word HOST, there was not a thing that resembled a ruby. She smiled vacantly at stranger after stranger with a growing sense of unease.

After the fourth group, she pulled him to one side. 'This is hopeless. We'll never find the ring at this rate.'

'I know, but what do you suggest?'

Janey thought for a moment. 'Well, the person wearing it must live here, so why don't you ask to meet the hostess?'

'Of course,' said Jack, nodding his approval. 'Which is exactly what I should have done anyway. Where are my manners?'

And he marched back towards the Ecuadorian minister, pulling Janey along with him.

'Actually, Jack, I think we'll cover more ground if we split up.'

'Yep. Right again,' said Jack, and he smiled cheerily as the crowd swallowed him up.

She watched his back disappear into the crowd, biding her time. What she'd said was true, of course – they would get more done if they separated. But there was something else, too. Somehow, what with the laughter that sounded as though it was directed at her and the prickle in her ribs that told her something was wrong, she couldn't help feeling that they were being watched. Sending Jack off on his own would allow her to become the spy, checking out who was following him.

She circled back to the doorway, watching carefully for anyone who appeared to be pursuing Jack – or Janey herself. Every single person nearby had their back to her, and she took the opportunity to scan for the ring while everyone was distracted. Jack was striding towards the back of the room, obviously in pursuit of the hostess, and as Janey's eyes charted his progress, her Ultra-Gogs flashed on something.

Not something.

Someone.

There was a girl. A girl about her own age, hiding at the room's edges where she couldn't be seen. Even more strangely, she was crouching on top of a large bookcase, up near the ceiling. Her eyes were trained on Jack in much the same way Trouble's had been skewered onto him, and as Jack moved out of sight, the girl coiled back onto her haunches and suddenly sprang across the room, right over the unwitting heads of the guests standing near the balcony doorways below. She landed noiselessly on a large French bureau on the other side of the door and surveyed the room.

Pausing for a second, the girl stared down at Jack with a strange expression on her face - a mixture of admiration and pure revulsion. Then, with a smooth movement that seemed to shimmy up from her feet to her strange silver-blue hair, the girl turned her head towards Janey, and winked.

Janey gasped and looked around her. There was nobody nearby. The girl had definitely winked at her. She stared back as the girl motioned towards Jack, mouthed something, then took another flying leap onto a set of library ladders. They wobbled slightly as the girl landed deftly on the top step, then settled back against the wall.

As calmly as anything, the girl then selected a book from a high shelf and climbed nimbly down the rungs into the crowd.

She was definitely watching Jack. And now she was closing in on him with a large, heavy book in her hand. What was she up to?

Jane Blonde let her instincts take over.

'G-Mamma,' she said under her breath, hoping the spy master also had BATS hearing, 'there's a girl here trailing Jack. She might even be about to attack. Yes, I know that rhymes and will pop up one day as a rap, but please just come and do some spy stuff while I go and find out what she's up to.'

Without waiting for a reply, she grabbed a steel platter of canapes from a nearby table, held it in front of her face, and slid through the throng towards the centre where Jack had been swallowed up.

'Miss Blon-Brown, do join us!' shouted the Ecuadorian minister.

Hoping she didn't sound as panicky as she felt, Janey thrust the platter at him. 'Thank you, Senor Litardo! Would you … mind these for me, and I'll just go and get Jack.'

'Delighted!' came the reply.

She was fairly sure Jack could have eaten the whole lot in a nano-second, plate and all. Concerned for her new friend, Janey prowled onward into the thickening crowd, overhearing shards of conversation about former and current athletes and races, performance enhancing drugs, playing fair, playing polo, playing games … and suddenly she was closing in on Jack's hoodie.

He was nodding studiously, as if he was taking in every word being uttered by the woman whose hand he was holding … a hand on which glinted a large, slightly tacky but nonetheless impressive ruby ring.

'Jack,' said Janey urgently, wanting to warn him, just at the moment in which a number of realisations collided in her brain.

That woman. She recognised her! It was the lady on the front of the newspaper that Gideon had sent – the one whose husband had died; the one who was part of HOST. Varley, she was called. Something Varley.

The World Community Games. Of course. That was why all these people were here - representing different countries, crowing about their polo horses and athletic achievements. It was a pre-games party, now that there were just a few more to days to go.

And then the most startling and worrying realisation of all – the girl, the one from the heights of the furniture with the silvery-blue shock of hair and a skull-crushing encyclopaedia in her hands. She was right behind Jack. Ready to attack in a horribly rhyming way. Even now she was reaching out, thrusting through the partygoers with the enormous book …

Janey ran. In one seamless movement she slid in beside Jack, gripping his elbow so that his hand fell away from the Varley woman's grasp, moving him subtly to one side so that the silver-haired girl didn't appear directly behind him, as she'd planned, but instead bolted into position exactly where Jack had just been standing.

Jack spluttered, confused. 'Janey! Ah, Mrs Varley, let me introduce my friend …'

He'd been about to say 'Jane Blon-Brown' again, she was sure, but before he was able to say more, the other girl nudged him in the ribs so hard that Jack coughed, then said, 'Well, I don't know if friend is the word. More like frenemy.'

And she snorted so hard with laughter that Janey knew, beyond a doubt, that this was the person who'd giggled at her earlier.

The girl pulled herself together. 'Hi, Mrs Varley, it's me. Matilda Peppercorn.' She popped the large book on the floor and stood on it so that Mrs Varley couldn't help but see her, as she wasn't exactly tall.

Mrs Varley looked momentarily confused, holding a finger up to her chin so that Janey could see the ring in all its glory. It was garish - a deeply carved rose-gold ring with a clumsy mount and an obscenely large ruby set it into it. Why anyone would want to wear it, Janey wasn't sure. Actually, it reminded her of something …

Mrs Varley's eyes cleared. 'Ah yes! Peppercorn. The kick-boxer.'

'That's me,' cried the girl with a grin. 'I just wanted to say thank you for making kick-boxing part of the World Community Games. About time, of course!'

'A pleasure,' said Mrs Varley, looking a little overwhelmed by Matilda Peppercorn's energy. 'We've received terrific sponsorship for the kick-boxing - which is how we got to hear about you, naturally - and we know it will be incredibly popular.'

'It will if I have anything to do with it!' The girl winked again, directly at Janey. Again. She appeared to be trying very hard to ignore Jack.

Mrs Varley extended her hand to offer it to Matilda, and she gripped it as if she was about to throw the woman over her shoulder.

'I'm so glad you could come tonight, Miss Peppercorn. I especially like to hear of strong young female role models like yourself. It's fitting that you should be in the Games.'

'Dream come true!' cried Matilda Peppercorn.

'Wonderful! And are there any other wishes I can grant you while you're here?'

Mrs Varley laughed heartily, as did all the people around her, and Janey held her breath.

For some reason, the atmosphere had changed. The chatter of the crowds seemed to quieten to a distant whisper – the tinkle of a stream dancing through woodland – and suddenly the crystals dangling from the chandeliers felt as if they were exploding with blinding starlight.

Matilda Peppercorn was still holding the woman's hand firmly between her own sturdy fingers, her eyes fixed resolutely on Mrs Varley's. The girl's eyes were vast and hypnotic, and Janey found herself having to look away.

Jack, of course, was mesmerised.

Then the girl spoke, in a strange lilting manner which seemed to match her pulsating eyes.

'Well, Mrs Var-ley, since you ask - it would be ver-y VER-y nice if you would …Ohhhhh … GIVE me this BEAUTiful ring?'

The woman blinked slowly, then nodded. 'Take it, dear,' she said robotically, as if a ventriloquist was throwing her voice into her body.

Matilda Peppercorn, smiling from ear to ear, slid the ring straight off Mrs Varley's gnarled finger, and pocketed it.

Then, with one last wink at Janey, she ran up the library ladder, bounded gracefully across the tall furniture, and disappeared through a sky light.

Chapter 9 – Cat Burglars and Other Thieves

As the window at the apex of the ceiling closed behind the thief, Jack burst out of his trance. And do did Mrs Varley.

'My ring!' she screeched, staring at her hand. 'It's gone! Who took it? Was it you?' she spat, glaring at Jack.

'Certainly not,' said Jack, deeply offended and sounding more than a little cross. 'I wouldn't dream of taking someone's ring. Anyway, I've got a museum full of them at home.' He was becoming increasingly flustered, and Janey could just see the tips of his ears developing a fine black fuzz of fur. If he got any more annoyed, his dog head would pop up in full view of everyone. 'Didn't you see—'

'I saw who it was, Mrs Varley,' she interjected quickly.

Security guards were moving in from all directions as the woman wrung her hands, shouting, 'Precious! It's precious beyond words! Find it! And activate security protocols.'

Janey was pretty sure she was shouting to the security guards rather than herself and Jack, but they needed to make their escape and find the ring first. Gideon was still waiting for it.

'We'll find it,' she said, with a firm nod at the approaching uniformed guard, putting a hand on Jack's shoulder and pressing down as it began to stretch towards the ceiling. 'Come on, Jack; she went that way. We'll be back in a jiffy, don't worry!'

It wasn't a second too soon. Jack was so upset at being accused of stealing a ring right off someone's finger that his head was blackening from the neck up. It probably wasn't the moment to remind him that he had actually come here to steal a ring – and someone had got there ahead of them.

'Stay calm, Jack,' she whispered, and he let out a small, unhappy yelp as they raced towards the doorway. 'G-Mamma, the girl took the ring,' she muttered, 'then she disappeared out onto the roof. And Jack's about to reveal himself to everyone in here.'

'Copy that, Blonde. Keep running and I'll improvise.'

Ahead of them, G-Mamma moved into position, placing an enormous ladder across the passageway with her can of paint balanced precariously on the top. The duo spurted forwards, aware of the confusion behind them as Mrs Varley screamed about the loss of her prized possession and the guards looked around helplessly for a thief.

Of course, the most likely candidates were the two people running away as fast as they could.

'You two, hold it!' shouted a guard.

'Stop them!' cried Simone Varley.

The Ecuadorian minister made a grab for Janey as she ran past, no longer looking quite so keen to get to know her. 'Hold your horses, Blon-Brown!' he cried rudely.

'No can do, sorry,' hissed Janey under her breath, not least because Jack was now a full half metre taller than her and about to burst out of his hoodie. 'Head down, Jack,' she warned him.

Senor Litardo shouted after them. 'And don't bother refreshing your mother's memory about me, Lord Bootle-Cadogan! She always preferred dogs to horses anyway!'

'What did we do to him?' whispered Jack, his canine teeth protruding over his upper lip.

'Take no notice of him and follow me,' said Janey, and they sprinted together beneath the ladder.

At the same moment, G-Mamma faked a surprised backward step and toppled the stepladder directly into the ballroom. Paint spattered across athletes and diplomats from countries of all kinds, and the two guards spearheading the chase slithered on the wet floor before crashing headlong into the tumbled ladders.

'Paints preserve us, I'm SO sorry!' yelled the strangely dressed painter and decorator. At the same time, she accidentally fell on top of the ladders and bent them around so that they seemed to form a metal barrier across the open doorway. More guards crashed into it as the uproar rose among the gathered crowds. 'So abjectly and totally sorry! I'll go and find my supervisor,' Janey heard G-Mamma telling the rows of angry party guests, and then she ran after Janey and Jack.

They assembled in the downstairs loo, Jack now completely dog-headed and enormous. He shook his canine head miserably. 'I just can't seem to control it at the moment.'

'Can you control your powers, though?' said Janey. 'Only we need to escape through this wall before the ladders give way.'

'Yes! Sorry. Right on it.'

'I've got the sitar,' cried G-Mamma. 'Go, go, go!'

Turning them around to avoid the loo and small basin, Jack planted a hand on each of their shoulders. Breathing in deeply, he sped them through the wall and out into the passageway beyond. Outside the house, he paused.

'Where did the girl go?'

Janey pointed upwards towards the roofline. 'Didn't you see her?'

'No. It was like I was hypnotised or something.'

'It was exactly like that, actually. Maybe my Ultra-Gogs saved me.'

'So what do we do?' Jack sounded utterly miserable. 'I'll never get paid now. We've lost the ring, and the girl.'

'No, you haven't,' said a familiar voice.

It came from beyond a gate in a high wall. Janey zoomed her Gogs onto it, and could see that the gate led into a small park behind the house.

'Gideon, where are you?'

'Come through to the park, quickly – they're about to storm out through the doors. Meet me in the ring of laurels in the centre.'

The gate wasn't locked, so Janey, Jack and G-Mamma coursed through it, easing it shut behind them. Security officers were surging out onto the street at the front of the house, imagining that they had escaped that way. All along the road, they were checking limousines and waking snoozing drivers.

For the moment, at least, they were on their own in a park that was amazingly spacious, considering that it was really just an extension of the gardens for the houses backing onto it. Passing a series of water features rather like the ones at Jack's castle, they threaded their way through a circle of benches to the laurel thicket beyond.

Shaded beneath their branches, Gideon Flynn struck a casual pose, hands in pockets.

Beside him was the girl.

'Who … who's there?' growled Jack, looking the two of them up and down, every bit as agitated as he'd been when Janey and G-Mamma had first met him. 'What are you up to?'

What was wrong with him? 'Jack, this is …' Then Janey realised something. 'Oh. You haven't met before.'

Jack's eyes flickered from Gideon to the girl and across to Janey. 'You see them too?'

'Yes, of course I see them.'

'Sometimes I see people who aren't … there,' said Jack with a shrug.

'They're here. This is your boss, Gideon Flynn, and …'

The other girl grinned heartily. 'Matilda Peppercorn. Tilly P. Living Legend. Take your pick on what to call me!'

'Some juicy names spring to mind,' said G-Mamma.

Janey shot her a warning glance, but Tilly laughed, unconcerned.

'Don't worry. I get that a lot. Usually for talking … or getting into trouble … or interfering where I shouldn't … or … You know,' she said with a shrug. 'All sorts. Having blue hair! That's a good one. They love that at school.' And she guffawed again as she had from her vantage point on top of the bookshelf.

Gideon's dark eyes observed them all closely, taking everything in although he remained silent.

What was going on? They appeared to be working together – but Gideon had sent them on this mission, hadn't he? Had he changed his mind? Didn't he think they were up to it?

'I ... I don't quite understand,' she said eventually, when even Tilly had finally stopped talking and the silence seemed to reverberate around the park. 'Did we do something wrong?'

Watching her carefully, Gideon shook his head. Cast in shadow, he looked paler and more jaded than ever, and Janey felt her heart twist for him. Whatever he was going through – whatever this condition was – it was obviously causing him a great deal of anguish.

'Nothing wrong at all,' he said. 'Everything right, in fact.'

'But we didn't get the ring,' cried Jack, his muzzle wrinkling. 'She did.'

And he pointed at Matilda Peppercorn.

'Who's she? The cat's mother?' said Tilly and G-Mamma together. It was something Janey had heard her parents say, too, if someone didn't use another's name properly.

Jack shuffled uncomfortably, aware of his rudeness, as G-Mamma and Tilly sized each other up.

Then, once again, Matilda Peppercorn laughed. 'Actually he's right. Well, not the mother part. But the cat bit, definitely.'

Gideon smiled slowly. 'You might call her a cat burglar.'

'And seeing as you're a dog, Freaky McFreakerson,' the girl said, staring pointedly at Jack's furred ears, 'I reckon you and I are destined to be enemies.'

'No. You need to get along,' said Gideon with a frown.

'Frenemies, then.' Tilly smiled at Jack, but it suddenly looked much more as though she was baring her teeth at him. 'Like I said.'

'Some cats worship me,' said Jack huffily.

'Yeah, not this one.'

'Please.' Filled with pain and a note of irritation, Gideon's voice cut across their bickering. 'Please at least try to get along. That was what tonight was about, seeing if you could work together. And you did it so perfectly – GM on standby, Jack with your excellent schmoozing, and Matilda grabbing the ring from Simone Varley's finger. That was superb.'

'Yes, how did you do that?' said Janey, intrigued. 'You hypnotised everyone.'

'Apart from you,' replied Tilly. 'And it wasn't hypnosis. More like a spell.'

'But … I'm sorry, but what kind of cat are you?'

Tilly screwed up her nose thoughtfully, and for the first time Janey could see that, when she wasn't being snippy with Jack, she could actually be quite … well, normal. Ish.

'It's kind of complicated,' said Tilly at length. 'I'm all sorts of cat and a little bit witchy, and sort of a legend. But mostly I'm a girl.'

'Are you sure about that?' sniffed Jack, but Janey laid a hand on his arm.

'So Matilda Peppercorn is another part of your team?' she asked Gideon directly.

He glanced from Tilly to Jack. 'Yes. If these two can bury their differences. No, not bury – bad choice of words. If they can learn to get along.'

'I'm sure they can,' she said. 'Can't you?'

She wasn't even sure why it was important to her that they did get along, but her spy instincts were bubbling like a geyser. They'd been selected for a mission. They'd been hand-picked by someone who believed in them, and now he'd trialled them by getting them to lift the ring directly from Mrs Varley's hand, and somehow … he was pleased. It was working.

And for Jane Blonde, it was … fun. More excitement than she'd had in forever, and she was sure it was the same for Jack and G-Mamma. Tilly looked as though she'd find the fun in almost anything, and then turn it into mischief. Still, there was no doubting that she had something special – and if they could all pull together there was no saying what they'd be able to achieve …

'The ring,' she said to Gideon. 'Did you actually want it, or was that just a test for us?'

Gideon stared at her in surprise. 'No, I really want it. Of course I want it.'

'Oh! Here you go,' said Tilly, fishing it out of her pocket. 'I'm not big on jewellery anyway. It's not allowed in kick-boxing in case you scratch someone and get an unfair advantage.'

'You're a cat, apparently,' said Jack. 'How is that not an unfair scratchy advantage?'

'Only some of the time, your dogness. You should try it. Can you take that big dopey head off whenever you like, or are you stuck like that?'

'You're so mean,' retorted Jack in a feeble little voice.

'Sticks and stones,' Tilly replied brightly.

And she held the ring out to Gideon as she and Jack glared at each other.

To Janey's amazement, Gideon recoiled. 'No!' he shouted abruptly.

Taken aback by the violence of his reaction, they all stared at him.

'No – I can't … I don't want to touch it. It's cursed.'

Or he couldn't touch it because it would hurt him to do so. Janey wondered if this was the problem, but actually it didn't look as though it was the same issue, this time. He was staring at the ring with revulsion, as if he hated it from the bottom of his heart.

'It's cursed?' Matilda Peppercorn rolled her eyes. 'Well, you might have told me! I might have put it on and subjected myself to cursiness.'

'Not traditionally cursed,' said Gideon. He thrust his hands into the pockets of his wide-legged trousers, scowling. 'But it was taken from an Indian holy man, and bad things happen around it.'

'And you took it so they'd stop happening?' asked Janey hopefully.

'Something like that.'

For long moments, they all stared at the ring balanced on the end of Matilda's startlingly long fingernail. It didn't look evil – more like the kind of cheap ornament usually found in a Christmas cracker – but it was quite evident that Gideon Flynn had no intention of going anywhere near it.

He shook himself out of his torpor as Simone Varley had shaken off her spell-like state. 'It needs to be kept safe.' His eyes turned to Janey. 'Could you hide it at your laboratory?'

'Of course.'

She reached out her Girl Gauntlet, and Tilly slid the ring onto her outstretched palm.

Then Gideon Flynn nodded towards the distant wall backing onto the Varley's house. 'They'll be here soon. We'd better all disappear. Thank you, everyone. I'll be in touch soon.'

Jack was calming down, now that he was no longer in immediate danger and Tilly had stopped needling him. As he shrunk back to normal teenager size, he held up a finger.

'Ahem, I don't like to be mercenary, but …'

'But you are a mercenary,' said Gideon with a quick grin. His smile was extraordinary: a full upward curve that flashed across his face and then disappeared just as quickly, as if it had been sucked back into his mouth. It was as if he wasn't accustomed to using it. 'You're a paid soldier, Jack. Don't worry; I've put a large deposit in your account. The same for the rest of you,' he said, nodding to G-Mamma and Matilda. 'Your help and loyalty are not going to go unrewarded.'

'Great, because I need a new kick-boxing helmet – like - immediately! Right, well, I'm off. Nice to meet you all. Mostly,' said Tilly with a wink, and then to their astonishment, she reached behind a tree, pulled out a long, knobbly branch with a raft of twigs at one end, and stepped on it. 'Home, Bronco, you brave little besom, you.'

The branch rose into the air with Matilda Peppercorn standing on its back and shot away above the treeline.

'Not bad,' said Jack reluctantly. 'Hypno spells, stealing stuff right from under the owner's nose, flying away on a broomstick. I've met some weird people - and some of them weren't even people – but she's about the weirdest. I suppose it's a little bit amazing.'

Janey nudged him. 'What you do is amazing, too. All of it.'

'I'm blushing, though you can't see it,' muttered Jack.

He was calmer now, and his dog features were softening.

'Would you zap G-Mamma home?' Janey asked quickly, before he changed back completely. Her spy instincts and spy-buys were calling her in more ways than one. 'I feel like a run.' It was many miles, but she'd cover it in a very short space of time.

'Don't wear those Fleet-Feet out, Girly-Girl,' said G-Mamma, lining up beside Jack. 'I don't know how long these new ones last.'

'I'll be careful.'

They disappeared, and Janey turned slowly. It was more than just wanting to feel the fields vanish beneath her soles as she flitted across the earth. She was suddenly very aware that she was alone, now, with Gideon Flynn. He hadn't emerged any further from the shadows, but she knew that he was watching her with his usual intensity.

'She isn't the ring's owner, you know.' Gideon's face sharpened again. 'She never was. She's just the … user.'

Janey nodded. 'And that's why you wanted it back – because it's yours?'

His dark eyelashes fluttered as if he was remembering something. 'More because of what it does.'

'It's a ring,' said Janey. 'What does it do?'

'You'll find out when it's time,' said Gideon solemnly. Then he glared at her, as if daring her to ask any more.

But Janey was used to objects that were more than they seemed, and people with agendas that weren't exactly like her own. Somehow she knew that he was telling the truth. When she needed to know what this evening had been about, he'd tell them.

Right now, though, there was something else she wanted to clear up.

'I wanted to ask you something,' she said.

He looked a little nervous at that, but finally he shrugged. 'Go ahead.'

'You didn't mention me,' she said, aware that she sounded sulky. 'G-Mamma was on standby, you said, and Jack did the schmoozing and Tilly … cat burgled. But what did I do? Why did you even need me on the team tonight?'

His bitter-chocolate eyes blinked as if he didn't understand the question, but then he laughed gently. 'I hadn't realised you didn't know,' he said.

'Know what?'

'You ran it. You ran the heist, Jane Blonde.' Gideon Flynn pointed at the ring, which now sat on top of her Girl Gauntlet, on her little finger. 'That's why I didn't just introduce you to Tilly first, in case you let her take over.

She's a strong character, but so are you. You were in charge.'

In charge? But that couldn't be right. Janey stared at the ring herself, trying to work it out. G-Mamma was always in charge – or perhaps it was Gideon himself, who had sent them on their mission in the first place. It couldn't be her, Jane Blon-Brown. Surely not her …

As she looked up to ask him more, there was a hefty rattle of the gate behind her. The guards had made their way to the back of the house. 'I'd better go,' she said, but when she peered more closely, she could no longer find him in the darkness. He was gone again, slithering back into the blackness like a startled fox.

With a sigh, Janey pushed the ring more firmly onto her gloved hand. Like the sprinters who would be running at the World Community Games, she leaned back and banged her heel into the ground. She was running. Running and free. And somehow – in charge.

As she vaulted the wall into a neighbouring garden, it was almost as if she was jumping for joy. She sped home through quiet streets and across playgrounds, keeping to the shadows so she wouldn't be seen, feelings of power and excitement raging through her. In no time, she was Fleet-Footing along her own street.

Knowing that G-Mamma wouldn't object to her sneaking into the Spylab, she crept up to her room, slithered through the fireplace tunnel and considered somewhere safe to keep the jewellery. That was what Gideon Flynn had entrusted her with – keeping the ring safe and running the mission. She'd been in charge! It was still hard to believe that she'd been slotted into such an important position right from the off set, but the more she thought about it, the more she realised it was probably true. Who was the one figuring out what to do? She was. Who had suggested all the next moves? She had. Even G-Mamma had just stayed out of the way, keeping things orderly – or rather, chaotic and paint-covered – in the background.

And now she was taking charge again, responsibly stashing the ring in a safe spot. There were a few choices for hiding things in the Spylab (as it was a place for secret spy-buys, after all) but Janey dismissed them all after looking around for a while. Actually, she'd really enjoyed the notion of hiding things in plain sight, and where could she stow a gaudy, oversized ring that looked like a child's toy?

Right with the other chunky, oversized rings that looked like a child's toys.

Removing an emerald-encrusted skull-and-crossbones knuckle-duster from the second rung of G-Mamma's ring tree, she slid the ruby ring towards the centre, placed the skull-and-crossbones back in position, and chucked a bit of G-Mamma's other jewellery around for good measure. It was almost buried behind a mountain of make-up, anyway, and she very much doubted whether anyone would dare to touch that without risking the mighty wrath of a large volatile spy.

Feeling strangely satisfied with the whole evening, Jane Blonder finally allowed herself to de-Wow and sidle off to her bed. Tomorrow was a whole new day – for a whole new spy.

Chapter 10 – A Mini Gift

Seeing the ring at such close quarters had unnerved him, it was true. The wretched thing had already caused such trouble that he could hardly bear to remember it at all. And now Simone was creating more mayhem with it.

Unbidden, a scene floated into his mind. It was the sitar player at the party his parents threw for his seventeenth birthday. He'd been thrilled, thinking the sitar was his gift - although a guitar would have been more practical - but he'd got that wrong. Gideon had been so ungracious, refusing to wear the peacock-blue silk band-master's outfit his mother had sewn for him by hand, sulking that the others would laugh at him - even though he loved it so much, really. His heroes wore them, so why shouldn't he? Well, because he wasn't beloved by millions, of course. He wasn't beloved by many at all.

Then the trick, the joke that wasn't funny: that the ring on the sitar player's finger was his actual gift, his birthday present. His father had researched it, bought it from Henry's father at huge expense.

'It's a genuine ruby from Burma, like the one George wore,' his father had whispered, talking about his favourite band member. 'One day it will be worth a fortune. When your studies are done, and you wander far from home ... well, the Indians believed it would protect you, so we'll let it look after you when your mother and I are no longer able to.'

'You're not that old,' Gideon said with a shake of his head, although he actually thought they were ancient. And a bit gullible. It was a wonderful present, but not for someone his age, and they'd probably mortgaged the house to buy it from Harry Wentworth, Henry's dad. Just like his son, Harry could be very persuasive. Why couldn't they have just bought him a car? A battered mini – that would have suited him down to the ground. They could all have squashed into it and blasted round the city, enjoying life.

And then it all went so wrong. The ruby wasn't genuine at all – still valuable, after a fashion, because it was one of the original Geneva rubies that had been synthetically created back in 1885 (by melting powdered aluminium oxide and chromium oxide together, a detail that Gideon had spent far too much time researching). But it wasn't worth what Mr Flynn had paid for it and they'd spent so, so much – so much on their only son, their pride and joy. Harry had refused to take it back or refund the *money, and anyway, it was his birthday gift, so Gideon couldn't complain, could he? If only they'd got him a Mini.*

Because then he'd discovered what more could be done with a fake ruby.

It was then that the trouble really began.

Chapter 11 – The Silent Spike

Alfie seemed to take forever to get away from soccer practice after school. She'd promised to wait for him, and as she watched him take out the guy he was marking with a filthy tackle, she wished she could share all this with him. But then the memories of the new team around her – this team of SWAG – filled her with such a sense of belonging that she cast the thought aside. She could keep it all to herself for now, and wait till she got home. G-Mamma would probably be desperate for a de-brief over a doughnut.

Luckily, although it was later than usual when she finally reached home, Janey's parents were still busily beavering away in their design studio, out in the office at the bottom of the garden. She took them each a cup of tea just to be sure, then zipped through the house and into the lab next door.

'Sorry!' she cried, giggling as she realised how much she sounded like Jack – always apologising, ever polite, apart from where Matilda Peppercorn was concerned. 'Just had to ply Mum and Dad with tea. They'll be set for a couple of hours now. G-Mamma?'

She wasn't here. The room was silent. Worryingly so. It didn't have the appearance of a room that had been infiltrated – nothing was suspiciously out of place, or anything … apart from G-Mamma.

No, it wasn't the look of the place that seemed odd. It was the quietness that was unusual. Everywhere G-Mamma went, even when she was spying, there was some accompanying sound: the tuneless humming of one of her lesser-known raps or Bigg Squid songs; the whirr of a smoothie machine as she puréed cakes and chocolate into a delicious shake, or the rhythmic purr of Trouble as she stroked his tummy with her foot and applied make-up to her face, or occasionally the cat's.

Now there was nothing … nothing apart from a very, very faint rasping sound that could easily have been mistaken for the electronic hum of a fridge.

Except that their fridges were silent, especially the thing that looked most like a fridge – the Wower.

The noise was coming from there, though. Had Janey left the door open like that when she'd de-wowed the previous night? She didn't think so, but there was no doubt that the Wower door was ajar, and the gentle rasping sound was echoing from the floor of the spy cabinet.

Janey proceeded with caution. She'd found hid-eous things in the Wower before now, and she didn't want to just assume she'd left the door open herself and that Trouble was in there having a snooze. She searched around quickly for a suitable spy-buy to defend herself with and seized upon an old ASPIC - an Aeronautical SPI Conveyor. If it came to it, she could jump on it and fly off, not as impressively as Tilly P had done the night before, but enough to stay ahead of her enemies. Or if it was really a crisis, she could thwack someone round the head with it.

Stealing forward on tiptoe, Janey peered past the Wower, towards the glass doors of the nearby storage cabinets, checking the reflection to give her a heads-up. There was somebody – or something – in there, pooled on the floor of the shower cabinet and spilling out across the Spy-lab floor. On hearing her approach, the rasping sound became quicker, more feverish, and suddenly Janey saw the thing she had feared the most.

G-Mamma was half-propped up against the wall of the Wower. The robotic hands were slightly extended as if she'd fallen before they got chance to work their magic, and a small pool of red liquid lapped against the side of her prone body.

'Blood! G-Mamma!'

She'd been shot or something, or stabbed or scratched or … Janey ran to her SPI:KE's side, where she lay with the top half of her body spooling out onto the floor of the lab, and her legs still trapped inside the Wower. She didn't move as Janey touched her, but the hoarse breathing became louder, more pronounced.

'Who did this? Where are you hurt?'

Janey scanned G-Mamma's body, wishing for her Ultra-Gogs, but there was no obvious reason for the puddle of blood in the shower tray, and the woman wasn't moving to point towards anything. She wasn't responding at all, in fact. She was just breathing in an increasingly laboured and terrified way as her round, blue eyes opened and closed in random, twitchy movements.

'What, G-Mamma? Can you tell me? What's wrong?'

The eyes flickered again, and this time Janey was sure they'd switched to her right, into the Wower cubicle. Maybe the Wower itself had been interfered with. Perhaps it had gone mad and attacked her mentor. Janey straddled G-Mamma to inspect the robotic hands, spattering the blood slick - which was when she noticed that the liquid that sprayed up the side of the Wower cubicle on contact with her feet was not red. It was clear. It was not blood. It was water. Just water.

And then she saw it.

The ring was on G-Mamma's right hand – the hand that now lay in a pool of water that had gathered as she'd struggled into it, trying to Wow up to combat whatever misfortune had befallen her. The ruby centre was reflected in the puddle, and that was the cause of the scarlet streak that looked like blood.

So if she wasn't stabbed or shot, what could have happened to her?

'Who did this to you? What's wrong?'

G-Mamma's eyes flicked towards her hand again, and with that flash in her brain that accompanied her best spying instincts, Janey knew that it was the ring itself that had harmed her mentor. G-Mamma appeared to be paralysed, and her breathing was coming in sharper and sharper rasps, more laboured with every passing second.

Janey was just about to reach out to grab the ring when she thought of Gideon the night before. Maybe it was cursed. G-Mamma had spotted it among her jewellery and decided to wear it; Janey should have warned her that she'd hidden it in plain sight but it still wasn't to be worn.

Moving G-Mamma's head out of the way of the spray, Janey stuck her hand under the shower head and barked: 'Wow me, now!' The multi-coloured droplets shimmered down from the ceiling and encased her hand and arm. She withdrew them instantly, and in the same moment as the shower stopped raining down on them, her Girl Gauntlet and part of her spy-suit sleeve shimmered into life.

Janey swallowed hard. She had no idea how the ring was harming G-Mamma – removing it might slice her finger off or something – but she knew that leaving it on wasn't an option.

'I'm sorry, GM,' she whispered, using her spy master's new title for the first time and noticing how easily it rolled off her tongue. 'This may hurt or make things worse, but the ring has to come off.'

She lifted G-Mamma's arm with her bare right hand, then eased the ring between the several other rings that the woman was wearing until it popped off the end of her finger and onto the palm of Janey's glove. Quickly, she inspected G-Mamma's hand. It wasn't severed or anything, which was what she'd feared, but there was definitely a vivid red wheal like a deep scratch along the top of G-Mamma's finger.

'Better?' Clambering into the Wower completely, Janey lifted G-Mamma's head onto her lap, waiting for her breathing to improve. She was huffing in hoarse little gasps now, and still seemed unable to move. 'No. You're not better. Worse, if anything. What shall I do?'

As soon as she spoke she realised it was hopeless to ask G-Mamma for advice. The woman could hardly fill her lungs with enough air to stay alive, let alone indicate how Janey should deal with it. The eye twitch had been a last attempt to save herself.

Grabbing the torch-taser from the edge of the Wower, she tried to prise open G-Mamma's eyelids and get a reaction. Her eyes barely twitched. Janey's heart fluttered as she wedged the torch in her pocket. This was literally a life and death situation, and she didn't have a clue how to handle it.

What would Gideon do? What would Jack do, or Tilly or any of them? What would G-Mamma herself do if she could speak, or even breathe?

'You'd call for help,' she told G-Mamma.

Only help was harder to come by these days. They no longer had the luxury of an entire SPI organisation behind them, or a SPI medical unit to swoop in and see to G-Mamma without anyone knowing. She couldn't even run to the garden and ask her parents, now that they were … ordinary.

Even worse, G-Mamma was blocking the Wower which would enable Janey to suit up and use her gadgets to call for assistance, or run to find it.

'Think, Janey, think!'

She peered around the laboratory from her awkward position on the Wower floor, still cradling G-Mamma's head and holding out the ring with the other hand, at a safe distance from anyone's flesh. Her eyes fell on the ring tree and the equipment beside it.

Of course. She'd just have to communicate like everyone else.

Placing G-Mamma's head gently on the floor, she tried not to notice that her SPI:KE's breathing was shorter and harsher than ever, and ran to the computer. She placed the ring back on the ring tree and located the email from Gideon, typing as fast as she could.

G-MAMMA PARALYSED, CAN'T BREATHE. HELP! JB

Then she texted Jack. 'Problem with GM, need to get hold of Gideon Flynn. Can you do anything?'

'On it,' came the reply within seconds.

For a long, tortuous minute, there was no response to her email. In case anyone else had the bright idea of putting on the ring, Janey quickly grabbed it from the jewellery stand and dropped into a beaker. Trouble was watching her with his hypnotic green eyes from beneath the bench, growling quietly as he did when either she or G-Mamma were in danger. 'Don't touch that, Twubs,' she warned him, and then just in case he couldn't resist, she snapped the beaker inside a cake tin, wrapped it in a sleeve of Invisibubble fabric that erased it from sight, and stacked it behind the computers.

The screen was flashing with a message from Gideon.

Call an ambulance immediately. She needs artificial respiration or she'll die, and we don't have the equipment. She'll have to go straight to a hospital. Do it now!

Janey's heart tremored as she bashed out a response.

But we can't use a normal hospital! They might expose us.

The answer came back almost immediately.

Okay. I know somewhere. Call the ambulance, get her on oxygen, then hijack it and meet me at this address.

Hijack it?!

If you want her to live.

This was nuts, completely nuts, but Janey knew she had no choice. G-Mamma's gasps were fainter, further and further apart. Even her fake eyelashes had stopped twitching.

There was nothing for it. With a shaky finger, Janey tapped out 999 on her phone and demanded an ambulance immediately.

To her relief, Jack ran up G-Mamma's stairs a moment later, transforming quickly back into Boy Jack and with Matilda Peppercorn hot on his heels.

'What's going on?' cried Jack. He looked over to where G-Mamma lay stretched out, half inside the Wower. 'Oh no. That's not good.'

'I know! That's why I texted. She was wearing the ring from last night and I found her like this – and now Gideon says we have to get her to a hospital.'

Jack shook his head, which was rapidly growing canine ears.

'I don't mean she looks sick. I mean … um, you know the processing stuff that I told you about? Well, I can see G-Mamma's ba – her spirit – trying to climb out of her body.'

'She's nearly gone?' said Matilda Peppercorn before Janey could say anything – or work out how Tilly had found out about it at all.

Jack nodded, completely dog-headed by now. 'Lie down,' he said sharply to the space above G-Mamma's body, and then he looked around at the girls. 'Her heart's about to give out, I think. She needs to be on artificial respiration, now.'

'There's an ambulance on the way,' said Janey, hardly able to breathe herself any more. 'Gideon said we're to take control of it and meet him at this address in Hertfordshire.'

'We've got to steal an ambulance?' Jack sounded incredulous, but then he raced over to G-Mamma and wafted both hands over her prone body. 'We've got to steal an ambulance!' he ordered. 'Now!'

'How do we do that? I'm not even in my spy-suit.' Janey felt as helpless as she'd ever felt in her life.

But Matilda Peppercorn rubbed her hands together. 'Leave that to me,' she said, rather more cheerfully than Janey would have expected. She'd mentioned kick-boxing – was Tilly going to take the ambulance drivers by force? It didn't seem very fair, somehow, when they were just doing their jobs and trying to save someone.

She didn't have much choice but to put her faith in Tilly despite her considerable misgivings about her, however, since the blare of the sirens was screeching ever nearer. As someone hammered on the door, Janey ran down the SPIral staircase and flung it open.

'Upstairs,' she cried to the man and woman on the doorstep, wondering how she would explain the Spylab to them.

But there was no need, as Jack was carrying G-Mamma down the stairs, his muzzle wrinkled with concern, or possibly effort.

Forget the Spylab. How would she explain Jack to them?

'Which one needs treatment?' said the male paramedic nervously.

'I ... I think it's both of them. Possibly all of us,' said Janey quickly. 'It's very catching.'

The female frowned. 'Have you all got a virus? We were only told about one patient.'

Then she caught sight of Matilda with her shock of blue-silver hair. Matilda slid the length of the banister down the staircase, then bounded to her feet with a whoop at the bottom.

'You too?' said the paramedics together.

'Noooooo,' replied Matilda, giving Janey and Jack a shove in the back. 'NOT meeeeee.'

Janey recognised the same creamy voice with which Tilly had persuaded Mrs Varley to give them the ring. In fact, yes, Tilly had taken the ring – the very ring that had now caused G-Mamma's paralysis. What was she up to? Could she even be trusted?

But then Tilly continued in her mellifluous purring: 'But YOUUUU look like you've had a shOCK. WOULD you like to sit ... on the stairs here ... and wait for ... oooo, THREE hours, un-TIL we're BACK?'

There it was - that same shift in the atmosphere that had taken place in Holland Park, as Tilly's voice soared and swooped and her luminous eyes fixed on the pair's faces.

'That sounds nice,' said the male medic.

'Nice? I've not had a day off in three weeks. It sounds fantastic!' The woman smiled hopefully at Tilly. 'Are there snacks?'

And before they knew what they were doing, the two paramedics parked themselves willingly on separate steps of the SPIral staircase, sandwiched a metre-long box of G-Mamma's doughnuts between them, and took absolutely no notice as three teenagers - two with wild heads and one carrying a large poisoned woman - made off with their ambulance.

Silently, the three teenagers carried the patient into the back as Janey located the oxygen mask and snapped it over G-Mamma's nose. Her breathing seemed to ease, but only for a second, as Jack stared in alarm at the inside wall of the vehicle.

'I told you,' he said firmly, in the kind of tone that G-Mamma herself might have used, 'you're not going anywhere. Lie the heck down in that body of yours.' He held up a hand. 'Nope. I'm not arguing, especially not in rap. It's not your time.' Then he rolled his eyes. 'Okay. Err … It isn't your time and you're going to be fine or it's no fault of mine, so … um … get back in the line.'

He shifted uncomfortably as both girls stared at him, but Janey understood. G-Mamma could be bossy – and rapping - even when she was close to death's door.

'I'll watch her,' said Matilda.

'I want to watch her,' Janey retorted.

'Okay, but I can't drive. Good with a broomstick, not so much with the brum-brums.' The other girl shrugged. 'Happy to risk it though?'

'Come on, Janey,' said Jack, and Janey sighed.

She wasn't old enough to drive either, but it had been part of her SPI training, and she'd never forgotten how to do it.

'You drive and I'll super-speed us,' Jack continued.

So that was how they travelled, with Tilly and Jack bickering over whether they should use the siren or not (Tilly was for, Jack against), Jack occasionally yelling, 'No! Back in your body,' over his shoulder towards the innocently sleeping body of G-Mamma, and Janey hanging onto the steering wheel with all her might, heading in the direction of the map points that Gideon had sent through.

Between arguments, Jack assisted by clutching the dashboard so that they suddenly slid through entire housing estates and across motorways without so much as a bump. Janey learned quickly how to compensate by taking her foot off the accelerator and focussing instead on the pinprick of light in the distance that showed where they were headed.

It would actually have been a giggle if her closest and greatest ally in the whole world wasn't lying inert in the back of the ambulance, fighting for her life, so stiff and white and cold that it was as if she'd already died.

Chapter 12 – The Host with the Most

W e're here.' Janey checked the sat-nav details against the numbers on the building in front of her, hardly able to believe that this was what Gideon had intended. 'This is definitely it, but I don't understand.'

The ambulance came to a barely controlled, slithering halt beside a large semi-circular forecourt on which stood a vast and impressive glass building. As Janey and Jack peered at it through the windscreen, the glass panels changed from transparent to a deep rose pink, as the whole building reflected the setting sun and the beautiful fuchsia clouds that rolled away across the hills.

'What is this place?' said Jack, switching back into his teen persona. 'It's superb!'

Matilda's voice interrupted them from the back of the van. 'Dying woman here! Where did Flynn say to meet him? Shall I march into Reception or whatever they call it in hospitals?'

'No,' said Janey quickly. 'We don't know it actually is a hospital. There are people walking around it in civilian clothes, for a start.'

'Patients? Visitors?' suggested Tilly.

'I don't know. It doesn't feel right.'

Janey looked around anxiously, wishing again for her spy-buys. Her Gogs would have told her far more about what was going on inside and exactly where to take G-Mamma, whose breathing was barely steadier than before.

Then she spotted him in the shadows at the edge of the forecourt, where the flax-filled flower beds ended and the angular, Japanese trees began.

With a finger to his lips, Gideon was waving them over.

'Over there,' she told Jack, pointing to Gideon.

Jack's eyes seemed to widen slightly, but then he nodded.

'Okay,' he said, checking out G-Mamma's status. 'Let's take GM on the gurney and get her straightened out. Her *ba* is practically standing up and jumping out now; there's no time to lose.'

Thrusting the ambulance into position beyond the flowerbeds, Janey hid it as best she could among the trees and then leapt out along with Matilda and Jack. Between them they lifted the stretcher on which G-Mamma had been placed and kicked the legs beneath it to turn it into a gurney. Then she turned to Gideon Flynn.

'This way,' he whispered, and they followed him around the thicket to a large ramp that led to the underground car park, sticking to the treeline so that they wouldn't be seen by the people inside the building. They'd have to be quick, though. Janey calculated that at this point between five and six pm, staff would soon start leaving for home, collecting their cars from the basement and wondering why four shifty-looking teenagers were wheeling a large, prone woman into the lift.

Because that was where they headed – or at least, that was what Janey assumed. However, as soon as they reached the shaft where the metal doors gleamed, looking for all the world like a Wower, Gideon peeled off to the left and nodded towards a slender doorway behind the lift shaft, almost invisible in the light-deprived corners of the building.

He reached out a hand to touch the keypad, then withdrew it quickly.

'I shouldn't with my condition,' he explained, turning to the others. 'Janey, would you mind?'

'No problem. What's the number?'

Gideon reeled off a string of digits. '0708 151 920.'

It sounded like a telephone number. Janey half-expected to hear a voice answering the call asking them what they were up to, but instead the door slid silently to the right and they found themselves in a long, narrow corridor.

Gideon ran ahead, urging them forward. 'Come on. I've seen this before. GM needs a full ventilation kit applied immediately, or she won't fight the poison.'

'Poison?' squawked Matilda from behind the gurney, her face purple with exertion as the three of them steered G-Mamma's trolley past door after door. 'Is that what this is? You got any toadst—'

Her words were drowned out by the pressurised blast of double doors opening automatically as they approached at full belt. Gideon ushered them into the room beyond, his dark eyes scanning the corridor.

'It wasn't toadstools, Tilly,' he said as they took in their surroundings. He had led them to a neat, square operating theatre, complete with tables of surgical instruments, towers of bleeping equipment and a pair of flat beds covered with blue sheets. 'It's called curare. It causes paralysis and then slow death through respiratory problems – and all the while the person who is suffering knows everything about what's happening.'

'Oh, poor G-Mamma! You mean she's been awake through all this?' Janey shoved the gurney into position near the equipment. She wasn't sure which apparatus would help G-Mamma breathe, but they had to get to it quickly – and even if she had to use it all at once, she'd find it.

Fortunately, Gideon seemed to know what to do.

'It's won't be very nice, but you're going to have to insert that tube down G-Mamma's throat and into her lungs,' he told her. She clutched the edge of the table, feeling queasy. 'Jack and Tilly, if you could attach –'

'I'll do it, Janey,' said Jack quickly. 'I do this kind of stuff all the time. It's a bit like mummification.'

'You can't mummify G-Mamma!' From the sudden blinking of G-Mamma's eyelids, the SPI:KE obviously agreed.

'No, this is so I won't need to mummify her.'

Janey spun around to Gideon. 'Shouldn't we try mouth-to-mouth or something before we go sticking tubes into her?'

'She's been poisoned. We can't risk it being passed on to someone else. Suppose the curare was in her lipstick or something, so that she'd ingest it without knowing?'

It was horrific to think of shoving tubes down G-Mamma's throat. Janey had imagined they'd use the defibrillators or something, not something this invasive.

But the alternative was even more horrific. If G-Mamma didn't get help, she'd die.

And soon.

'Do it,' she whispered to Jack; then she watched bravely, gripping G-Mamma's arm and talking to her the whole time in case she could still hear what was going on, and waiting until Jack nodded to show he'd finished so that she could switch on the machine behind her.

For a moment they all held their breath along with G-Mamma … and then finally the plastic pipe shifted slightly as air was forced down it and into the SPI:KE's lungs. She was breathing again, her abdomen rising up and down as the machine took over her oxygen intake for a little while. Almost immediately, G-Mamma's colour improved, and within a few moments she was able to open her eyes and give Janey a weak thumbs-up.

As one, they laughed and huffed out a great sigh of relief.

'So I suppose that was cool,' said Tilly to Jack, rather reluctantly. 'Though a bit alarming that you know how to mummify people.'

Jack sniffed. 'It's not just people. I can mummify cats, too.'

'Okay, it's alarming that you know how to mummify FULL STOP.'

'It's a bit alarming that you know to hypnotise FULL STOP.'

'I told you, it's not hypnosis, your dogness. It's magic.'

'Well, whatever it is, Matilda Peppercorn, it's freaky, and believe me, I know freaky when I see it.'

G-Mamma's suddenly reached out a finger and prodded Jack in the side with it. It was a definite sign that her breathing was improving – and her hearing.

'I think she wants you to stop arguing,' said Janey with a laugh.

Jack's eyebrows shot up in indignation. 'She started it!'

'All right, children,' said Gideon in his low, calm voice. 'Janey, while these two are sorting out their differences, I'd like to talk to you outside, if I may. I think GM's on the road to recovery now.'

The woman's cheeks were almost back to their usual pink now, so Janey turned to follow him.

'Make sure she's okay, will you?' Jack and Tilly both nodded, even though they were still throwing vicious glances at each other.

Janey gestured to Gideon. 'After you.'

The doors swished open again as they stepped towards them, side by side, and then they were once more out in the corridor. Rather than going back towards the car park as she'd half-expected, however, Gideon turned the other way, passing a few more doors before drawing to a halt beside an office.

It was labelled with a brass plaque bearing the title Chief Executive Officer above the name 'Oscar Sullivan'. Janey remembered it from the newspaper article about the World Community Games.

'Gideon, where are we?' she said, suddenly as alarmed as she was confused. 'What kind of offices have a complete surgery underneath them?'

He stood back so that she could operate the door's keypad with the number she'd memorised from earlier, thanks to her spy training – 0708 151 920 - and waved her in ahead of him.

'Perhaps that will answer your question,' he said, and he pointed to a photograph adorning the wall behind a large mahogany desk that gleamed as if it was shot through with flames, surrounded by several glowing LCD screens and a panel of knobs and buttons.

Janey stared at the picture, instantly recognising the woman they'd met at the party the other night.

'That's Simone Varley,' she said. 'And I've seen those two before – Oscar Sullivan and someone whose name I can't remember.'

'Henry Wentworth.' Gideon's sombre eyes, always so full of the pain of his condition, swivelled to the other man.

The figure was smaller than the other men, just about the same height as the woman. Unlike the others, he was looking off to the left rather than directly at the camera. He was the only one of them who wasn't grinning broadly. In fact, thought Janey, he appeared to be rather uncomfortable.

'That's Trent Varley, Simone's husband. Her dead husband,' Gideon added drily.

'She didn't seem very sad the other night,' Janey observed, 'considering her husband had just died.'

'Exactly what I was thinking.'

Janey, meanwhile, was thinking about something else. 'So hang on – we're in the office of Oscar Sullivan, CEO, and there's a picture with three other people on it, just like in that newspaper article. Is this … is this the head office for HOST?'

For a second, Gideon's eyes cleared, and he glanced at her with a touch of admiration. 'Correct. And to answer your question about what kind of company has a surgery beneath its canteen – well, a dodgy one.'

Janey frowned as Gideon circled the desk. His voice had grown hostile and hard, and she realised once more that she knew very little about their strange client. Was she in danger here?

Her panic increased as she spotted what Gideon was advancing upon.

It was a rifle.

It looked pretty old, and it was mounted on the wall beneath an internal window in a sturdy Perspex case, so he wouldn't be able to do anything to harm her without smashing its box first, but still …

While his back was still turned, Janey quickly assessed the desk. There was nothing on it apart from a cable which would be attached to a laptop, a green desk lamp, a letter in a trembling hand-writing starting 'Oscar, there's something you need to—' that looked as if it had been read quickly and thrust aside, and a jug of water with a paper cup beside it. Silently, she pulled the cable towards her. It was no use on its own, but if anything happened she could possibly drench Gideon Flynn with the jug of water and see if the cable would produce an electrical charge, or perhaps she could use it as a garrotte of some kind …

To her surprise, though, Gideon just dropped down, squatting on his heels, and stared at the rifle with a reverential sigh. 'There you are,' he whispered to it. He almost seemed to have forgotten that Janey was there. 'You shouldn't be imprisoned in there.'

'Gideon, are you okay?'

He sat upright with a start. 'Yes! Yes, quite all right, thank you.'

'For a moment there I thought you were going to shoot me.' Janey laughed, but she could see by Gideon's expression that he knew she was serious.

'Oh, Janey, I couldn't …' The pain in his eyes had returned. 'I understand that you don't know me very well, and I suppose I don't really know you – any of you – other than what I've researched. But please know that I could never shoot you, or hurt you in any way. Not intentionally, anyway,' he said with a sideways glance towards the door.

Janey looked over her shoulder. He'd seen something behind her, she was sure of it.

'Is there someone there?'

Gideon frowned. 'I'm not sure. I'll check in a second. Before I do that, though,' and he dropped his voice to such a tiny whisper that Janey had to lean in close to hear his words, 'I wanted to tell you that this rifle is your next mission.'

Had she heard him correctly? 'My mission?'

'The next heist. It was my great great … great … grandfather's,' he hissed. 'It belongs with my family, not here in this … terrible place. And I can't get it out of this case.'

'Because of your … condition?'

Gideon laughed under his breath. 'No, actually. This time it's not my hands that won't work – it's my brain. There's some kind of code, or a clip to unlatch, or … something that I'm not able to work out. I need your spying abilities to liberate it.'

'You think that I'm some kind of safe cracker?' Janey shook her head, confused again. 'You seem to have a strange idea about what I've done in the past as a spy.'

Gideon's eyes darted over her shoulder again, back towards the corridor. He stood slowly and leaned towards her ear.

'I do know you're not a thief, Jane Blonde,' he whispered, the sound so tiny that she couldn't even feel his breath on her skin. 'But you have an excellent skillset, and more importantly, you know right from wrong. This rifle doesn't belong here. It should be with my family, not with HOST. Please say you'll try.'

Janey's stomach clenched, and it was only partly because she knew she was going to say yes – of course she was, because she couldn't resist a challenge, a new spying mission, even one that felt a little peculiar.

It was his closeness that really unnerved her, however, and those anxious glances towards the door. There was more going on here than Gideon was saying, and she desperately wanted to know what it was. To help him. To help the strangely quiet figure of Gideon Flynn.

'Yes,' she whispered eventually, feeling the dark eyes upon her. 'I'll try.'

Gideon nodded gratefully. 'Thank you. I must go and see what that disturbance was. The offices are still open, after all – anybody could be out there. I'll be back as soon as I can.'

He whisked out of the door before she could say anything.

She hesitated for an instant, wondering whether she should check on G-Mamma and the others, perhaps even ask one of them to help - but something stopped her. She wasn't sure which member of this new team that she'd found herself in would be the most help to her, for a start – or which one would be a strong companion for G-Mamma when she came around fully.

Beyond that, however, was a frisson of excitement that felt like old times. She was on her own again: Jane Blonde, on a secret mission, relying on her spying instincts, her carefully extracted skills and training. And this time it was to help Gideon Flynn, who, she guessed, hadn't been helped in a long, long time …

So without calling for back-up from the others, Janey dropped to her knees in front of the case containing the rifle.

It was a simple enough box, with five sides fashioned from heavy plastic, and the wall into the next office forming its sixth side at the back. Each Perspex edge fitted tightly and seamlessly into a ridged metal strip, rather like double-glazing. The clumsy-looking rifle with a heavy wooden butt and long blackened rod for a muzzle appeared to be mounted directly onto the wall, though Janey couldn't see any visible fixings. Of safe-cracking dials and cogs, there was no sign.

But Janey knew this meant nothing. There were all sorts of tricks for disguising different types of openings. She'd seen many and could usually work out any that she hadn't seen before.

It was time to get to work, Janey thought with a shiver of anticipation. It had been a while, but she slipped into it as easily as the Wower had encased her in her spysuit ...

First of all she lay on the floor and inspected the box from beneath, and then from above. Next, she peered into the Perspex case from either end, searching for any notches or springs that she might be able to trigger to open the case. Nothing. She stared directly into the front of the box, and just to be sure that she hadn't missed anything obvious, she grabbed the desk lamp, flicked it on and ran the light all over the plastic, looking for smudges, chips in the smooth panels, an eyelash … Anything that might indicate how the case opened. There was nothing.

Remembering that she was still wearing what was usually a very useful gadget, Janey pressed every finger of her Girl Gauntlet in turn. If she could freeze and shatter the box, that would make life very simple. Unfortunately, though, it seemed that the Wower had been powered off before it could install all the Gauntlet's functions. A nice duel-nibbed invisible ink pen shot out of her little finger like a pair of ears, and her thumb glowed with a strange light with intricate patterned whorls flashing across it – some kind of device to fake fingerprints, Janey guessed – but the three fingers across the middle didn't so much as twitch, and Janey gave up when she realised that neither of the other two spy-buys in the glove were going to help. Instead, she unscrewed the bulb from the desk lamp, removing it along with the green glass shade before smashing the lampstand against the plastic box. It achieved nothing, apart from leaving a serious dent in the lamp's brass base.

'This is ridiculous,' she muttered, breathing onto the surface in case fingerprints emerged in the mist so that she could at least try to use her new magical thumb. They didn't. There was no sign of a keypad, but she chose a suitable spot in the middle top panel of the case and entered the number they'd used on each of the door entry systems, first in a line as if it were on a computer screen or

QWERTY keyboard, and then in the shape it would form on a phone's keypad. Still nothing. When she'd exhausted all options and any other ideas had disappeared from her brain, Janey placed a hand on either end of the case, planted her feet on the wall beneath it, and pulled as hard as she could possibly pull without bursting an eyeball.

The box didn't even budge. It was as if it was moulded to the very wall itself.

If it was, she would just have to tell Gideon she couldn't retrieve the rifle without her spy-buys - possibly a Boy-Battler glove as she needed a sledgehammer to shatter the case or the wall around it. Just to be sure, however, Janey wanted to try one last thing.

She turned to the desk which seemed to buzz beneath her fingers as she yanked open a drawer. Pens and pencils. They weren't sharp enough. The second drawer yielded better results. Grabbing a long metal paper clip, Janey wrenched it apart with her fingertips to create a barb that could penetrate the angle between the case and the wall. If it really was moulded into the wall, then she wouldn't be able to find a gap. If it wasn't, then a spike might reveal something.

She dragged the prong along the top of the case, directly next to the wall, trying to slice through the paintwork. The clip seemed to leap beneath her fingers, and she wondered for a second if she'd caught it on something – a hinge, perhaps.

'Yes!' she cried, and took hold of the extended paper clip for a second assault … but then the strangest thing happened.

The clip wrenched itself out of her grip, flew towards the case and attached itself resolutely to the metal bar which held the plastic in place.

Janey stared at it for a second, then grabbed another paper clip from the drawer and tossed it towards the case. In exactly the same way, it snapped itself onto the metallic surface as soon as it came even close to being in contact with it.

Janey looked around frantically. Sure enough, there was a noticeboard nearby with flyers and leaflets stuck onto it - not by pins, but by small, round enamel blobs. Grabbing one, Janey eased it close to the metallic strip and opened her palm. It jumped out of her hand, landing on the case edge with a satisfying smack.

'It's magnetised!'

No wonder the rifle didn't appear to be held up by anything. Magnetic forces were pinning it to the wall. If she could find the source of magnetic energy, she could divert it or even remove it, and then the metal framework of the case would simply fall apart.

Janey thrust her ear to the wall. Even without her BATS hearing, she could just about make out an indistinct hum, so low that it was not so much a sound, but more like a vibration that she felt in her chest – and buzzed through the table. It was coming from the next office, and Janey suddenly made sense of the window in the wall above her head. It had appeared to go nowhere, but presumably it looked onto the next room, and the knobs and dials operated something within it.

Dashing to the door, she checked for people in the corridor. Gideon was standing beyond the operating theatre with his back to her; behind him Jack was just emerging from the room, murmuring something to Gideon in a low voice. Just her own team-mates, having a chat – presumably about G-Mamma's improved state.

Well, that was fine. Without further hesitation, Janey raced in the other direction to the next door along the corridor.

The door slid open obediently after she'd punched 0708 151 920 into the entry system, and she slipped into the room on high alert – it was always possible that someone might be in there, hiding.

The room, however, was completely devoid of people. In fact, all it contained was a vast white cylinder that stretched along the centre of the room. It emanated a weak violet light that reflected off irregular patches on the wall. From the middle of the cylinder, a stretcher-type bed covered in surgical paper protruded like a pale, sickly tongue, and some electrical, headache-inducing pulse throbbed rhythmically throughout the entire room.

It was another of those odd rooms that wouldn't usually exist in a head office building. Janey had seen several, and even spy organisations' central offices didn't usually house an advanced hospital wing.

Because she was sure that this was yet more medical equipment. She'd never had cause to go in one, but Janey was fairly certain that this was an MRI machine, used to scan people for whatever might be going on beneath the surface, inside their joints and organs and in the core of their bones.

'Strange,' she whispered as she searched around for the switch to turn it off.

A cable ran to the edge of the room and she followed it to the plug socket, but suddenly she was distracted by the ghostly purple patches spattered across the walls. What did that remind her of?

It was only as she seized the plug and pulled it from the wall that she realised. It was like Gideon's Garbo message, illuminated by the UV light that G-Mamma had created in the Spylab. Fumbling for the piece of kit in her pocket, she shone the blacklight across the walls.

Something had been cleaned off the walls, but the eerie blacklight could still make it out. Slowly, she drew her finger through the nearest patch and held it up to her face. Janey's heart sank. It wasn't invisible ink.

It was blood.

All over the walls.

Stumbling, Janey backed out of the room, only just remembering to close the door behind her, then she ran back to Oscar Sullivan's office with its evil window that overlooked the horrible MRI room.

Her hunch had been correct: now that the magnetic force had completely disappeared, the case pulled easily off the wall. The rifle fell to the floor, for all the world as if it had shot its own way out of its ... what had Gideon called it? Its prison.

What terrible deeds had been carried out with this gun? Janey hardly dared to think. She didn't want to touch it, but she had to decide whether she should trust Gideon Flynn who had urged her to know right from wrong, or the HOST organisation who seemed to be hiding some monstrous secrets in their basement.

Taking off her jumper, she wrapped it carefully around the rifle and then walked, with a heavy knot in her stomach, to join the others.

Chapter 13 – B is for Bad Basement

Jack and Tilly were wheeling G-Mamma towards the theatre door as Janey approached, while Gideon was nowhere to be seen.

'Up and at 'em, Blondette,' said G-Mamma, her voice weak and halting, but nonetheless with some of her usual verve.

Janey raced to her side. 'You're better!'

'It's going to take more than a bit of poison to get rid of me, especially when, at long last, I've stopped being the Bigg Squid and can be the Big G again.' G-Mamma turned her head towards Janey. The mentor's eyes were bloodshot and sore, but they were as wide and blinking as ever, and right now they were focussed on the parcel in Janey's arms. 'A gun might do it, though, if you were planning to finish me off.'

'A gun?' shouted Jack and Tilly together.

'It's an old rifle.' Janey peeked into the corridor, then waved them forward. 'I'll explain later. Where's Gideon?'

There was someone else who could also do some explaining, and not very much later at all. In fact, if she could find him, there were a few questions she would like Gideon Flynn to clear up straight away – like, why was there blood all over the wall of the MRI room, and why was he so interested in this rifle, and just what was the HOST organisation up to in these dark basements that contrasted so starkly with the streamlined glass of the main offices?

Jack swung the gurney out into the corridor, ignoring G-Mamma's outraged squeaking. 'Flynn took off after that man, the one who was lurking outside the operating theatre. He said to meet him by the ambulance.'

'Which we'll have to return to its owners in less than half an hour, before the paramedics come to and wonder why all the doughnuts have gone,' added Tilly, springing along beside the trolley like a spaniel and fronting up to every door they passed like a silvery-blue haired ninja, checking for enemies to fight.

G-Mamma's squeaking became even more outraged. 'You gave them my doughnuts?'

'Erm, in exchange for your life?' Tilly pointed out reasonably. Spotting something in the glass front of one of the offices, she dropped into a defensive position, screaming 'Kai-aiaiaiaiaia!' at the top of her voice. 'Oh!' she said suddenly. 'That man's no danger, with his eyes all bandaged up.'

They all peered in through the glass. A tall, slender man was sitting up in bed, the upper half of his head entirely swathed in bandages. He cocked his head towards the door, calling, 'Sullivan? Is that you? You can't just keep me here. Sullivan!'

Tilly threw open the door. 'Sorry! Not Sully. Tilly!' she yelled across the ward. The man slumped back against the pillows, defeated. 'I'll get someone for you,' she called sweetly.

'The poor man's blind, not deaf! You're very loud,' barked G-Mamma, and Janey almost laughed.

'Takes one to know one,' replied Tilly.

She was right. There were definite similarities between Matilda Peppercorn and her SPI:KE – both self-assured, both larger than life, both ready to take on anything and anyone, and both exceptionally chatty. Janey caught Jack's eye and they both grinned, but deep down she was starting to wonder about Tilly. They were so different that she wasn't sure they'd ever truly get along – and she wasn't entirely sure why she had to in the first place. What was Tilly doing here anyway?

Yet another of those questions that Gideon could answer for her, when they found him again.

'The man Gideon was chasing – was it a security guard?' she asked Jack. They were nearing the car park now, so they needed to be sure the coast was clear before they revealed themselves in the bright subterranean lighting.

Jack shrugged. 'Not sure. I only saw him for a second when I came out to report that G-Mamma's *ba* was firmly back in her body. He clocked Gideon, looked furious and then turned tail and ran. He was heading out here.'

They were in the car park. Half the cars had disappeared as the staff had gone home, and Janey suddenly realised that she had very little idea how long they'd been here. If Tilly had given the paramedics three hours and they had half an hour to get back, it must be about six thirty. With an anxious flutter of her heart, Janey thought of her parents. She hadn't told them she was going out. They'd be getting dinner ready, assuming she was in her room, then discover that she wasn't there and hadn't even left a note. They'd be terrified about what might have happened to her – although perhaps not as terrified as they would have been if they'd still been spies. There was no time to lose – which was ironic, given that they were in the head office of the HOST organisation. What was their motto again? Helping Others Save Time. The only time-saving equipment she knew of was back in the Spylab …

… but then there was also Jack Bootle-Cadogan, who could speed things up rather significantly. And Tilly, who seemed to be able to pause time while she got on with whatever wrong doing she fancied. They could be a very useful team if it suited them.

And right now, it did suit them.

From a dimly lit recess of the car park came the screech of an engine. They all turned together to see a large transit van careering towards them, and before they could register what was going on, a khaki-clad arm appeared from a window, letting loose shot after shot from a gun that certainly wasn't an old rifle, as the gap between them and the van decreased at an alarming pace.

Jack yelped, his dog head popping up almost instantly as he positioned himself between the approaching vehicle and his patient. Janey scanned the exits; they were all blocked by more vans, more guards in khaki uniforms. Tilly's hair was standing on end so crazily that it almost appeared to be radiating blue light. 'They mustn't see me!' she cried, then she dived onto the bottom section of the gurney below G-Mamma.

'Off!' shouted the SPI:KE, and in the same moment she rolled herself sideways and landed solidly on both feet, almost her usual self. She grabbed Tilly's arm, hauled her off the trolley and thrust the girl behind her. 'Blonde, use the gurney.'

Janey had already worked out what she was planning. She nodded immediately.

'The exits are a no-go,' she said quickly, 'so the only way is back down the corridor. You go and find Gideon, and give this to him.' She could try firing the rifle, of course, but she wasn't sure it was in very good shape, or even whether she'd be comfortable using a gun. 'Take the ambulance if you have to. I'll distract the guards. Don't wait for me!'

'Of course we'll wait for you.' Jack was hopping from one enormous foot to the other, very undecided on what to do for the best. 'You can't fight these people on your own!'

The van was barrelling around the nearest corner of the car park, scraping along an entire row of tiny electric two-seater smart cars that were hooked up to their chargers, before wrenching the bumper off an executive-looking BMW. Bullets ricocheted wildly off the concrete pillars.

'Go!' she screamed. 'GM needs help.'

With one last desperate glance, Jack nodded and rushed away, grabbing Tilly and G-Mamma by the shoulder and evaporating them through the wall and back along the corridor.

Wishing she had her spysuit on, Jane Blonde faced the vehicle that screamed directly towards her. She'd have to improvise. The gurney on its own wouldn't do much, but if she could motorise it in some way …

Grabbing two fire extinguishers from either side of the lift, she smacked the button to call the double-sized lift down to the basement. In the same movement, she banged both extinguishers on the floor and leapt onto the gurney. The pressure from the exploding fire equipment was almost uncontrollable, but she managed to hang on as the jet-propelled trolley veered towards the van. It was upon her. She'd crash into it any second! But just as she could clearly see the stunned faces of the driver and passenger of the van, could feel the flare from the muzzle of the revolver as shots were fired, Janey leapt to her feet, spun the fire extinguishers around and sprayed the van's windscreen with cascades of white foam. The two men shouted, their vision completely obliterated and chemical foam spurting through the open windows into their faces – and, Janey hoped, their guns.

As she flung herself from the gurney, the transit van swung sideways and crashed into a skip, ripping the hospital gurney in half and springing the car's alarm so that the noise brought the other guards running.

Janey landed with a crash on the bonnet of the BMW, behind the van and away from the main door to the car park, where the HOST security forces were now gathering. A bolt of pain shot through her arm as she tried to lever herself up, and she fell back again. She'd broken it, or dislocated her shoulder or something, but the means to her escape was not going to hang around for her to investigate it. She could hear it now, trundling to a stop, the lights blinking above it. Around the car park echoed a loud ping, and then the double doors of the lift slid apart.

The lift was twenty metres away, and the guards were only a little further on. In her agonised state, she'd never be able to run across to it before the doors closed again. A shot rang out past her ear and she turned her head to avoid it – and saw her chance.

Letting her spy instincts take over completely, Jane Blonde slid off the side of the BMW, wrenched open the door of the neighbouring Smart car. She smacked what she hoped was some kind of ignition button and slammed her foot on the accelerator, cradling her arm at the same time as waves of pain surged through her. She could hardly steer, but with her left hand she dragged the wheel down as the little car shot forward, tearing itself free of the charger. It hurtled towards the lift, rocking wildly as Janey tried to control the steering one-handed, and then, just as the light above the lift turned red and the doors began to roll back into view, the tiny car powered into the metal cube. Janey hit the brakes and the car practically stood on its nose as the lift doors slid shut behind her and it bounced off the back wall of the lift.

Janey released a breath of relief, even though she knew the fight wasn't over. She might be in the lift, but the car doors were jammed up against the sides – she was trapped in the Smart car, and if the lift didn't move the doors would open again and she'd have to face the whole angry guard mob straight on.

Just as she was searching for a way to operate the sunroof, she heard a noise – that ping again. Someone had called the lift. Immediately the metal box began to shift, and Janey looked around desperately for a way to get out. Otherwise she'd have to reverse out into the corridor in the main offices, and she had no idea who might be waiting for her up there. Even worse, there might be ordinary HOST staff there who could be mown down, injured or worse, by a careering Smart car operated by someone who only had a sketchy idea of how to drive at the best of times.

Then she spotted the illuminated numbers on the lift's panel. G for Ground Floor sat above B for Basement – and indeed, she could see the word 'Reception' beside the G and 'Parking' next to B. Above the G, the numbers 1 to 5 were just about visible – because the illumination of the numbers was going in the other direction.

'I'm going down,' Janey hissed.

She peered more closely at the numbers. There seemed to be just as many floors below the Ground Floor as there were above it, although it appeared from the fact that they glowed a dark and ominous red, unlike the cheery green of the upper floors, that there might be limited access to these floors.

The lift halted at B5. There was no helpful description on the plate beside the light display, and Janey ducked down as the lift doors glided apart in case she'd been set up. When nobody appeared, and before the lift could be called to another part of the building, she reversed the car as gently as she knew how and parked in the corridor. It was tempting to drive the car the full length of the passageway and make her escape that way, but she was fearful of being trapped in it if the corridor narrowed. Wishing she'd kept hold of the rifle, if only for a show of strength, she opened the car door gingerly and stepped out into the passage.

It was even darker than the corridor containing the operating theatre, but Janey could see a faint light from the far end – an exit, hopefully. She set off towards it, trying to jog but feeling the jagged jolts of pain through her arm as her feet hit the floor, so she slowed to a fast walk, taking in her surroundings. The passageway was unlit, but at intervals she could see a dark, blood-red glow oozing out beneath a door. Remembering the walls of the MRI room, she shivered and tried to hurry along.

Then suddenly she heard it – a woman's voice. 'This way! She's trapped down in B5.'

The sound of the HOST henchmen's pounding feet filled Janey's ears. Staggering back towards the car, she thought again about driving along the corridor, but if it truly was a dead end and she was trapped, then she could crash it or get herself completely stuck. She had to hide.

But talking of crashes … Hobbling to the car door and thanking the stars that she'd left the engine running, Janey reached through the door with her good arm and slammed it into DRIVE. The car set off on its own, slowly at first but gathering momentum as it scraped haplessly along the corridor. That should distract them for a moment, at least. Looking around, Janey raced towards the next sliver of light along the corridor, for all the world like a demonic eye peering at her from the floor. She pressed her ear to the door. There was a deep humming sound from within, and for a second her heart thumped again – more MRI machines? But this was different – less like a pulsating beat and more … mechanical. It sounded rather like the Smart car being charged – the car that was currently careering towards a dead end. As it smashed into a wall in the distance, Janey pushed the door open a little, then shoved it open fully.

It was a factory of some kind. Twenty or thirty long cabinets hid some kind of machinery from view, churning away before spitting out their product onto a conveyor belt at the end. The red glow was emanating from these belts, so Janey shut the door as footsteps and the same woman's voice penetrated the air close by, and moved silently to the nearest cabinet. Seeing lights and symbols that she couldn't understand, she stole past it until she was standing beside the vast rotating belt on which something sparkled and gleamed.

The products were something worryingly familiar. The machine, to her astonishment, was churning out rubies – tiny, beautifully formed rubies cut into flat lozenge shapes, not like the stone in the Simone Varley's ring but more like … what was it? Janey stared. They reminded her of something, but she couldn't think what. She certainly couldn't think of any jewellery they'd be used for, unless they were joined together to make a necklace or bracelet.

Further along the conveyor belt, the rubies were tipped onto a tray in neat lines before being swallowed up into a black hole at the belt's end.

Janey was just about to investigate that when her text alert buzzed. 'Where have you gone? We just tried Alfie but you're not there! Dinner went cold an hour ago.'

It was her parents, fretting as she'd known they would. How quickly she'd forgotten, now that she was caught up in an adventure again. She texted back quickly 'Sorry! Needed book from Bree at school. Back in a few!' Then she slid her phone back into her jeans pocket - along with one tiny lozenge-shaped ruby – as she headed back towards the door to make her escape.

But suddenly it banged back on its hinges. Trying not to gasp aloud, Janey flung herself beneath the nearest machine, but it wasn't far enough. Her arm was sticking out, and meanwhile a troop of khaki-clad marines were stomping into the room, pelting towards her. They'd see her any moment, see her stupid arm that acted like it no longer belonged to her, screaming with pain and refusing to bend so that she could drag it back under cover.

And then she remembered. She didn't have to drag it under cover. It was already under cover. Her arm was the most spy-like part of her. She was wearing most of a Girl Gauntlet – and what was it G-Mamma had said? It now had a new feature.

She angled her head towards the gap, spotting a shoe only a few metres away.

'Invisibubble,' she whispered.

Holding her breath, she hoped fervently that this would work better than the rest of the glove … and then she watched as her arm disappeared.

Her heart raced beneath her tee-shirt; she placed her other hand over it, urging it to be quiet as the shoes approached. They weren't steel-toed boots as she'd expected, however. They were women's shoes, with a slight heel and a gently rounded toe in a shade of green of which even G-Mamma might have approved. The left foot was close to her arm – if the woman took too short a step, she'd kick Janey's hand and then it wouldn't matter that it was invisible. Holding her breath to combat the pain, Janey carefully curled her hand into a fist … and the foot touched down, just millimetres from where her fingers had lain, less than a second ago.

The feet stamped by, and then a sharp voice cried, 'She must have got out. I don't know how. Get the car into forensics, and check the load stone.'

Load stone? What was that? The female voice sent such shudders down Janey's spine that she wasn't really sure she wanted to know. It was Simone Varley, she was pretty certain of it, once more sending her security men after her. Which meant one thing for sure: the woman would recognise Janey if she saw her again.

From now on, she'd have to tread very, very carefully.

For the moment, there was nothing she could do but wait for the sound of the car wreckage being removed. At long last the corridor fell silent, and Janey slipped out of the room and ran to where it had crashed. Maybe she could text Jack to come and get her, or something. When she reached the end, however, she discovered that the dull light she'd seen earlier was an exit of sorts – a long steel ladder leading up to a manhole cover, somewhere in the grounds of the HOST offices. Janey clambered up it slowly, trying not to use her injured arm, until she found herself being hauled out by several welcome pairs of hands.

'You shouldn't have waited!' she said sternly, although she was very glad to see G-Mamma, Tilly and Jack.

Tilly laughed. 'Don't worry. We didn't.'

'What she means is,' said Jack, elbowing Tilly in the side, 'is that we powered back to your laboratory, gave the ambulance back to the poor confused paramedics …'

'… and they had eaten all my doughnuts.' G-Mamma glared at the three of them. 'So I put that rifle in the empty box and left Trouble in charge of it.'

'Then we came back for you, in G-Mamma's mad squid van,' finished Tilly.

'It's the Octobus,' said G-Mamma with a sniff. 'Invisibubbled, naturally.'

Janey almost cried with relief. 'Oh, thank goodness! I can use the Wower and fix my arm. Dis-located, I think.'

'Half of it's missing!' cried Jack, turning a little green. 'That's not dislocated. That's … chewed!'

'Oh, I forgot. That's not the injured bit. It's just Invisibubbled.'

'Wower? Octobus? Invisibubbled? muttered Tilly to Jack. 'I don't understand half of what you people say.'

Jack shrugged. 'You'll get used to it. I have. Just about.'

'Yes, but have they got used to you, Jack BC with the ancient head?'

It looked as though another argument was brewing between Tilly and Jack, so Janey interjected instead.

'Where's Gideon?'

'He's minding the mad squid … the Octobus,' said Tilly with a roll of her eyes. 'He wanted to make sure you were okay.'

And Janey was very glad about that – not just because he was concerned enough to wait for her, of course, although she had to admit that she was more pleased about that than she possibly should be, but because she'd now seen and heard so much more than when he took them on.

It was time for Gideon Flynn to start talking.

Chapter 14 – Catty Comments

Gideon appeared to be standing randomly among the low-branched Japanese trees. Only the twin tyre tracks that ended near his feet gave away the presence of the Octobus, and Gideon himself, in his burgundy suit and with his dark hair and eyes, was nearly invisible in the lengthening shadows.

'You made it,' he said as Janey approached with the others. 'Good.' He gestured to the space in which the Octobus stood. 'It looks as if you could do with a Wower.'

'Yes!' cried G-Mamma brightly. 'I don't know if you're Wowing up or down, but if you don't get into the magic gadget soon, your arm might need re-breaking.'

Janey felt faint at the thought of it, so she waited until the van had been de-glamoured of its Invisibubble covering and hauled herself into the back. 'Could you … could you guys wait here?' It was one thing Wowing in a spacious Spylab with other people sitting in the same room; quite another when they would be just the other side of the Wower door.

The rest of the 'team' shuffled uncomfortably, both Jack and Gideon snapping 'Sure!' in a vaguely embarrassed fashion. G-Mamma raised an eyebrow at them, then gave Janey a strange smirk. 'Go make yourself beautiful then,' she said.

'It's not that, it's … never mind.'

This team business is challenging, she thought as the Wower worked its magic on her pulverised shoulder. She wouldn't be throwing any javelins any time soon, but at least it wasn't pure agony to lift her hand to scratch her nose. Trying it out for strength, Janey stared at the silvery-white sleeve which now extended all the way up her arm. The Wower had encased her in full spy regalia, seeing as she'd climbed into it in normal clothes. She sighed. There was no point de-Wowing now – though it might be time for a bit of de-briefing.

She opened the side door to the Octobus's side door and stood back to allow everyone to climb in. With five people lined up among the screens and surveillance equipment it was rather crowded, so after a moment it was agreed that Jack and G-Mamma should get in the front and drive home while the other three discussed matters in the back.

'It was you two I needed to talk to anyway,' Janey explained, although her SPI:KE and canine friend would be able to hear what they were saying. Perhaps with Tilly and Jack separated like naughty kids, they'd be able to get down to business more quickly.

Once again, Gideon shuffled uncomfortably and insisted on standing because of his 'condition'.

Matilda Peppercorn, too, preferred to stand. Whatever Gideon did, she seemed to do it too, thought Janey a little peevishly. It was like they were the original team, and Janey and Jack were bolt-ons.

Tilly caught her eye and grinned. 'I've got broom butt,' she announced.

'You ... What's that?'

'Broom butt, you know, from sitting on the broomstick.' She pointed to the offending area. 'I prefer to stand on it like a skateboard but sometimes it's not practical.'

'Like when you're flying over treetops,' said Janey with a nod.

Tilly winked at her. 'You're catching on. Get it? Cat ... ching on. Cos I'm a cat.'

'Well, actually, that's what I wanted to ask about,' said Janey, glad of the excuse to jump into the questions. She tried sitting down on one of the stools at the surveillance bench, but was suddenly aware that both Gideon and Tilly were looming above her. She stood up again, and they both gazed at her expectantly.

'I ... um ... well, I saw some funny things in that HOST place, and then when you said you couldn't let the guards see you, Tilly, I wondered why. Surely they shouldn't have seen *any* of us? And Mrs Varley had already heard of you when you ...' Janey searched for the right word. Not hypnosis. 'When you magicked the ring off her hand. You have to admit, it's all a bit suspicious, and I think now that the game is hotting up and people are actually shooting at us – well, me, specifically – that we deserve an explanation.' Janey stopped short, feeling very warm around the neck of her spysuit as she realised what a huge speech she'd just delivered. For her, at least.

Tilly glanced at Gideon. He gave her a small, almost imperceptible nod, and she began.

'Well, Jane Blonde, I think there's probably a lot you need to tell me too, you spy girl you, and one day you and I will just hang out like BFFs – although not really as we probably both already have actual BFFs - and then we'll spill ALL the beanios,' she said airily, hardly pausing for breath. Unlike Janey, she was evidently very used to talking. A lot. 'But for now, you said the games were hotting up and that's just about the truth of it. That's why I'm here. For the games.'

'The World Community Games,' Gideon said, in case they'd forgotten. 'It ties in with what you've just seen, Janey.' She glanced at him for a moment. How did he know what she seen? He hadn't been with her at all, while she'd scraped the rifle off the wall by de-commissioning the MRI machine in the blood-spattered room, or when she'd checked out the ruby manufacturing set up in the lower basement. 'I'm guessing, of course,' he said quickly, his familiar tight smile flitting across his face.

'But why?' she said. 'Why is Tilly involved because of the Games?'

Tilly hauled in a great breath for her next instalment. 'Because of my kickboxing,' she said. 'You see, it's really hard to get noticed for kick-boxing and they've only just started covering it as a full sport in competitions like the World Community Games. It's even been hard to get ordinary belts and stuff in kickboxing. It's just not treated like the other martial arts, which makes me incredibly cross!'

'I bet.' Janey imagined that a cross Tilly would be very formidable indeed. 'But I still don't understand how that involves you, Gideon, and …' She tried out the name of Gideon's creation – his team. 'How it involves us. SWAG, I mean. And you shouted, Tilly, that they couldn't see you – but they'd already seen you at that reception party.'

Tilly was obviously preparing herself for another volley of words, but Gideon held up a hand.

'I paid for her,' he said simply. 'I needed an athlete accepted into the games, one who nobody knows or has seen before. If she happens to be a living legend with special powers, well, so much the better for me. Us.'

'Oh, stop it!' cried Tilly, although she sounded as though she was actually quite pleased with the flattery.

Gideon laughed, then turned back to Janey. His penetrating eyes were watchful, searching for her reactions, and once again Janey felt her neck flushing uncomfortably.

'I paid a large amount of sponsorship to the WCG committee to get Tilly admitted as a contestant. That's why she was happy to be seen at the Games Reception – because she'd been invited, although she sneaked in via an open skylight just to suss the place out first. The only other thing they might have suspected was Mrs Varley willingly handing over a ring to her but they didn't, because of her spell. But Tilly definitely couldn't be seen in the basement of the HOST head office, wheeling a body around the car park. They'd smell a rat then, and they would have vetoed her acceptance.'

'You want her to win the Games?' Janey felt her anger rising. 'But that's not even ethical or … or fair. She's magic, and a … a cat, apparently, although we haven't seen that yet. She's bound to be able to win.'

'I do want to win, it's true,' said Tilly with a laugh.

Gideon shook his head slightly and Tilly stood back, but not before Janey's voice had risen another notch.

'Is it to get more money? Is that what we're doing stealing rings and rifles and helping you smuggle a sure-fire winner into the Games? I can't believe we fell for it. Jack!' she cried, pretty certain that the lovely Jack wouldn't have wanted to be involved in cheating at sports. 'Are you hearing this?'

A tousle of fair hair appeared from the front seat. 'Actually I am, and that's really not on,' he said evenly.

But Gideon was shaking his head again, his expression more pinched and pained than ever. 'No, of course not. I don't care if Tilly wins or not – I just needed someone on the inside, going through whatever it is that HOST is planning.' His eyes meet Janey's. 'You know they're up to something. Why else would they have a security detail guarding the basement car park? They shot at you all, Jane Blonde. You know it's not right!'

As Gideon railed at Janey, they all fell silent, only the quiet thrum of the Octobus engine permeating the air. Gideon continued to stare at her, and it was only after she'd managed to calm her temper a little that Janey realised he wasn't *angry* with her. He was deeply, deeply sad – and he was imploring her to believe him. To share this with him. To say what she'd seen.

And the thing was, she knew he was right. She'd known it hours now, or even days.

She had to break the awful silence and put Gideon out of his misery, even if she didn't agree with his methods.

'Something *is* going on in there,' she said. 'Something not right. There was blood all over the wall of one of the rooms on the same corridor as the operating theatre, and on the fifth level down …'

She reached into the pocket of her jeans for the ruby, then stopped when she found her pocket wasn't even there.

She was in her spysuit. Without explaining, she brushed past Tilly to reach the Wower, wrenching open the door.

The stone lay on the floor of the cabinet, now a vibrant blood-red and roughly the size of her thumb. Reaching out her left hand, she'd only just touched it when she noticed that it was pulsing, vibrating gently rather like the MRI machine. 'Ouch!' The sharp edge of the sliced across her thumb, a droplet of blood spilling out onto her skin. Instantly her head spun. It was almost as if the malevolent hum was inside her head, filling her brain with noise and sensations that caused her ears to ring and her vision to blur. She withdrew her bleeding hand instantly and grabbed the stone with her Gauntlet instead.

'They're making these,' she said, holding it out for the others to inspect. 'They're much smaller – the Wower has increased its size, its colour and … well, everything, I think. I didn't know it was buzzing like that.'

Gideon stared at it, repulsed, then he pointed to the open window beside G-Mamma. 'Get rid of it,' he spat.

'But it's beautiful!' cried Tilly. 'Like the ring.'

'It's vile.' Gideon could hardly bear to look at it. 'Please, Janey. Throw it out. Besides, we don't want them to know we've got it. Not yet anyway.'

Janey frowned. 'But there were hundreds of them. They won't miss one. We could take it to the Spylab and test it—'

'No!' Gideon's retort echoed around the van. 'We'll be able to inspect them soon enough, but that one has had its powers increased by the Wower, and we don't know how much and what it can do. It could have a trace on it. It has to go! Just ... do as I say.'

The bitter silence multiplied a hundredfold as Gideon rapped out his order. Janey swallowed, her cheeks flaming. How could he talk to her like that? How could anyone talk to ... well, anyone like that?

But then she looked at Gideon's face and saw the horror upon it, and suddenly worked something out. Whatever harm this stone could do was nothing compared to whatever had happened to Gideon. 'Did it ... did you get your condition because of a stone like this?'

'More or less,' he replied, calmer now.

Not saying another word, Janey simply trained her Ultra-Gogs on the crack in the window to work out the exact trajectory to get the stone as far from them as possible, then flung it out of the van. It glanced off G-Mamma's neck, causing a round of violent rapping before it flew like a missile between the top of the open window and the frame of the car, and was gone.

As soon as it had disappeared, the atmosphere inside the Octobus cleared slightly, but Janey still felt shaky, somehow, and she finally allowed herself to sink onto one of the stools.

'Thank you,' said Gideon, so quietly that she suspected she was the only one who'd heard it. They'd all heard him yell at her as if he was a prefect and she was some lowly year seven, but not that he'd thanked her for it.

And they definitely didn't hear him as he mouthed, directly at her: 'Sorry.'

She nodded to reassure him that it was okay - and somewhere deep in her being she knew that it probably would be - but right now she was angry with him, possibly angrier than she had ever been in her life. He might have persuaded her to get rid of the stone, and she certainly felt massive sympathy for anyone who had obviously suffered as much as he had, but it was going to take a very, very long time – and a whole lot more positive evidence – before Jane Blonde would trust Gideon Flynn again.

'We're at your home,' called Jack from the cabin. 'Need a lift inside?'

'No thanks, Jack. I'll de-wow, grab a book that I've supposedly been out to get, and then go and pretend to my parents that everything's normal.'

'And I,' said G-Mamma, rubbing her neck, 'am ordering at least three takeaways and testing that evil ring, once I've made sure that the flying ruby didn't slice through my jugular.'

Jack laughed. 'Well, I feel like a run, if that's okay?'

He addressed this to Gideon. Janey almost yelled out that they didn't need permission from Flynn, any of them, but Gideon just smiled sadly at Jack, then nodded.

'If you're running, Dogboy, then I'm racing you. It will be good training for the Games,' said Tilly.

'You'll never catch me with those little legs,' said Jack kindly.

'Hey! They may be short but they're mighty powerful. And anyway, I won't be using these legs.'

Tilly stretched up to her full, not terribly great height, and arched her back. 'Here we go,' she cried, and then Janey and Gideon watched in awe as she changed before their eyes into a large brown cat with leopard-like markings on its pelt. Winking a distinctive amber eye, Matilda Peppercorn bounded smoothly out of the van window and waited for Jack to follow.

If she hadn't been in such a bad mood, that was a race that Janey might even have enjoyed.

'How about you?' she said stiffly to Gideon Flynn.

He shrugged. 'I've got some … research to do in about an hour's time. I might just stay in here in the meantime, if that's all right with you, GM?'

'Fine by me.' G-Mamma was obviously already thinking about crispy duck and green beans. 'You paid for the Octobus anyway! Only right that you should get to use it.'

Janey almost scowled. He'd paid for the spy upgrades, and Jack's castle upkeep, and Tilly's entry into the games. What else did he think he could buy his way into?

Maybe that was the research he was doing – in their spy van.

So perhaps she should do some research of her own – like, where was he getting all the money to shell out for gadgets and games admittance?

'Bye then,' she said to Flynn, not sure why she was so torn between feeling pity for him at the same time as being volcanically furious.

He regarded her warily. 'Good night, Janey.'

Oh, it will be, she told herself. It really will.

An hour later, with her parents placated by the sight of a hastily grabbed textbook that she *insisted* on reading in her room, Janey slipped back through the fireplace into the Spylab under the pretence of checking on G-Mamma. No – not a pretence, she reminded herself. Of course she was concerned about her. She genuinely wanted to check that the Big G had fully recovered.

It certainly looked as though she had. The SPI:KE was surrounded by takeaway trays, littered among several hard, crusty ends of spring rolls which Trouble was eyeing up hopefully.

'Are you feeling okay now?'

'Yup. Much better now I'm breathing. I like breathing, I've decided.' G-Mamma looked her up and down. 'Have you come to de-Wow, Blondalicious?'

Janey puffed out her cheeks. 'Oh, actually, I thought I might just check … you know, on Gideon.'

'Did you now?' said her SPI:KE in that strange tone of voice again. 'Well, I'm sure our patron can manage on his own.'

She had to come clean. 'Okay, G-Mamma, I mean that I want to follow him. He's only telling us part of the truth, I know it, and besides, he was so … so rude! I don't trust him, and I'm just tuning in to my spy instincts like you always said I should.'

G-Mamma nodded. 'Following your gut?'

'Exactly,' said Janey.

'Feeling a little peculiar, is it? Your gut, I mean.'

'No, just …' Actually it was, but she wasn't about to tell her mentor that. It was as though her spy instincts were on fire, working overtime; if G-Mamma knew that, she'd suspect Janey was in danger and not let her go after Gideon. Or … maybe she *was* in danger! Perhaps her spy instincts – her gut – had been compromised. Maybe she'd been poisoned too – by the super-sized ruby. It had certainly made her feel strange.

'I just think I ought to find out what he's up to,' she spluttered, aware that G-Mamma was patiently waiting for an answer, with her arms crossed and her eyebrows meeting her hairline. 'And you … you should investigate where that poison came from! It must be the ring.'

'Actually that's exactly what I should do, Blondette,' said G-Mamma. 'Where did you put it?'

She'd been distracted, to Janey's relief. It wasn't that she didn't want G-Mamma with her on this particular part of the mission - it was just that she moved faster and operated better on her own. Sometimes. Whisking the Invisibubble covering from the cake tin with the ring in it,

Janey grabbed a cold spring roll and headed down the SPIral staircase.

As she stepped out into the moonlight, Janey remembered something about her newly refreshed spy-suit. Like the Girl Gauntlet, it contained Invisibubble technology – but she didn't know where or how it worked.

'Invisibubble switch,' she hissed to her Ultra-Gogs, and instantly a diagram popped up on the mini screen before her eyes.

In reality, it wasn't a switch - it was the label in the back of the neat neckline of her suit. She reached over her head and pulled it up and over her shoulder like the ripcord on a parachute, then watched as her shoulders, arms, stomach, thighs, knees, ankles and finally her feet disappeared from sight. Her head could be seen, but she was still holding the Invisibubble napkin with which she'd hidden the ruby ring. She draped it over her head, tucking it into the collar of her suit along with her ponytail, and checked in G-Mamma's front window. She had no reflection at all.

'Like a blood-sucking vampire,' she told herself.

But the only blood she was worried about was the stuff sprayed around the HOST office. And the blood that had thumped in her ears and trickled down her thumb when she'd held the massive gemstone in her palm . There was a whole lot of mystery needing further investigation. Time to get going.

As she turned around and strode across to the Octobus, wondering how to get into it without Gideon noticing, she suddenly spotted him. He was walking away from the van, sticking to the edges of the pavements where the streetlights wouldn't give his presence away. Janey trailed him at a safe distance. Even though he wouldn't be able to see her, she didn't want him to hear her footfall.

After a mile or so she realised where he was going. As she had done herself on many occasions, and once or twice in a very spectacular fashion on a SPIcycle, he was taking the Tube. It was late; the barriers were open and unattended, so he breezed through the gates and made his way down the stairs to the District Line. Feeling bad for not buying a ticket, Janey hesitated at the barriers – but then recalled that she'd spent the day stealing rubies and avoiding evils with guns. Was one train ticket going to make a difference? Besides, nobody could see her.

It was as if she wasn't really there.

She crept down the stairs behind Gideon, then perched on a different bench to await the train's arrival. He let the first one go by, perhaps because it was destined for Ealing Broadway, and then drifted onto the second train bound for Richmond. He moved with his head down, eyes cast towards the floor, as sad and quiet as Janey had ever seen him, making eye contact with nobody and avoiding the seats and rails because of the painful condition that made physical contact so sore. Instead, he remained in the doorway, swaying gently.

Through the next set of doors, Janey slipped, undetected, onto the same train.

They alighted, separately, at the Richmond terminus, whereupon Gideon started walking again, tucking his head into the unusually rounded collar of his shirt and giving any people he passed a very wide berth. It was as if he was ashamed, Janey thought – as if he felt they would stare at him with his illness on view for all to see, like some kind of deformity. For a moment she wanted to run up to him and tell him that nobody saw him like that. He was just pale and tired-looking, that was all, and there were plenty of people around them who were the same – Alfie, for instance, and Janey herself sometimes. Before she could decide to give up her disguise and offer her kind words, he turned a corner, stepped sideways through some tall iron gates, and disappeared into the blackness.

She'd lost him! Janey took to her heels, kicking the Fleet-Feet into action and surging onwards towards the gates. She could see he wasn't directly behind them, and with her Invisibubble outfit he wouldn't be able to see her anyway, so she took a risk and slammed down onto her soles. The spring action of the Feet didn't get her completely across the gates, but she landed near the top, hung on with both hands and swung herself over, landing neatly and silently on the tarmac with her toes together and her arms out to balance herself. See, she thought, I'm like a gymnast. It could have been Janey herself in the World Community Games – although she would have to compete in her spy-suit …

Suddenly she spied him ahead of her, striding through the trees past startled deer and the occasional indignant-sounding owl. They appeared to be in some kind of gardens, although it was slightly wilder and certainly a lot larger.

'Where am I?' she asked her Gogs under her breath, and the answer came up immediately. 'Ah. *Richmond Park*,' she read. '*The largest of London's eight Royal Parks and the biggest enclosed space in London.* Interesting. Thank you!'

Gideon was speeding up now, hurrying through the trees as a nearby church clock chimed eleven thirty. Janey closed the gap between them, afraid he'd whisk out of sight as once more he stepped sideways through a set of gates that Janey vaulted, this time in one smooth leap.

They were in a different part of town, with smaller terraced houses – cottages, almost – that edged the Thames. Finally, Gideon began to slow. The houses had almost petered out and they were reaching the end of the terrace. Light shone from a low window in the last house, shifting in the darkness – someone watching TV, Janey guessed. Beyond the house there appeared to be a small park, and other adjoining terraced houses set out around a small triangular green. It was almost like a tiny version of the grander gardens they'd seen at Simone Varley's house.

She drew to a halt suddenly. Gideon had stopped. Standing before the blinking window with the flickering shafts of light, he stuffed his hands further into his pockets and peered inside. Janey edged closer so that she could see past him.

He was staring intently at an elderly couple who leaned against each other, side by side on a neat sofa. The old gentleman was probably in his nineties, and Janey could see that he was actually nodding off, although he would wake with a start occasionally and pretend he'd been concentrating on the screen. Beside him, the elderly lady completed her crossword, took off her glasses and laid her head on her husband's shoulder. Together, they continued to watch the TV, although Janey was sure that neither of them was far from sleep.

As she hung back near the hedge, a familiar face was projected onto the window pane as Simone Varley and her fellow HOST executive told the world about the upcoming World Community Games. Mrs Varley's face was wreathed with smiles and solicitous concern, but Janey knew better than to trust them. So far the woman had owned a dangerous ring, told her henchmen to shoot at them all, and ordered her destruction in a mysterious basement – for Janey was convinced that the voice and the green shoes had belonged to Varley. As for the man, Janey recognised him from two photographs she'd now seen of him: it was Henry Wentworth, a handsome man in his fifties or sixties who grinned too often and too broadly for comfort.

Janey zoomed in quickly.

'… a global first,' the woman was saying. 'Through the power of technology we will be able to – ahem - *host* every event, from skiing to tennis or curling on ice to beach volleyball, with all events occurring concurrently over just three days. Athletes will be convening in a tiny handful of locations around the world tomorrow, and the viewer will never have had so much choice. They'll be able to watch multiple sports at the same time. They'll be able to attend "live" via fan-led forums on a scale such as you've never before seen, and the piece de resistance … every single athlete will have fan-cam capabilities so you can join in the match, run the race, play the game along with them, from the athlete's perspective.'

'This is state-of-the-art technology.' The interviewer cocked his head. 'Are these athletes the first to try it?'

'Of course not.' Simone Varley's response seemed a little snappy. 'As all great inventors do, we tried it on our own people first.'

'Your own people? So are you saying—'

'And let's not forget, Simone,' Henry Wentworth interjected smoothly, his toothy smile encompassing the woman, the journalist and the camera alike, 'you can even sponsor your favourite athlete as you watch. Many of them are not professionals and need funding to continue towards their dream. So Andrew, it's a truly mind-blowing, multi-sharing, viewer-centric experience.'

'Which brings us,' said Andrew casually, 'to the athletes we won't be seeing – Vance Kettering, and now Olympian diver, Karen Fallows, who dropped out with crippling migraines just this morning, citing HOST as the cause.'

Wentworth wrinkled his brow thoughtfully. 'It's a very sad state of affairs, Andrew,' he crooned, 'when people who've served their country well don't just retire gracefully, but rather insist on blaming others for the end of their career. Everyone knows how much your head hurts when you hit the water. That's obviously the cause of her migraines. Nonetheless, we are having Fallows tested in our own top-class facility with the very latest in medical technology.' He grinned again, directly at the camera. 'We promise not to live-stream that though, Andrew, as we will with forty plus different events shown simultaneously and then sequentially from the Games.'

'Extraordinary – and just thirty-six hours to go until this all begins in …' Andrew the journalist laughed. 'Well, it doesn't matter where, viewers, because it's all in your own hands!'

The camera panned out to show a vast arena, decorated with HOST material with the now familiar logo of a bejewelled 'O' in the centre of the company's name, and bristling with satellite equipment and antennae. Men and women of all shapes, sizes and nationalities were warming up, practicing with or against each other, or simply gazing into space as they reached for the Zen-like state they needed to hone their physical performance.

In the darkness outside their window, Gideon watched the old people watching TV, apparently not interested in the information about the Games despite being so desperate to get Tilly involved in them. He didn't move or attempt to knock on the door. In fact, the couple would have had no way to know that he was there at all. In the beams of light dancing through the low window, Janey could see that Gideon Flynn's weary eyes were heavy with tears.

He stayed in his covert position, his head scrunched down into his neck, his eyes more pained than ever before until they finally switched off the television set and the lights and went to bed. Then he turned away and walked to the triangular patch of grass, staring at the ground, once more alone in the shadows.

Janey watched him until she felt like the worst kind of spy – more like a sneak. It was too late now to reveal herself to him. He'd know that she'd been there for ages, and she wouldn't be able to explain why in any satisfactory way. She wondered now if she understood a little more – were these his great (or however many greats it had been) grandparents, from whom the rifle had been stolen? Or perhaps his condition meant he couldn't go near his relatives as they were so elderly and frail and it might be fatal for them if they caught it. Maybe that was why he gazed at them with such intense sadness.

Whatever the reason, she knew that this was a part of the mission from which they were excluded. This was private. She'd overstepped the mark, and she wanted no more of this overwhelming sense of despair.

In fact, like Tilly and Jack, suddenly she wanted to run. Disguised by her spysuit, Janey set up the directions on her Ultra-Gogs, and raced, fleet of foot, across the city and back towards her home.

All at once, she couldn't imagine anywhere that she'd rather be.

Knowing someone was there from the moment he arrived at the house, he'd adapted his actions accordingly.

His sense was that whoever it was posed no kind of threat. They appeared to be just watching him. Which meant that he couldn't suddenly leave when he'd obviously come all this way to achieve something – and anyway, it was his gift to himself, standing in the garden like this, feeling so close. He'd continued to wait there for so long that he'd almost forgotten the presence of the second person standing just metres away.

But then the Games were projected onto the window, right before his eyes, and once again he curbed his reactions. He could have no reaction, in fact. Whoever it was could have no knowledge of the way the news item disturbed him. Actually, worried him to the core. They might be a HOST member, somehow able to keep tabs on him, like the one he thought he'd seen at the offices the other day. He'd given chase, but the figure disappeared before he could catch up.

So despite the sense of panic filling his chest as the news report continued and the double act of Varley and Wentworth shamelessly plugged the games and their own technology (and what a joke that was), Gideon Flynn simply trained his eyes on the elderly pair through the window — the impossibly elderly couple - never letting his gaze even flicker to the TV screen.

But just because he wasn't staring at the screen didn't mean he couldn't hear it. He heard all of it. Heard what they were saying and understood it more than anyone else could possibly know.

Which was only natural, when he was the one who had discovered what the ruby could do. He was the one who'd tested and experimented and played until he uncovered the stone's amazing wave-transmitting properties, from short UV waves that could read invisible ink, to the long infra-red rays used for lasers and masers. Then, like the prized fool he was, so proud of his own *cleverness, he'd invented a way to create more, finding the means to mix $AI^2 O^3$ with $Cr^2 O^3$, creating fake rubies like the Geneva stone in the birthday ring. Loving the science and the numbers. Always loving the numbers.*

And now they were mass-producing rubies in that crypt beneath the HOST offices and it was his fault. Someone had died while testing the new batch – because he was now pretty sure that this was the reason for the twitching eyes, the jerking body. That was his fault too. What was about to happen – it was his fault. He had to stop it. Poisonous anger surged through him, just as it had for all this time. All this time that he'd spent researching, learning, finding solutions. They must pay for what they'd done. He'd waited long enough.

So that meant hiding his emotional response to the news piece from whoever was observing him. He held on fast to his neutral stance, although he was fairly sure his eyes filled up from time to time. Then, when they went to bed, he turned the other way and marched off across the green, making for the trees which always made him feel wholesome again, somehow, strenuously hoping that the other person in the garden wouldn't follow this time.

They didn't, so when he'd walked far enough away, Flynn chanced a quick look over his shoulder. At first he saw nothing, but then, reflected in a shaft of moonlight, he caught a momentary glimpse of two silvery-white soles as the observer ran off in the opposite direction.

So that was it. Blonde was his pursuer.

His heart felt heavier than ever as he stared at his useless hands. His useless, pointless hands that just wouldn't comply, couldn't contribute to what his mind could imagine.

Yes. He really had to stop it. It was time.

Chapter 16 – Ring, Rifle, Rock

Just to avoid suspicions, and also to give herself the chance to process what she had seen the night before, Janey tried to keep her day as straightforward as possible. As she had de-Wowed in the Octobus before bed the previous night, she was completely ready to go down for breakfast in her dressing gown and assure her parents that she really didn't hate them (as they worried why she was spending so much time in her room) and that she was just studying hard for exams. They seemed to buy it, fussing around each other making sandwiches and tea like they were going out of fashion. Janey watched them fondly, remembering Gideon's expression as he'd surveyed the scene before him. She'd never really known her own grandparents, let alone any other kind of 'greats', but his face had shown what she imagined she would feel if she did.

With a sigh, she pushed away her muesli and packed her bag for school, wishing once more that she could share at least a tiny bit of this with Alfie. If only it wouldn't blow his mind, she thought. He'd probably be very concerned about her mental health and have serious chats with his parents and then her own. She wondered about confiding with Jack instead. He was certainly very sweet, and from what she'd observed he'd witnessed about as much craziness as she had, if not more. But he wasn't a spy, and that was the language she spoke.

As for Matilda Peppercorn – well, Janey still wasn't sure. She found the other girl overwhelming at times, and somehow Tilly's overt confidence made her own shrivel into nothingness. There was the disconcerting way she just kept on turning up, everywhere and anywhere, whether she'd been invited or not. And if Janey was completely honest, she was uncomfortable with how easily Tilly got along with the guys. The others. She couldn't imagine teasing Jack or bantering with Gideon the way Tilly did. Sometimes she felt as though she could hardly get a sentence out in front of Gideon – maybe because he was older, and so … observant.

It was a very good job, she decided, that there was still one person who always understood her – sometimes when she didn't even understand herself. So much for keeping the day straightforward. Now that the Spylab was open for business again, Janey couldn't keep away …

There were only a few minutes to go before she had to leave for the bus, but Janey figured it would be just enough time to see if G-Mamma had any updates. She dressed quickly and shimmied beneath the mantelpiece into the tunnel. 'It's only me,' she called breathlessly, brushing down her school skirt.

'It's only me too!' cried a chirpy voice – but not the one she was expecting. 'Me, Matilda Peppercorn.'

Janey looked around, but there was no sign of the blue-and-silver crest of hair that usually heralded Tilly's presence. Trouble, however, had discovered a friend. Two cats were perched on top of the spy-buy cabinets, out of reach and ready to cause mayhem. Trouble had even Wowed into his uber-cat form, with a gigantic bushy tail and a golden go-faster stripe down the length of his body. The other cat was fluffy and beige.

'Tilly, is that you?' Janey shielded her eyes against the glare of two sets of eyes like laser beams. 'I thought you were a leopard cat.'

'Bengal, not leopard,' the fluffy cat said quite clearly, before explaining, 'only not all the time. Right now … well, not sure what I am. Persian, maybe? I was trying to match the Fluff Fiend here.'

She leapt down onto a bench, her body morphing into Tilly's sturdy frame as she coiled downwards. The girl strutted up and down the bench. 'Look! I'm on a catwalk,' she said, striking a pose at the end. 'Like a model. See? Which is funny, because—'

'You're a cat,' said Janey.

'No, well, yes.' Matilda Peppercorn pointed to her own crazy head. 'But I meant it's funny because I'd be probably the worst model ever! I've got blue-grey hair like an old lady, and stocky thighs from kickboxing. I'm like a short, female footballer.'

Janey couldn't help smiling. 'And then there's the broom butt,' she reminded her.

'Don't even mention the broom butt.' Tilly tried to turn around to inspect her own behind, but gave up after a moment and plonked herself down on the benchtop. 'Off to school?'

'Yes,' said Janey, although suddenly she wasn't so sure. Why was Tilly here? And where was G-Mamma? 'What about you?'

Drawing in the great gulp of breath that indicated a long speech was about to pour out of her, Tilly began. 'No, I'm not on the way to school today, although I usually would be. Sometimes I have normal school and sometimes I go to … well, a special place for kickboxing and stuff. I thought that was where I was going today, but then I got a message from Gideon Flynn and it turns out I have to go and be an athleticy person today. In Kazakhstan.'

'Where?'

'That's exactly and totally what I said. It's right in the middle of central Asia, apparently, with China on side and Russia above it and Europe sort of to the left, especially Eastern European places like Romania. The Big G – does she really want us to call her that? – well, the Big G has been explaining it all to me. She's coming too.'

'To … to Kazakhstan?' said Janey, experiencing a small chill of alarm as she thought of G-Mamma disappearing across the world with Matilda Peppercorn. She wanted to pretend that it was strictly professional because she still had her suspicions about Tilly – which she did – but in reality, she couldn't help recognising that she was probably just a tiny bit jealous.

Tilly held up her hands. 'I know! I wasn't expecting it either, but the Games start later today so I've got to be there, obviously, and the Big G is masquerading as my coach as I'm under-age and I can't just turn up on my own. As if I couldn't handle a bunch of lightweight gymnasts on my lonesome! Anyway, them's the rules. She's just getting ready now,' Tilly said, jerking a finger towards the Wower.

Before Janey could approach the spy shower, however, there was a curious rumbling sound from the downstairs hallway and then Jack Bootle-Cadogan's black, hairy head emerged through the door. He withdrew it, opened the door properly and entered with his teenage boy hair in place.

'Have I missed anything? I got here as soon as I could,' he said cheerfully, folding himself onto the opposite end of the bench from Tilly.

The Spylab was starting to feel very crowded.

'Don't you have school either?' she asked Jack.

He wrinkled his nose. 'Hm. Don't know what you call it. Compassionate leave, or something like that? I'll go back in a couple of weeks, if I can't get my own thing set up at home.'

'Where's that, super-posh boarding school?' said Tilly.

'Nope. Ordinary neighbourhood school. I tried Eton for a while but it wasn't me.'

'But you're all posh.'

'I'm also all ordinary.'

'You're a dog and, err, a god; I don't think that's ordinary.'

What was it with these two? Janey steered them back towards the more important matter.

'Jack, why are you here?'

'Oh!' He stopped glaring at Tilly. 'Gideon told me to come here. According to his message we're going somewhere. I want to say … Afghanistan?'

'Are you sure? You're not a contestant. What kind of message?' said Tilly, looking a little put out that her starring role in the Games was turning into a group activity.

'Just a …' Jack squirmed uncomfortably. 'Just a message. Like you.'

'Okay. Mine – which specifically said I had to do some superbly excellent kick-boxing at the World Community Games - came via a small warlock named

Horace,' said Matilda Peppercorn. Janey wondered once again about where Tilly lived. 'Did Horace visit you?'

She obviously knew that he hadn't, as Jack started to wriggle even more. 'No, not Horace,' he mumbled.

'Come on, Jack BC.' Tilly folded her arms belligerently. 'Now I'm intrigued. I get my messages by magic and stuff. Jane the Blonde, I'm guessing yours come by some spy-type means, yes?'

Janey nodded. 'Yes, actually. Via the Wower, or through Secret Service invisible ink. Even codes and encryptions.'

She hadn't thought about it before now. It had never occurred to her that Gideon didn't inform them all about their missions – or heists – in the same way. Now she was as curious as Tilly.

'Go on, Jack,' she said gently, in the calm way she knew he responded to. 'Tell us how Gideon contacts you.'

Then Jack jumped off the bench, glowering at each of them in turn. 'He sent a dead person, okay? A spirit. Someone's ba.'

Oh no. 'It wasn't G-Mamma's, was it?'

'No. Her ba's all safely locked up back in her body. It was actually Percy. He used to be a gardener at Lowmount. About a century ago,' he added under his breath.

'You reckon you go to an ordinary school?' Tilly shook her head slowly. 'You are so not ordinary.'

'Well, as far as I know, they don't have schools for dead people and their ba processors!'

'I think,' said Janey carefully, stepping between them before a full-blown row broke out, 'that we're all missing the point here. The real question is …' She paused, wondering how phrase it without being insulting to their paymaster. 'I guess it's this: who is Gideon Flynn? How does a teenaged boy who's not much older than any of us have enough money to pay for everything he does, and the means to contact Tilly by magic, and Jack through dead people, and me and G-Mamma in codes and puzzles?'

The others stopped short, gazing at her. Then Jack nodded. 'Actually, you're right. In fact, I didn't get any messages to begin with. They all came through you, Janey.'

'Tilly, when did you first hear from him?'

She scrunched up her face, thinking about it carefully. 'Just before that party,' she said eventually. 'Yes. I got a phone call telling me about the Games, and then I met him in that park we all went into, while he explained that he knew all about me. It was a bit of relief to hear that, to be honest. The whole of witchkind knows about me, but not many humans.'

'Aren't you a human?' said Jack nervously.

Tilly shrugged. 'Mostly. Like I said. Like you.'

'That's true as well.' Janey's senses were prickling beneath her skin. 'In fact, the only ones who are completely human are me and G-Mamma. So how does he do that? I mean, what do we actually know about him?'

The three of them were all staring at each other, trying to figure out anything that they genuinely knew for sure about Gideon Flynn, when G-Mamma emerged from the Wower.

She was definitely prepared for coaching. Decked out in head-to-toe lime green polyester, she wore a tracksuit with go-faster stripes to rival Trouble's circling her body at intervals; orange trainers which Janey guessed were actually Fleet-Feet; a baseball cap that she wore backwords to keep her Nordic plaits out of the way, and finally, around her neck, a whistle the size of a coconut that could kill someone with a single swipe. Which was probably the intention. She looked like a gangsta rapper who was once a Russian gymnast – which again, was probably the intention.

'Having a little conflab here, are we?' she said, closing Jack's jaw which had dropped open at the sight of her. She picked up a bag of sports equipment (and possibly a few spy-buys). 'Only we're on a deadline.'

Janey glanced at her watch. She had about four minutes before she needed to say goodbye to her folks and skip off for the ordinary school bus to her distinctly ordinary school. 'We've just been talking about Gideon and how little we know about him,' she told her SPI:KE.

'Did you find out anything more last night?' said G-Mamma with a wink.

Janey felt herself blushing to the roots of her hair as Jack and Tilly both turned their heads towards her with interest. 'No. Nothing really. But ... but what we've discovered today is that he contacts us all in different ways – ways that most people could never access, like *dead* people for Jack. And we know nothing about him, really.'

'You do have a point, Girly-Girls and Boysy Boy.' G-Mamma paced the room, thinking. 'So he's gathered us all up, sent us all messages in scary freaky ways, and also tried to poison me.' She nodded when they all stared at her. 'Yep. The ring was the source of the poison.'

'That could have been me!' cried Tilly. 'Not that poisoned you, obviously. The one that got poisoned, I mean.'

'You didn't wear it, though. It was probably injected through the bottom of the stone. G-Mamma, you had a long scratch on your finger.' Janey paced the other side of the bench from G-Mamma so that they moved along the room together. 'So we don't know who that ring was intended for, or why it didn't affect Mrs Varley.'

Tilly jumped up. 'She was wearing super-thin latex gloves, I bet that's why – probably because of all those germy hands she had to shake.'

'How did you get your message this morning, GM?' asked Jack, his eyes casting around her body as if he was expecting her ba to clamber out of it at any second.

'Encrypted email.' The SPI:KE opened up her laptop. 'Accompany Tilly to Kazakhstan for the World Community Games. Once cleared, divert to Transnordia and acquire the Rock.'

'That's the same message I received by Percy-gram,' said Jack.

They were all staring at each other, intrigued, but Janey could feel her anger rising. Suddenly she was outraged again. 'And … and I was just supposed to go to school, while you go to Central Asia and wherever Transnordia is, and Tilly's entered in the most important Games the world has ever known?'

G-Mamma peered at the message. 'It doesn't say that you *shouldn't* come, Blonde and Brainy Janey Zaney,' she said at length, but Janey could tell she was trying to pacify her.

'Gideon Flynn,' she said venomously, 'can tell us in whatever way he likes to do whatever he wants, but there is no way on this planet – on several planets, actually, because I've been to more than one! – that he is sending anyone on a mission or a heist or whatever he calls it, without me being there. No way at all.'

Janey stared the other three down, daring them to say anything. When they all simply nodded, she said, 'Give me five minutes.' Then she raced back through to her own house, rushed off for the bus as she always did, told Alfie she was horribly ill and would have to go home, then rounded back on herself and re-entered the spy-lab by way of G-Mamma's front door.

For a moment she thought the room was empty, and she almost cried with frustration. Even Trouble had disappeared. They'd gone without her. 'What is going on?' she screamed, even if nobody was there to hear it.

'The ladies have gone on ahead,' said a muffled voice.

Jack's ebony, dog-eared head shot into view at ground level from behind the furthest bench, and Janey rushed round to see what had happened to the rest of him. He was standing on a narrow ledge that surrounded a meter-wide crater in the Spylab floor. So deep and dark was it that Janey couldn't even see the bottom. Her heart leapt; this indicated some form of travel by spy-buy. She just knew it.

'GM thought there probably was some cause for concern about Gideon,' Jack explained. 'She's taking Tilly to the Games in Kazakhstan as ordered, and then she's going to double back and keep tabs on Gideon. You and I are going to Transnordia to get this rock he's after.' Holding up a scrap of paper, Jack grinned cheerfully. 'These are the coordinates, and although I offered to whoosh us, it seems we'll take less time and be at less risk if we shoot through this hole practically through the centre of the earth.'

'ESPIdrilles,' whispered Janey, remembering the last time she'd travelled this way.

'No, an upgrade, apparently. GM had her Chinese takeaway on it the other night – I think they call it a Lazy Susan?' The object was a round wooden platform positioned on a smaller wooden disk, rather like a spinning breadboard. 'But this one's not lazy at all. She called it a Lazy Spisan.' Jack shrugged helplessly, still unfamiliar with the inexplicable ways of G-Mamma.

'She would,' said Janey with a laugh. 'Right, let me Wow up and we'll get going.'

In mere moments, attired in her spysuit, she was back at the edge of the hole the floor where Jack waited patiently with the Lazy SPIsan clutched under his arm like a vast Frisbee.

'You punch the coordinates in the bottom,' he explained, 'and then we both have to stand on it.'

'Back to back?'

Jack shrugged. 'Depends how much mud you want in your face.'

But Janey had done this kind of thing before, and although some of G-Mamma's gear could be at the prototype stage, she guessed that this wouldn't cause too much mess. Taking the piece of paper from Jack, she inserted the coordinates for the place in Eastern Europe where they would find the rock – probably another ruby, or possibly a diamond? – and pushed the hovering Spisan out into the middle of the shaft.

'Ready?'

'Can't be any worse than much of the stuff I've already done,' replied Jack with his usual affable smile.

So they stepped onto the circlet together, turned back to back, and linked their arms together. After a tiny pause, the SPIsan began to spin, and their journey began, down and round, down and round into the depths of the earth, until they could see no more, and darkness and fire enveloped them completely.

Chapter 17 – The Gates of Hell

It was astonishing to consider that both she and Jack had been through something like this before. Churning earth spat up beside them, plastering itself to the walls of the tunnel so that it smoothed and grew into a towering castle turret around them. The opening they'd climbed into vanished into a pin-prick of light as they tunnelled ever deeper; tree roots and grubs simply evaporated under the devilish spinning of the SPIsan; mulch and moistness increased into a fine mist and then a dense fog and then a liquid, running in rivulets down their skin until they were passing through the beds of underground lakes and even oceans, ploughing ever onwards.

'Doing okay, Jack?' she screamed into the vortex that whirled around them, unsure whether her words would whip around to him or would simply disintegrate in the roar of wind that swallowed them up.

In response, Jack pressed down with both elbows where their arms were interlinked.

She laughed. 'Twice for yes!'

There it was – one, two distinct feelings of pressure on her elbows as he signalled to her.

If she was honest, Janey was glad he was there. This kind of adventure had been fairly commonplace for her at one time, but since she de-spied everyone, it had been a while since she'd travelled on anything more adventurous than a roller-coaster at the fairground. And she was also just bringing to mind that the last time she had done this particular journey, she had bored her way through the molten core of the earth, protected only by her spysuit ... and a helmet? Surely she'd had some kind of helmet? Otherwise her face would melt, wouldn't it? Maybe she should warn Jack that his face might liquefy like a burnt-down candle ...

Then it struck her, firstly that Jack seemed to be fairly relaxed about passing through solid structures of any kind, including car engines and fireplaces, and secondly that theirs was a different destination to the one she'd been travelling to before. Then she'd been zooming off to Australia. This time they were just winding east to a more distant part of Europe. A very distant part of Europe, by all accounts.

No sooner had she clarified this in her mind than the Lazy SPIsan slowed, rotated backwards for a moment or two to slow down, then tipped them on their side as it drilled out an underground tunnel far beneath the earth's surface, under France and Holland according to her Gogs, then parts of the Czech Republic and goodness only knew where else. It was an even stranger sensation being on her side, and Janey was just starting to feel rather queasy when she noticed they were slowing down again, not by rotating in reverse this time, but in a steady decline in speed that suggested they were reaching their end point. A few moments later, the SPIsan erupted through the earth's crust so that they emerged feet-first, plopping out onto the grass like a couple of gophers.

Jack leapt up immediately, offering Janey a hand to help her stand. It was shaking slightly.

'Were you really okay?'

'Yes, honestly, done way worse,' he whispered, but as soon as he'd helped her to her feet, he shoved her slightly behind him, dog ears swivelling back and forth at an alarming speed.

'Then what's wrong?'

'It … it's this place.' He growled deep in his throat. 'There's something very odd about it. And I've--'

'You've been in some very odd places,' finished Janey. 'It's probably just shock after that journey, but … I know what you mean.'

Instinctively the pair moved themselves into the back-to-back position as they checked out their surroundings. There wasn't really anything sinister in the immediate vicinity – just a village that appeared to be fairly affluent and well-kept, judging by the lights gleaming out through polished windows, even though it was hard to see in the dark.

'Jack!' hissed Janey suddenly. 'Why is it dark?'

She could feel him shaking his head. 'I don't know. I can only hope that the sun rises later than at home. Two hours later. Otherwise there really is something very wrong here.'

'Sunrise, Transnordia.' Janey waited for her Ultra-Gogs to inform her, and then relayed it to Jack. 'According to my Gogs, sunrise should be in about ten minutes.'

'Good. Then I suggest we wait until then to go and investigate. Maybe they'll have disappeared by that time.'

'Who will?'

Jack tossed his head upwards, and Janey followed his line of vision. At the peak of a craggy mountain above the village, a castle clung to the cliff edge, brooding and black. Even more brooding were the shapes that swooped across the skyline.

'Are they bats?' Janey tried focussing her glasses on them but they were too far away for the Gogs.

'If we're lucky,' said Jack ominously. It didn't sound as if he expected much luck.

Scampering into a small wooded area while they waited for sunrise, Janey crouched down and ran her fingers through the earth. Maybe they should dig some up and cover the Lazy SPIsan hole …

As she bent, however, she felt something sharp beneath her feet. It was an iron arrowhead. She scanned ahead of her. A trail of them lead to a row of hills behind the village, and from deep within them, they could hear the clank of machinery. Last time she'd heard that sort of sound she had uncovered the ruby factory. Maybe this was another one? She gestured to Jack and they crept forward.

This time it wasn't a factory. It was a mine of some kind, with a network of railways and tracks winding up into the air and vanishing into the heights of the mine. Upon them, trolleys carted tonnes of ore in great chunky nuggets up to an enormous furnace at its centre.

'Do you think that's the rock we're supposed to collect?' said Jack.

'I don't know, but … oh. I don't think that's it.'

The dark, gritty iron ore was obviously just feeding the furnace. Maybe it was coal, not ore. But Janey had spotted what was coming out of the tunnels at the other side of the mine.

'I think that's probably the rock,' she said with a sigh as she turned Jack's shoulders in the right direction.

What was emerging from the fiery depths of the mine was something else entirely.

It appeared to be solid gold.

'Ohhhh,' whispered Jack, in a tone that said both 'Wow' and 'Bad news' at the same time.

Her heart sank a little. She had really hoped that Gideon was going to prove to be less predictable. He obviously just wanted things that created more money – or madness. Ruby rings, antique rifles, and now lumps of gleaming gold freshly hacked from the Transnordian mines – that was all he was after. Presumably, there was something about Tilly at the Games that would bring him a fortune too – winnings, perhaps, or maybe his investment would bring him dividends from all that sponsorship the duo had been talking about on TV. Whatever the case, Janey wasn't at all sure that she wanted any further part in it.

'Let's get it over with,' she said, suddenly sick of the whole set-up … because that was what it felt like. A set-up. Flynn just getting them to do his dirty work for him. 'Can you turn back into Jack with hair instead of Jack with fur? You might frighten the miners otherwise.'

Ever obliging, Jack concentrated hard, bringing down his anxiety level sufficiently to grow back his own fresh face topped with fair hair. 'I don't know how long I'll last,' he said. 'This place makes me very nervous, for some reason.'

'Me too,' she told him. 'We'll grab the rock and get out of here.'

Pale fingers of sunlight stroked the treetops as she and Jack crouched low and ran around to the far side of the mine. They had quickly agreed to take one clump of the ore and one of the rough bricks of gold, as they didn't actually know which rock Gideon was after. As soon as they'd seen a couple of the miners move away behind the machinery, they separated. In synchronised movements,

Janey scuttled to the golden lumps piled high on a nearby trailer, as Jack skirted the vast clanging machinery and made for the carriages filled with the unidentified grey stone.

Ducking behind the trailer, Janey checked that nobody was looking and then grabbed a small chunk of the golden rock. Not only had Gideon failed to say what rock he wanted; he'd also omitted to tell them how much he needed. She chose a medium-sized piece that she decided to call Goldilocks because it was "just right" and turned to make her way back to the entrance of the mine.

As she half-stood, she glanced across at Jack. With his back to her, he was inspecting the trays of metallic ore, studying them as she had done to select the best piece. He was concentrating so hard that he hadn't noticed the miner creeping up behind him with a large shovel raised above his head. If she didn't do something quickly, it would clang down on Jack's crown so hard it might split it in two, and while she didn't know if that would damage him much, she knew it might startle him so much that the whole mine would come running.

The spade was being heaved into position, just as Jack was nodding over his piece of rock and moving to stow it in his pocket. Janey had no choice. In an action that looked very much like the miner's, she raised Goldilocks-the-lump-of-gold above her head and whammed it across the mine, shouting 'Jack!' as the missile cracked into the skull of the villager. Jack whipped around in time to catch the poor miner as he fell forward, his face a picture as he saw the gold lying beside the man. He laid the miner across the trailer he'd been inspecting and dropped the gold into the other pocket. 'He's okay,' he mouthed. 'Just unconscious.'

Unfortunately, though, the miner had been missed – either that or Janey's shout had been overheard - because suddenly men were appearing from all sections of the mine, yelling and brandishing their functional but very deadly weapons: shovels, picks, axes and vicious balls of metal ore.

Janey and Jack ran for the door, meeting at the entrance, then looked left and right. The path was blocked on either side by armed villagers streaming towards them, throwing missiles of stone. Gritty rock and gold rained down on Janey and Jack; she batted it away as best she could, but then grabbed Jack's elbow as the villagers got nearer.

'Head for the castle!' she hollered as the clang of metal clubs rang out around them. 'We'll get lynched if we go back towards the village.'

By some miracle, Jack had managed to hang onto his boy appearance, but immediately he heard Janey's suggestion, he pelted straight forward for the trees, his body lengthening even as he ran. Janey flanked him, matching his loping stride step for step with the aid of her Fleet-Feet, the cries of the miners fading only slightly as they lunged into the forest and slowed for a second to get their bearings.

It was no use – the villagers knew the terrain better than they did and were pouring through the trees towards them. Jack took one look at the advancing horde and transformed instantly into Doghead.

'Need a hand?' he growled softly, nodding towards the clifftop.

Janey grinned. 'No, thanks. I'll run.'

'See you up there.'

As if they'd agreed it beforehand, they set off in two different directions, Janey zig-zagging through the trees as G-Mamma had once taught her, cutting straight across the forest to confuse the villagers and allow Jack to make his escape, before stamping on her heels and leaping in just a few enormous bounds towards the scree-covered lower slopes of the mountain. A hundred metres away, Jack was surging upwards through the shingle, his tread barely leaving a mark as he ploughed on through boulders and gnarled, bone-dry trees as if they weren't there.

Before long, Janey had cleared the scree and was now forced to clamber, hand over foot, up the face of the mountain. She gripped with her Girl Gauntlet and found, to her relief, that it held fast so that she was able to reach out with the other, searching for a suitable grip. It was hard work and she didn't have the equipment for it, and even Jack, she could see, was starting to struggle, his feet disappearing into the rocky surface as his ability to evaporate through solid objects turned rapidly into a curse. Where was Tilly and her broomstick when they needed her? At this rate, they were going to fall, and with the Spisan passage probably blocked off to them now, she wasn't at all convinced they'd ever get back.

Then suddenly, just above her outstretched right hand, Janey spotted a hole. It was a perfect circle so it appeared to be man-made, which would suggest that it might be a drainage tunnel of some sort. With some effort, she leaned back and trained her Ultra-Gogs on it.

'X-ray,' she called, and the Gogs' viewers penetrated the rock-face.

Good. The tunnel ran from the surface of the mountain to … well, she wasn't sure exactly where, but probably somewhere inside the castle. She viewed the skies above her head. The enormous circling bats had disappeared, she was very glad to see, and suddenly the castle seemed much less scary.

'Over here,' she called to Jack, before levering herself into the mouth of the tunnel.

It was as she'd suspected: liquid pooled around her feet and she detected the aroma of something sweet - fruit perhaps - in the air around her. With any luck, that would mean that it ran to and from the kitchens, where they could emerge without too many eyes on them. The tunnel ran upwards in a very gentle slope that even Jack should be able to manage without disaster.

He slid into the passage mouth behind her, the lower half of his body buried deep in the cliff. Jack thrust his hands down flat and heaved himself fully into the space, as if he were climbing out of a swimming pool. 'Good call,' he said, crouching to fit beneath the roof. 'I was beginning to go backwards.'

They trotted up the tunnel as far as the height would allow, then belly-crawled for the last few hundred metres to where a gloomy light funnelled its way towards them by way of an iron grille. Janey pulled herself towards it and peered out.

'Some kind of staircase,' she whispered. 'Stone. There's a door up to the right and another below us. Nobody on the stairs. Honestly, it's like something out of Robin Hood,' she said, grinning at Jack.

Suddenly, though, he frowned. 'Did you see that?'

Janey peered out onto the staircase. 'What—' she was about to ask, when she did see something – a shadowy figure running down the stairs, swiftly followed by another. 'Yes. I saw that.'

But she didn't get an opportunity to say what she'd thought it was, because before she could gather her thoughts again, the grille beside her clattered to the ground and a pair of skeletal yet powerful hands grabbed her by the wrists. With very little effort on her captor's behalf,

Janey was yanked out of the aperture and onto the stairs. The person who'd pulled her out, an immensely thin and startlingly tall man whose skinny frame matched his hands, waved to Jack to climb out voluntarily. Jack did so, sniffing suspiciously.

'I must get that tunnel sealed up, forsooth,' said the person behind her assailant. 'People are always jumping out of there. And other … things.' This was obviously aimed at Jack.

'Am I allowed to stand?' said Janey, and the person peeked around the tall man in surprise.

'Gadsbudlikins,' he said, 'you're a girl.'

'It's obvious she's a girl, isn't it?' said Jack, his muzzle wrinkling with scorn. 'I would have thought the outfit and the hair would give it away.'

'We're dressed in quite a similar fashion, I'm afraid, my canine-headed sir, so it wasn't obvious at all,' said the boy addressing them.

They both turned to look at him properly, and Janey saw that what he said was true. His outfit consisted of tight-fitting velvet trousers that ended just below his knee and segued neatly into a pair of white stockings finished with buckled shoes, and a matching velvet tunic that reached to his thighs. It could easily have been a spysuit. The boy's hair was long and flowing – or at least it would have been if it wasn't tied back in a neat ponytail.

'Are you a scientist?' he asked politely. 'I tie my hair back for those purposes.'

Janey shook her head. 'No, I'm …'

There was no explaining what she was, actually, and there was definitely no explanation for what Jack was, although neither the boy nor the man seemed particularly perturbed by him. If anything, it was the other way round. With his lip curled in distaste, Jack's eyes were darting between them as if they might vanish before him in a puff of poisonous smoke.

'I'm Jane Blon-Brown,' she said in the end, and stuck out her hand as she'd seen Jack to at the reception.

'La!' cried the boy, quite delighted with this turn of events, although he simply stared at her hand as if it was a specimen in a display before turning to Jack. 'And who is your friend?'

'Jack Bootle-Cadogan,' she said as Jack simply growled. 'Actually, *Lord* Jack Bootle-Cadogan.'

'Gadzooks, more royalty!' the boy exclaimed.

The tall, skeletal man clapped his hands. 'More royalty, my prince!'

This was getting stranger by the second. 'Are you … royalty, then?'

The boy stepped forward and bowed his head slightly. 'My apologies, fair lady. I am royalty, indeed. Prince Stein of the Huckenbeck Dynasty, once of the fair shores of

England and now of Transnordia. This is Lord Viggo. Do you hail from England?'

'Um, yes,' said Janey.

'And you, Lord Bootle-Cadogan? Are you from England, or perhaps the land of the Nile?'

Jack scowled. 'Yes, both of them, actually.'

'I thought so,' said Stein with a studious expression. 'I have seen you in one of my books. I have many books,' he added as if he needed to expand on this, 'and have studied widely for many, many years.'

He looked about thirteen, so Janey suspected this was the kind of exaggeration normally saved for parents and teachers.

'Would you like a tour of the castle?' he then asked politely. 'That would be acceptable, Viggo?'

'Indeed! The pom juice is drunk, and all is well among the ramparts. Come!'

The man gestured down the stairs, and as the prince hopped merrily after him, Janey and Jack followed.

'Try to escape,' muttered Jack into his chest so that only Janey, assisted by her BATS, would hear.

'Why? They seem nice, and besides –'

'They're UNDEAD!' he spat. 'It's all wrong up here, and we need to get out.'

Undead? What was he talking about? 'Are you sure?'

'Believe me, I know my deads – and they are UN.'

They emerged into the courtyard, where the prince led them in a stately procession across the cobbles as people shambled out from their rooms – dungeons, probably, judging by the state of them - to stare at the pair of infiltrators.

'What about them?' Janey smiled brightly at the nearest person about their own age. He looked strangely canine, rather like Jack, and rather than smiling back, he sniffed the air and frowned.

'All of them,' warned Jack under his breath. 'Every single one. All undead. We should run for it.'

But Janey knew that they couldn't – not because the castle-dwellers would stop them, although that might well be the case, but because she knew that someone else was here as well.

One of the shadows that she had seen running past the tunnel …

… she was pretty sure that it was Gideon Flynn.

Chapter 18 – The Pom Juice Equation

Before too long they arrived at an immense pair of double doors, screened with velvet curtains of such a rich red that Janey was reminded of the blood on the walls of the MRI room. Lord Viggo parted them, ducked his bald head and waited for the prince and his two unexpected guests to pass through.

A couple about her parents' age were poring over a map spread across a banqueting table. 'Stein-Stein!' cried the woman as the trio approached.

'Good morning, Mother, Father,' said the prince, sounding rather embarrassed.

Janey suspected that if he wasn't undead as Jack believed him to be, he would have been blushing to the tips of his ears at being called Stein-Stein in front of strangers. G-Mamma's names definitely had that effect on her. And … undead? Could that really be? She stole a glance around the room beneath lowered eyelashes. It was certainly true that all of them were extremely pallid with dark shadows around their eyes, and they were all dressed in strange outfits that didn't bear any resemblance to any Janey had seen in her own century. The prince's father was in a silk outfit rather like his son's, and both the mother and Viggo were hidden in head-to-toe robes in a stiff grey fabric, the only difference being that the woman's featured a clinched waist and low-cut bodice.

Apart from their appearance, however, they were the liveliest bunch Janey had ever come across, with the exception of G-Mamma and Tilly. When Stein announced: 'They're from England,' the couple – presumably the king and queen – clapped their hands in delight and shouted 'Zounds!' and 'La and forsooth!' in great excitement.

The queen rushed to clutch Janey's hands with her own cold fingers. 'Art thou male or female? What wearest thou? Do they still hang witches?'

'Mother,' groaned the prince. 'Nobody says "thou" any more.'

Or Mother, thought Janey, but she held it back. 'I'm female, wearing … um … Lycra, and I hope they don't hang witches because we just sort of met one.'

At that the woman looked desperately crestfallen. 'Witches are safe now?'

'Well, I'm not sure about that, and I'm not even sure she's properly a witch, but …'

'Greetings. I am Darius Huckenbeck, formerly Penhaligan, and this is my good wife, Lavinia. And thou … pardon me, sir, *you* art hound-headed!' The man in the silk suit strode over to Jack and pumped his hand, not at all concerned for his safety. 'God's truth, art you a demon?'

'Are, Father,' said Stein with a distinct roll of his eyes. '*Are* you a demon?'

'No, I'm not a demon,' Jack replied. He was relaxing now; Janey could see pink skin appearing through the fur and he appeared to be shrinking. 'I'm part-boy, part Egyptian god.'

'Anubis!' cried Stein triumphantly. 'God of embalming and mummification! That is why you are not afraid among us – you have seen much death, I expect.'

'Much,' said Jack, his eyes narrowing, 'but nothing quite like you.'

The atmosphere suddenly seized up in the most awkward of awkward moments as the four undead castle-dwellers eyed each other with concern. Viggo appeared to be especially uncomfortable, shredding the edge of the map with the tapered nails of his long, bony fingers.

Jack pressed on. 'You're *un*dead, aren't you?'

Stein stared at the floor, suddenly sad. 'Are you here to tell the world of our state?' he asked quietly. 'We had been told by the villagers that the world is coming almost to our door for these community games in the neighbouring country. Are you part of that?'

'No, we're not,' Janey declared, more firmly than she'd actually intended to. 'The people running the World Community Games are up to no good, and we're going to stop them.'

'No good?' shrieked Viggo, skewering the country of Kazakhstan with a nail. So that was why they were studying the map. 'Do they plan to invade?'

'I don't think so,' said Janey honestly, 'but the truth is that we don't really know what they're up to. Someone has … well, hired us to gather some things together, and every single one of them has been something to do with these Games. We're going to get to the bottom of it and stop them in their tracks, even if our boss doesn't like it.'

'We are?' said Jack.

'We are.'

Janey folded her arms defiantly, shocked at how determined she suddenly felt. This hadn't been the plan, but now it was – with or without Gideon Flynn.

Viggo was drawing nearer, however, and suddenly Janey could see the terrifying irises of his eyes. Red. Dark, blood red. 'Regretfully, it may not be possible for you to leave,' he said with a tinge of genuine sadness in his voice. 'The world cannot know that in Transnordia there is a castle harbouring the undead.'

Jack's dog head materialised instantly, and Janey found that she was curling her Gauntlet into position to attack. What good it would do against … a vampire, she suddenly understood … she wasn't quite sure. Didn't they need a stake through the heart? The blade in one of her fingertips might not be up to the job.

But Prince Stein stepped in between Viggo and the visitors. 'Lord Viggo, with respect, this girl in boy's garb and hound-headed lad clearly have secrets of their own. They're not going to tell anyone of ours, I'm sure. Are you?' he said, frowning at Janey.

'No,' she confirmed. 'Definitely not. I don't even know what the secrets are.'

'And you wouldn't believe the stuff we've both seen and had to keep to ourselves.' Jack waggled his ears. 'This is just the tip of the iceberg. For example, to get here we tunnelled through the earth beneath Europe on a Lazy Susan.'

'Lazy Susan! Is she a witch?' asked Lavinia hopefully.

Janey couldn't help herself. She really liked them. They might be undead, or vampires − and probably werewolves and goodness knew what other forms of monster − but they seemed harmless and sweet. They just wanted to be left to themselves, and who could blame them for that?

She held up her hands so that Viggo could see they contained nothing, then asked Jack to turn out his pockets. 'Look, we don't want to tell anyone about you. Your secret is safe. But our …' She didn't quite know what to call him. Leader? Manager? Client? 'Gideon Flynn sent us to here to grab some rock or other, so we've taken a lump of ore and a chunk of gold. Is that okay?'

She'd meant to assuage their fears, but now the family seemed even more concerned.

'He sent you to grab a rock?' repeated the prince.

Janey shrugged. 'Yes. He didn't say what kind, though, so we're going to take these to Kazakhstan. Our friend is there competing in the Games.'

'He wishes for you to take a Transnordian rock to the World Games?' Darius Huckenbeck paced the floor uneasily, pulling at his pointed beard. 'No. That … that cannot be. You must stay here among us and not return to this Gideon Flynn.'

'We … we can't take these stones?' Janey took them off Jack and held them up one after the other. Walking over to the map, trying not to shudder as she passed the vampire, she placed both chunks on the table. 'Then that's fine. We won't take them. I don't know what he wants them for anyway. I don't know what he wants any of this stuff for, actually. So we'll just leave them here with you, and we'll … you know, disappear.'

Lavinia was chewing her nails. 'What doth he know, thinkest thou?' she muttered to her husband.

'I know not, dearest, but it will remain our secret.'

The tone of the conversation had turned again. Jack's fur was bristling ominously and her own spy instincts were filling her gut with a growing sense of doom. If they weren't allowed to leave, they would have to break out of the castle – a castle on a cliff-top peopled by … well, non-people. Undead things.

She was just about to try to negotiate with them when a familiar shadow filtered past the window, swiftly followed by another, taller one.

'That's him!' she cried. 'Gideon Flynn – he's here!'

The undeads all gasped. Jack swivelled on his heel, heading for the diamond-shaped slot in the wall that acted as the window. 'I knew I'd seen him! When we were still in the tunnel.'

In an instant, Janey had followed him, grabbing onto his shoulder. If it worked when he grabbed her shoulder, hopefully it would be effective the other way around too.

'Wait!' cried Viggo. 'We have not yet decided your –'

Fate? Death? Hotel room? There wasn't time to find out.

'We didn't know he was here,' she shouted, gripping Jack's shoulder as firmly as she could. 'Come with us if you want!'

'You cannot … the door …' Prince Stein called plaintively.

'Don't need it, thanks!' cried Jack, and then he whooshed through a metre of solid granite with Janey fastened tightly to his back so that she wouldn't get buried in the wall. It was as if he'd walked through air; in a mere moment they were out in the courtyard, scanning the walkway that ran all the way around it to see where Gideon was.

Jack paused. 'No sign of him.'

'He passed just seconds ago,' said Janey. 'He must be close by. I'll set the Gogs on heat-seek.'

'Good idea. With all these undeads around, they should zone in on him in no time.'

Running around the courtyard as the prince, his parents and his vampire tumbled out of the door behind them, Janey zoomed in on every room, but still she couldn't see Flynn.

'Upstairs!' she called, sprinting for the stairs where she and Jack had first entered the castle. Jack followed instantly, hastily pursued by the family and a growing number of castle dwellers, who did appear to be a whole range of undeads: werewolves, vampires of all varieties, a large number of lumbering bodies with ill-fitting heads and occasional missing limbs, and a young man even bigger than Jack who hollered 'Steiny!' and lurched after them with open arms.

At the pinnacle of the small army of strange folk, Janey located the tunnel opening and peered along it. Nobody there. She cast her vision left into the two rooms opposite the tunnel. They appeared to be devoid of people – live ones, anyway. Yet for some reason she could see in her heat-seeking Gogs the outlines of tables and shelving lined with equipment, some of which was bubbling on an ancient Bunsen burner like she used at school. Laboratories – they were both labs like the Spylab, only cooking up something different than spy-buys and with only one small computer screen visible in either.

Of Gideon Flynn, though, there was no sign.

She ran backwards up the stairs, calling out to the young prince. 'What's up here?'

'Ramparts!' he replied, stumbling up the stairs behind Jack. 'Very high! Be careful!'

They spilled out onto the towering castle defences which were mostly just a narrow and slippery stone ledge, edged by a crenelated wall on the side facing out towards the village. On each corner was a small circular turret, but again, each one was empty.

Then suddenly she saw him, slithering on the ramparts across the opposite side of the courtyard. He had his arms up in front of his face and was jumping to and fro, as if trying to dodge a blow from an invisible assailant – but then the assailant leapt out from behind one of the turrets, raining blows on Gideon's head so that he ducked his head, wriggling his shoulders out of the way as the punches jabbed at him from the side, below his chin. He struck out helplessly but it was evident, even from this distance, that his opponent was getting the best of him – and no wonder, as he was much taller and with greater body weight, a fully grown, hefty man beating a slender teenage boy remorselessly. Gideon was trying to remonstrate with him; Janey could hear him crying out 'Don't! It's nothing to do with them, it's all me!' But his words had no effect. He was forced back against the low wall, unable to slow the advancing fists with his own useless hands. 'Jane, he's after you! Get out of here!' he screamed.

'Go!' she called to Jack, and he leapt into action, running around the left walkway as she took to her heels and raced off to the right, her Fleet Feet holding her steady on the treacherously worn surface of the castle defences. She rounded one corner and then the next, Jack moving on an identical path across on the other face of the castle as if he was her mirror image. They were on the same pathway as Gideon and the man, whose face she could now see as she pelted towards them. Over Gideon's shoulder, he spotted her, his mouth opening in surprise. He looked familiar, but she didn't have time to work out where she'd seen him before as Gideon noticed Jack and shouted out to him: 'No! This is my fight.'

It was all the time the man needed. With one hammer blow of a curled fist, he punched Gideon in the ribs and sent him sprawling against the low wall. Flynn's body hung off the ramparts, a thousand metres above the sharp shale at the foot of the mountain. He was slipping. In the last moments he finally used his hands, reaching out to grip the man's trouser leg, and just before Janey and Jack managed to get to them, the grappling pair slid over the edge of the parapet and plunged into the vast open space below.

'No!' she screamed, thrusting out her Gauntlet, trying to recall which finger might hold a grappling hook, rushing to fling herself over the wall to reach Gideon Flynn … but Jack stilled her hand with his own enormous one.

'There's no point. They couldn't survive that fall, Blonde,' he said gently.

She rocked back on her heels, horrified. She didn't know anything about Gideon, really, or why he was there, but to watch someone – anyone – plummet to their death like that was truly horrific. And seeing Gideon remonstrate with the man, trying to stop him as much for their sake as for his own, or so it seemed – well, the ache in her heart was impenetrable.

'I'll go and find … them,' said Jack. 'Do my thing so at least their *bas* are safe. I still don't like all this undead stuff so I don't want to leave their b*as* floating around.'

Unable to speak, Janey nodded, hardly able to watch as Jack ran back along the ramparts and down the stairs, shouting, 'Scuse me, 'scuse me' to anybody in his way.

'You need some pom juice,' said a voice behind her.

She turned to find the prince standing behind her, sandwiched between his parents.

'We've had battles of our own from these ramparts,' said Stein, 'and pom juice is the only thing that ever helps afterwards.'

'As well as the not dying because we're undead,' said his father helpfully. 'That helps too.'

Janey offered him a small smile. 'That would be an advantage.'

'Pom juice,' they all uttered together, nodding.

Whatever it was, it was a popular cure-all.

She let Stein lead her back along the walkway and down the stairs, making for the castle kitchens. The crowd had melted away once the action was over, leaving just Viggo, the man-sized boy and his parents to accompany the prince in search of the mysterious pom juice. What had happened, she asked herself. Why was Gideon here rather than at the Games? And who was the man he was fighting with? She'd definitely seen him before. Was he one of the guards from the party or the others at the HOST car park?

Slowing down to avoid the chatter of the Huckenbecks, who were clearly more used to people diving to their deaths from the castle walls, she zoomed in again on the laboratories. Strangely, she could still make out a heat-source from various spots inside the room. It was almost as if something was alive in there. She passed the second lab door and noticed the same thing in that room, though less marked, before walking beneath an enormous moose head nailed to a plaque on the stone wall, and a massive family portrait of the Huckenbecks of the type she'd been taken to see in the National Gallery.

In the painting, they all looked exactly the same as they did in the – well, flesh - although with a bit more sparkle. She thought she knew why. This, presumably, was painted before they became undead, for whatever reason that had happened. Back before they became the Transnordian Huckenbeck Dynasty. When they were simply - Janey read the tiny brass plate on the mahogany frame – 'Darius and Lavinia Penhaligan, and their son, Petroc, Year of Our Lord 1725.'

'Come along, Mistress Blon-Brown!' called Prince Stein from the kitchen doorway. 'Pom juice awaits!' He was holding out a goblet of some gungey brown liquid that had dribbled a little down the outside of the cup.

'That's not really my name,' she started to say, and then she realised something.

Three things, actually.

Firstly, the liquid in the chalice that Stein was holding out was glowing as she looked at it. According to her Gogs, it gave off a heat source like the stuff in the laboratories, as if it was … alive.

Secondly, the dribbles down the outside of the dull metal goblet had caused it to change colour. Change its very nature, in fact. Where the gunge had flowed across it, the goblet now shone like the sun.

And thirdly, she'd noticed that, in the same way Blon-Brown wasn't her actual name, so Prince Stein Huckenbeck wasn't the boy's name either.

He was called Petroc. Stein was his name in another language.

'Translate Stein,' she whispered to her glasses.

STEIN, she read. Germanic translation for stone or rock.

So that was it. No – *he* was it.

The rock they'd been sent to collect was Petroc Penhaligan - a scientist who had studied many books for three hundred years, and had somehow managed to work out how to turn lumps of iron ore - or whatever came out of the mines - into gold.

They'd come to steal the prince.

But before she could work out why, Jack ran across the courtyard, calling, 'I couldn't find them!'

She was about to reply when, to her astonishment, the necklace around the collar of her spysuit vibrated. It was a SPIV or SPI visualator, an invention which G-Mamma complained constantly had been stolen by various people – but mostly Steve Jobs - and turned into Skype and Facetime.

Janey held it up before her. 'G-Mamma?'

A flustered face appeared, blowing hair out of the way – slightly blue, silvery hair. 'No, it's me, Matilda Peppercorn.'

'Tilly! What are you doing?'

Tilly's eyes appeared in the SPIV. 'You'd better get to Kazakhstan quickly,' she said. 'I think we've stuffed

up.' Her face contorted into a guilty wince. 'The Big G –
your G-Mamma – well, she's been arrested.'

'Arrested?'

Tilly nodded. 'Yep. And apparently it's for murder.'

W hat's the fastest way to Kazakhstan?' Janey demanded, waving away the goblet of pom juice. 'You said it's the neighbouring country?'

'You are leaving?' Stein sounded horribly disappointed. 'I'd hoped we were going to be friends! Of course, we won't make you stay if you don't want to …'

Janey paused, weighing it up – weighing *him* up – then decided in a rush. There was no time for delay with G-Mamma holed up in jail somewhere. No matter what Gideon had wanted Stein for (and she had a horrible feeling it was to turn metal into gold in yet another money-making scheme, probably the most successful so far), his other choices of team-mate had turned out to be quite useful. Even quite nice. Even … and she almost hated to admit it … kind of fun. Stein looked as if he needed that kind of fun, and he might also turn out to have some hidden skills that could winkle the Big G out of a cell.

'Come with us,' she said, ignoring Jack's disapproving grunt. 'You're a scientist, aren't you? You actually make that … pom juice?'

Stein glanced at his parents, and then nodded.

'Well, a dear friend of mine – my teacher and mentor, actually, kind of like your Lord Viggo, I'm guessing – is in very big trouble in Kazakhstan. Our witch-type person is with her, but that isn't enough. She needs us there, and Gideon had chosen you too, so I think you could come.'

'How?' bleated Jack. 'How has he chosen the undead prince too? Flynn asked for a brick, didn't he?'

'A rock. I'll explain on the way.' She nudged Stein's shoulder. 'You're obviously already dead, so you can't come to any harm, and nobody will guess your state so they won't come back looking for the rest of your people.'

'Oh, Stein-Stein, no!' Lavinia wrung her hands wretchedly. 'You're so young. Forsooth, how will you manage without us?'

'Gadsbudlikins, Mother, I'm over three hundred years old. When do you think I'll be ready to manage without you?' Stein held a hand up imperiously. 'And don't say never! I'd … I'd like to go,' he continued more kindly. 'I've made new friends, they're in trouble, and I'd like to go beyond the golden village of Rustnuts at least once in my life. Non-life.'

Darius slipped a hand across his wife's shoulder. 'We should probably let him spread his proverbial wings,' he said. 'And it could indeed be useful to discover what lies beyond our borders. Dost thou agree?'

'Thou must take a goodly supply of pom juice,' said Lavinia reluctantly, her bottom lip wobbling. 'And cometh home directly!'

Stein looked from one to the other of them as if he could hardly believe what he was hearing, and then he burst into a tiny, Scottish-looking dance, with lots of pointed toes and arm flourishes. 'I'm off! Moose and Frank, look out for each other. Mother and Father, take care of each other. Lord Viggo, keep control of everybody. And servant,' he cried to a nearby wolfish creature, 'bring me a week's supply of the pom!'

The juice was hastily stowed in a flagon (although Janey was secretly sure that once he'd tried cola at the World Games, he'd never drink the gunky goo again by choice) as Stein explained that he wouldn't need a change of clothes as he was undead and didn't sweat.

'Do you have alternative clothing, Mistress Blon-Brown?' he asked politely.

'Actually no, not here. And it's just Janey.'

'That would never do, unless we were betrothed,' said Stein with a smile.

'Then could you just call me Blonde? Like 'Servant'? It will save time.'

Stein tried it for size. 'Blonde. Blonde! Yes, I can use that, just while we're away.'

'Come on,' said Jack, starting to yawn. 'We've got to get across the border into Kazakhstan yet, and find these wretched games.'

That was true, and they hadn't thought that far ahead yet. Luckily, someone was doing it for them. Janey's SPIV rattled with an incoming message, and she picked it up to find an upside-down Tilly in the visuality screen. She shook it, and Tilly turned the right way up.

'Are you on the way?'

'Any second,' said Janey as Stein stared in awe at the SPIV.

'Good, because the Big G's disappeared without trace so I've had to make my own arrangements. You and Jack—'

'And Stein!' added the prince.

'What? Well, whoever you're bringing, you have to pretend you're my replacement coach and physio or something. As soon as you arrive, I'll magic the guys on the gates into seeing you on the list and letting you in. And be quick, because it's not just the Big G's disappearance that's weird.'

Jack leaned into the SPIV. 'How long do we have?'

'Well, Scary Hairy-face,' cried Tilly, recoiling, 'no time at all if you turn up like that. And less than an hour if you turn up looking half-normal.' She rattled off some coordinates and then turned her head sideways so that they were staring into her ear. 'Gotta go,' she hissed. 'I'm being called up for the band.'

She zoomed out of focus before they could ask whether she was singing or playing an instrument, although frankly, nothing much that Tilly did would surprise Janey any longer. Reading out the coordinates to the others, Janey felt her heart sank. She had seen Kazakhstan on the map in the library, and even with Jack's help, there was no way they could get from Transnordia in only half an hour or so.

'The Lazy SPIsan is too small for three, and too slow anyway. We'd need a jet to get there that quickly,' she said mournfully.

Lord Viggo peered at her with his piercing red eyes. 'Or perhaps … a bat?'

And that was how they came to be travelling across Transnordia by vampire. Viggo had roused three of his colleagues from their coffins and issued instructions. 'Straight there and back, no harassing the locals and definitely no stopping for a drink.'

'Aren't they going to shrivel in daylight?' said Jack, with just a shade of hope in his voice.

Stein shook his head. 'They'll have their pom juice. Nearly all our undead people eaters go out and about by day. Some of them are miners, for instance. Zombies are spectacularly strong.'

'What about people spotting us?' said Janey.

Lord Viggo turned to Stein. 'That is indeed a fair point, my prince. You must be at the vanguard, and lead the group above the clouds as much as you can. If you're high enough up, you might look like birds. Again, no stopping.'

The three vampires selected to fly to the Games shuffled together. 'What about landing?' said the shortest one. 'Or do we just drop them?'

'If there are no observers, then you may land. Otherwise, yes, find a good spot and drop them. One is undead, one possibly immortal, and the other …'

'I have a spysuit,' said Janey, though she wasn't sure it would save her if they let go of her at thirty thousand feet. Still, she'd fallen further and survived, and that was without Jack and Stein at her side. 'Can we go? I'm getting worried.'

So after the vampire squadron each chucked a flagon of pom juice down their scrawny necks and donned a pair of aviator sunglasses, they all ran to the castle heights and lined up along the wall. Hardly daring to look down, Janey thought of Gideon with a painful pang. What had happened to him to make others track him down so violently? She might not approve of his money-grabbing ways, but she really hadn't wanted any harm to come to him.

And talking of harm … 'Ready,' she said firmly, wondering if the vampire behind her had a strap like a tandem parachutist.

Jack nodded as the tallest vampire moved in close to his back. It would be strange to see someone else with a hand on his shoulder, guiding him this time. 'Set,' said Jack.

Stein could barely contain himself. 'Go! Oh, adventure! Oh, wide blue sky! Oh, new friends! Go, go, go!'

And suddenly they were each gripped around the middle by a pair of vice-like arms. The vampires spread their capes and from beneath them emerged sinewy black wings, veined throughout with the faint pulsating glow of pom juice. It really was amazing stuff. With a simple nod to the vampire on either side, Stein's vampire pilot launched himself from the parapet. For a moment they swooped towards the ground as he adjusted to Stein's weight, and then they soared into the pale grey sky, wings beating slowly and steadily as they pierced the cloud cover and disappeared.

It was Janey's turn. 'Good luck!' she cried to Jack, and then her vampire friend – a young undead man not much older than Gideon, with deep auburn hair and startling hazel eyes that glowed against his stark-white skin - jumped away from the building. Janey felt as though she were being carried by an enormous eagle. There was a jolt as he extended his wings and thrust upwards, completing a full barrel roll into a current of air before chasing Stein up through the clouds.

Across the mountaintop, she heard Jack shout out for joy. 'I've never been able to do up! This is fantastic!'

'Secret mission, Jack BC,' she called back in warning, but she gave him a big thumbs-up and a grin before the clouds swallowed her up.

The span of the vampires' wings was massive, each beat taking almost a minute as they stretched the tips forward and drew them back effortlessly and rather majestically. Their grace was incredible, and if she didn't think too hard about the fangs that were positioned only a short space behind the back of her neck, she could enjoy the flight. They swooped and swept across the skies like dolphins arcing through the sea, Stein always slightly ahead, darting below the clouds for occasional reconnaissance before re-joining them to lead the flock. Were they a flock? It was hard to tell.

Just as Janey had actually started to relax so much that she felt like dropping off, Stein shouted from up ahead. 'We're going down!'

They were beneath the clouds; the skin on her face felt damp although her spysuit, ponytail and Gogs had protected her from the worst of it. She trained her glasses on the terrain below. It was almost like a desert – just a vast dustbowl that stretched on for ever, flat and unyielding.

The vampire carrying her suddenly spoke into her ear. 'There is no cover, Mistress, so we cannot land.'

'No, that's fine,' she shouted, her heart thumping with the shock. 'You can drop me on one of those marquees.'

'As my lady pleases,' he said, his mouth just above her neck. 'It has been my pleasure to serve you.'

Suddenly she felt ashamed for what she'd been fearing. Why couldn't she trust anyone? Why was she always judging people – or non-people? She didn't even know her saviour's name. 'Thank you so much, err …'

'Ambro.'

'Thank you, Ambro.'

For a moment she feared once again that he was baring his fangs to sink them into her, but he was merely smiling, gazing into her face with his intense green-brown eyes. He nodded to the others as they lined them up high above the immense tents on the outskirts of the Games venue, and they all let go at the same moment. As she dropped like a stone he swooped down beside her, as upright as if they were both standing on a platform. Then, with a gracious bow of his head, Ambro powered his way upwards, back among the clouds.

And now she had to concentrate. To her right, Jack was flailing like a windmill with his canine features horribly visible, while Stein was rushing towards a tent in a free-fall position, eyes closed as the wind buffeted him this way and that. At least she'd been dropped feet first; she was slicing through the atmosphere like a dart. The white slope of the marquee was sailing into view with alarming speed, and Janey realised that her Fleet-Feet would have nothing to grip onto if she landed this way up.

Jack would be fine as he would simply sink into the ground to whatever depth the velocity took him before struggling upwards through the earth, but she had a strong suspicion that both she and Stein could shatter on impact.

There was only one thing for it. As Ambro had flown along she had watched with interest, and now she mimicked his movements. She found this put her in the same position as Stein, spread like the letter x across the sky. Once she'd stabilised, she pushed off with her legs and reached out with her arms, swimming towards Jack. From the corner of his eye he appeared to notice what she was doing, and for a moment he stopped wheeling his arms around. His speed increased immediately, so he followed Janey's lead and tipped himself so that he was lying across a cushion of air. Janey swam towards him once more, and this time she glided through the air as Ambro had done. Jack copied her, and as the white mass below turned out to be not one big marquee but many smaller oblong tents, rather like greenhouses in a market garden, Janey reached his side. She pointed to the floor, unable to speak as the wind pushed against her face, and to her relief Jack nodded, grabbed her shoulder, then stretched an enormous arm out towards Stein who was rocketing past on his right. There was just time for the three of them to link up in a line as a snowy surface rushed up to meet them, followed by a row of tables and a layer of grass before a familiar loamy smell filled her nostril. They'd stopped, but they were submerged several metres into the earth.

Stein clambered to his feet, reeling and dazed, then slowly an enormous grin spread across his pale face. 'Zooks and zounds,' he hollered, 'that was AWESOME!'

Janey put a finger to her lips. They hadn't yet worked out where they were. They could be surrounded, for all they knew.

But the coast was relatively clear. They were evidently in one of the outer holding areas for the Games, as the HOST insignia was emblazoned on every possible surface, from the inside of the tent walls to the tabletops which stretched as far as the eye could see. A security guard was seated outside the door at the very far end, but judging by the way his chair was tipped back on two legs, he was indulging in a spot of sunbathing in the weak midday sun. Their arrival had gone unnoticed.

Silently, they climbed out of the pit they had just created and then crawled beneath a table on Janey's mimed instructions. She turned to Jack. 'That was brilliant, thank you so much.'

'Gadsbudlikins, it most certainly was,' agreed Stein.

Jack nodded modestly.

'But the thing is, if we're going to pass ourselves off as coaches and so on, you're going to have to …'

'Lose the head,' said Jack. 'I know. Bear with me.'

They turned away politely as Jack calmed his pulse down enough for his canine ears to shrink against his head into the pink question marks of his human ears, and once that was achieved he transformed readily into Lord Jack Bootle-Cadogan. 'Getting easier,' he said with a smile.

'Good. Then let's find Tilly.'

They crawled beneath the tables for a while, then when they were well clear of the guard they got to their feet and trotted towards the door. It was only then that Janey noticed the tables were covered in something other than the HOST logo. Every one of the sixty or seventy tables sported a flag – she could see the Ecuadorian one across the room, and the Union Jack not too far away from the Chinese pendant – and beneath each flag lay a line of bracelets, individually named for the athlete who was going to wear it. Janey picked up the nearest one, for a member of the Georgian National Ballet.

'These Games really are weird,' she whispered. 'They're including ballet!'

She was just about to return the bracelet, which was little more than a black leather wristband, when she noticed how the bracelet fastened. The stud at one end obviously popped into the slot at the other, but as it was too small a slit for the stud, the bracelet would have to be clipped on with a machine of some kind. She ran her fingers down the leather towards the stud, holding it up to her glasses so that she could see.

The stud was a ruby. A miniscule, lozenge-shaped ruby, glued to the end of the strap in such a way that, once it was secured, it would surely press into the flesh of the athlete wearing it. And finally Janey worked out what it had reminded her of: it was the same shape as a SIM card for a mobile phone, only with all four corners cut off instead of just one.

'These aren't just identification bracelets,' she said to Jack and Stein. 'They're communications devices.'

'That's a bit odd, but I suppose that HOST is a technology company.' Jack looked at the nearest table. 'These are all missing. Norway must have had theirs put on already.'

'As with this one,' reported Stein from further along the room. 'I believe from my studies that this must be the Union.'

'The Union of who?' said Janey.

'Of England and Scotland, of course.'

'He means the Union Jack. The United Kingdom.' Jack trotted over to the UK table. 'Yes, all gone.' And he held up a tiny name card. 'Including this one.'

'Matilda Peppercorn,' they said together.

'So that was the band she was being called for – a wrist-band.'

Janey sighed. It could well be that Tilly was in some kind of trouble, but more than anything she needed to get to G-Mamma and find out about the murder charge.

'You two find Tilly,' she said quickly. 'I'll look for G-Mamma.'

'Who is this Jeem-Amah?' asked Stein. 'Is she a housemaid from the colonies?'

Jack grabbed his arm. 'I'll tell you on the way, but don't you dare say that to her if you value your life. Death, I mean. Oh, just come on.'

They hurried out through the back door, bursting into a very passable training routine as they neared some visiting athletes. Janey stared at the competitors. They were all wearing bracelets, along with the vacant zoned out expression she'd seen on the TV the other night. This was obviously where they'd been located as she watched – right here in Kazakhstan. So hopefully G-Mamma was here too – but she had no idea where.

And then she recalled the first rule the SPI:KE had ever taught her: surprise, surprise, surprise. Sometimes, to surprise someone, it paid to do the obvious.

Grabbing a coat from a nearby rail, Janey covered her spysuit and twisted her hair into a top knot, hoping she looked like a Kazakhstan policewoman, albeit a young one. Without pausing to check, she marched across to an official-looking booth and stomped up to the guard.

'I am interpreter for prisoner,' she barked, hoping whole-heartedly that they didn't reply in whatever the local language was. 'Take me.'

Luckily, they spoke English. The guard looked her up and down then gazed at his phone. 'What is the prisoner's name?'

'G … Rosie Biggenham,' snapped Janey, sighing as if she had much better things to do than chat with mere guards.

'And she is charged with?'

Janey tutted. 'With murder. As I may be also …' she intoned darkly, raising her brow to indicate that the guard would probably be her next victim.

The guard nodded quickly. 'Fine. This way.'

She trailed him through a maze of tents, marquees and prefabricated buildings from which the shouts and thumps of practicing athletes rang out, until she was almost sure he was leading her on a wild goose chase to confuse her. At long last, he stopped at the back of a row of what seemed to be earthen mounds. Was this a grave? Fear mounting, Janey followed his finger to the far side of the mound.

A temporary prison had been dug into a bank of earth. At the side near to her it was much deeper – deep enough for a woman to stand in, just about, railed in by a massive iron gate. In the first cell was a woman half the size of G-Mamma, wearing two eye patches. She had scratched out a word in the dust at her feet. HELP. Janey turned to her instinctively.

'Don't touch,' warned the guard, miming instant electrocution.

'Of course not!'

With a heart beating so fast it was a wonder the guard hadn't seen her coat moving, Janey stepped in front of the next gate and addressed herself to the woman within. 'Biggenham. I am interpreter.'

G-Mamma stared at her with tears in her enormous blue eyes. 'Blonde!' she hissed. 'Get me out of here! They're feeding me nothing.' She actually did look thinner, Janey was alarmed to see. Maybe the other lady had been bigger, too, before they locked her in here.

Janey felt the guard's eyes on her, so she blinked rapidly at her mentor and snapped at her again. 'What is crime?'

'They're framing me for murder,' said G-Mamma with a sob. 'Me? Murder? Haven't killed a soul since S ... Sol's Lols folded. But they found all this evidence at our ... my lab. They ransacked it!'

She had a horrible feeling she knew what the answer was going to be, but Janey was forced to ask. 'And what was found?'

'The poisoned ring and that stupid old rifle.'

The very items that Janey had put there. G-Mamma had been framed, and Janey had unwittingly done it herself.

'But who were you ...' She stopped herself quickly. 'Who is victim?'

G-Mamma shook her head, and for the first time ever Janey could see that she had absolutely no idea what to do. 'I don't even know the guy. Never met him.'

'Which guy?'

'Trent Varley.'

'Trent Varley? Simone Varley's husband?' Janey could feel her accent slipping again, but she wanted to know more. G-Mamma nodded. Hoping it would sound like a Kazakhstan curse, she said insolently, 'Ach, Gogs! Who is zis Trent Varley?'

The information spooled out on the mini screens before her eyes. He was one of the HOST leaders, married to Simone Varley, the other man in the picture behind Oscar Sullivan's desk.

'And how did he die, Rosie Biggenham?'

G-Mamma was nearly shaking. 'This is the weirdest bit. Apparently, Blon … Interpreter, he was shot. Shot in an MRI machine.'

And then Janey stepped right out of character. 'But he can't have been, G-Mamma,' she cried. 'Trent Varley isn't even dead, or at least he wasn't at that stage! He might be dead now, but you're right – it's a set-up.'

Jane Blonde knew it for sure, because the image of Trent Varley being displayed on her glasses was completely familiar to her.

Only a few hours before, that man had knocked Gideon Flynn off the castle ramparts in Transnordia, before falling to his own death over the edge.

'I haven't time to explain, but I'm going to get you out,' she hissed urgently.

But then the guard stepped up to her, pressing a remote control on his belt.

'You've got all the time in the world,' he said, not very kindly, 'because you're joining her in there. I heard accent. You are no interpreter.'

With a foot in her back, he propelled her into the cell where she sprawled alongside her teacher. The gate slid shut behind her, humming with electrically evil power.

'Good work, Blonde,' said G-Mamma sardonically.

'It's all right. We'll just have to wait for the others.'

'Others?'

The guard was right. She did need a lot of time to explain it all. All the time in the world.

She heaved in a deep breath as Tilly would. 'So there's this place called Rustnuts,' she began.

Chapter 20 – The Great Escape

G-Mamma listened with a slack jaw as Janey described everything that had gone on Transnordia, interjecting with occasional shouts of 'Spies alive!' and 'You flew with Fang Airways?'

When Janey told the tale of Gideon and – apparently – Trent Varley grappling on the battlements of the castle, she reached across and grabbed Janey, folding her into her capacious lime-green bosom. 'What a thing to see, Blondey Baby! How are you coping?'

'Okay. I'm mostly confused, though,' said Janey, but then she paused.

She really was confused, about matters like Gideon and Varley falling off the castle walls but their bodies not appearing on the ground below. Had the villagers taken them? Had they somehow fallen out of sight where not even Jack could find them? Although surely he'd have spotted their *bas* ambling about with his x-ray death vision or whatever it was he had. Added to that was the complication that Trent Varley was missing-presumed-dead at that point, judging by G-Mamma's arrest. Well, he could certainly pack a punch for a dead guy.

It was all completely bewildering, but nothing was more peculiar than the terrible sadness and feeling of loss that had swept over her when Gideon Flynn tumbled to his death. Actually, she'd wanted to cry when relating that part of the tale. And yet she didn't like him or trust him and she suspected him of some truly hideous things – theft and avarice and possibly murder ... She blinked up at G-Mamma from where she was squashed into her chest, and said again, 'Yeah. Confused.'

'I know, Zaney Janey,' said G-Mamma with a sigh.

'So what happened to you?' Janey righted herself and leaned her back against the cell wall. It was pitted, hard and uncomfortable, but the only other options were the electrocuted gate or G-Mamma's well-padded tracksuit, so she shuffled in closer to the wall and settled in for a long tale.

G-Mamma was surprisingly brief, however. 'We arrived in good time and checked in with the other athletes. Tilly said hello to Mrs Varley to see if she'd accuse her of stealing that ring, but she barely remembered the girl at all. I introduced myself as Tilly's coach, and she just hurried off to deal with some technological issue. Ha! Technological issue my behind. Framing-me-and-locking-me-up issue, more like.' She glared venomously at her orange trainers, as if she was visualising planting one in Mrs Varley's mid-riff. 'Then these goons in khaki – and I mean, what kind of colour is khaki? – grabbed me and hauled me off to speak to these policemen, English policeman, and it turned out they'd been tipped off that Trent Varley's death was suspicious because he was,' – she mimed air quotes – '"poisoned" with curare and then shot with an old-fashioned rifle in the HOST basement.'

Janey nodded. 'The MRI room. I saw it when I was collecting the rifle. The walls were covered in blood.'

'AND,' cried G-Mamma, 'my lovely locks! One of my hairs was found near a plug socket, and both the ring and the rifle were found stashed away suspiciously in my home, as if I'd been trying to hide them.'

Janey gulped, forcing back tears again. 'That was all me! I'm so sorry. I must have had one of your hairs on my sleeve from dragging you to the operating theatre, and I suppose it fell off when I unplugged the MRI machine. The rifle was in that long doughnut box, and the ring was hidden in a cake tin.'

'So not only do they believe I'm a murderer, but they think I'm a pig too! As if I could have eaten all those doughnuts,' huffed G-Mamma crossly.

'Well, you could …'

The SPI:KE glared at Janey. 'Not all at *once*! Seriously, Blondette – I've been poisoned myself and left for dead with some sheep creature trying to climb out of my body, according to Jack Booty-Delicious, and now framed for murder. Give me a break!'

Janey apologised quickly, diverting G-Mamma as fast as she could. Provoking an angry, hungry G-Mamma in a small space was not a great idea. 'So what did Tilly do?'

'She tried her best,' said G-Mamma with a shrug. 'Did that slidy voice thing on the policeman, which is why they left me here instead of taking me back to the UK. She wanted to try out her kick-boxing on a few of the guards but we couldn't compromise her position in the Games, so she grabbed my SPIV and headed back to the arena.'

'She called me with it,' said Janey, thinking hard.

'Well! Maybe she's not just loud and annoying.'

'I don't really trust her either, but I think she's just … well, fun. She seems to enjoy everything.' Janey stopped herself before pointing out that G-Mamma was a lot like that, too – even, occasionally, loud and annoying. 'And she did manage to let us know what had happened. But where is she now? And Jack and Stein, of course. I'm guessing she's had that bracelet stuck on her wrist, but what does that mean?'

'More poison?'

Janey's innards squeezed tight. First G-Mamma, then Gideon's plummet from the ramparts, and now Matilda Peppercorn. They were falling like flies. 'I don't know, but I'd hoped they'd be here by now. We need to get out of here and find them.'

'Sure, if you want to be fried alive on a big griddle,' scoffed G-Mamma, jabbing a finger towards the gate.

'Well, there's a keypad. Maybe I can find something to put in the code.'

'You know the code?'

'I know one code, but I'm not sure it's the right one.'

Scrabbling around on the floor of the earthen cave in which they were imprisoned, she tried to find something that would extend between the bars of the gate to touch the keypad. The cave was completely empty, presumably as it was newly created and hadn't had anyone living in it. How she longed for some cavemen's tools - a mammoth bone, or something. She took off her glasses, wondering if they would stretch out into a long prong, but as she approached the gate with them, they started to vibrate in her hand.

'They're made of metal, I suppose,' she said, shoving them back on quickly. 'They'd just send the current right through me. G-Mamma, what about your trainers? Do they have a rubber sole?'

With her usual surprising dexterity, G-Mamma pulled her shoe in front of her nose and sniffed. 'I think so! That will protect you from the electrical charge. Did I teach you that?' she finished, preening slightly as she handed Janey an enormous orange sneaker.

'No, I learned it in physics.'

She placed her hand inside the trainer, realising instantly that G-Mamma was not undead like Stein, and evidently did sweat rather a lot. Why had she not persuaded her SPI:KE to do this? As carefully as she could, ensuring that not even a dangling lace could wobble against the fizzing metal gates, Janey eased her hand through the gap. 'Good! I can reach it,' she told G-Mamma, before turning the tip of the trainer towards the keypad.

'O-7-1, oh! It's not working. The toe isn't pointy enough.'

'Squash it!' suggested G-Mamma, so Janey pulled it back through the gate and flattened the front of the trainer into an angle. Then she tried again.

'O – yep, got that one, 7 … no, missed. I think I hit the 8 by mistake, and …' She hunted around the keyboard helplessly. 'Now I can't find a correction key. I daren't carry on, or we'll trigger some alarm somewhere. That's if it's even the right code.'

'Well, we can't just sit here!' G-Mamma scrambled to her feet. 'Give me my shoe back and I'll try it.'

'It won't work,' said Janey despondently as she held out the trainer. 'Unless …'

She felt that tingle of anticipation as an idea occurred to her, accompanied by a tiny flash in her brain, like a camera going off. 'Are your shoes equipped with Fleet-Feet?'

'Of course,' said G-Mamma, still holding her hand out for her missing trainer.

'And so are mine. Which means that we have two pairs of matching spy devices. And they built this cell in a hurry which means some of the walls might be weak.' Her eyes brightened as she X-rayed the cave wall through her spy glasses. 'Here!' she cried, running to the corner nearest the track she'd come down earlier. 'It's thinner here.'

'Sometimes, if I say so myself, you're quite brilliant, Blonde.' G-Mamma cottoned quickly to what Janey was planning; she seized the shoe from her other foot and handed it to Janey.

She was now holding – well, effectively a couple of small bombs. Scooping earth out of the cave wall with the trainers, she then planted the shoes in the hollow with the soles towards her. Without force, though, they couldn't be detonated, which was where her own Fleet-Feet came in.

'You'll have to hold me up, GM,' she said quickly, 'and be careful not to fall back against the gates.'

'I've got ya,' the woman replied, positioning herself in the middle of the cell and linking her hands under Janey's arms so that she was facing the wall.

'On three,' said Janey. 'Three, two, one ...'

They moved seamlessly like a piston, Janey lifting her legs to waist height as G-Mamma leaned back to take the strain, just avoiding connecting with the gates. In one mighty shove, Janey rammed both legs out in front of her and slammed her feet against the soles of G-Mamma's trainers, implanted in the earthen wall.

The explosive impact was immediate. Janey and G-Mamma were thrown backwards but the SPI:KE held her ground. Before their eyes, the trainers emitted a dull 'whu-whump' then ploughed through the packed earth to the outside of the dirt cell and burst out into daylight in a trail of smoke. Janey looked down — her own feet were shrouded in vapour too, and she realised how lucky it was she was wearing her spysuit, or else her ankles would have been broken, or possibly worse.

Now a tunnel lay between them and the outside world, rather like the one at the cliff-top castle in Transnordia.

'Come on!' she shouted, throwing herself into it, head and elbows first.

She was out in seconds, then she turned to help G-Mamma who squeezed herself through the tube, shovelling earth to either side to clear the way. 'Now I know what a mole feels like. Ha! A mole, like a spy mole … oh never mind.'

They stood for a moment, working out which way to go. Around them, televisions the size of cinema screens were directing the athletes to the bracelet tents, or to the arena, or for their screen-test for their sponsorship telethon. Half of every screen was dominated by a huge clock which counted down to the opening of the games. There were less than four hours to go.

'Where do you think they'll be?' said G-Mamma, hastily shoving on her trainers.

Following her lead, Janey threw off the coat she'd borrowed and untied her topknot. Hopefully they'd just be mistaken for an athlete and coach if anyone spotted them. She gazed at the screen again, working it out, working it out, with something niggling away at the back of her head.

'Tilly's team have been in the arena,' she read from the directions, 'and now they're on the way for their screen test for their sponsorship telethon, so we need to find out where those two things are and check in between … oh no.'

'Have we been spotted?' G-Mamma jumped from side to side, trying to make herself invisible.

Janey shook her head, her heart sinking. 'No, it's not that. It's that I've just realised what this might all be about. The rubies in the wristbands are like SIM cards, and each individual athlete is asking for sponsorship through their own telethon, so there must be some connection. That code!' she remembered with a start. 'It's like a telephone number – 0708 151 920. Maybe it's a trick that will destroy all the athletes, or steal all their money, or …'

'You've worked it all out very well,' said a low voice behind them, and Janey froze. That was impossible. She knew that voice. She'd heard it just hours ago, before he toppled from a cliff-top onto the unforgiving spikes below.

They turned around slowly.

'The thing is, you've only solved half the problem,' said the person before them. 'And you're running out of time.'

'But you … you're meant to have died.' She looked him up and down. 'Twice.'

And Trent Varley just smiled coldly – so coldly that Janey felt ice penetrate her spysuit – and then he turned and ran.

Was that the man I'm meant to have murdered?' shrieked G-Mamma.

'Yes, and I saw him plummet to his death yesterday, too.' Janey began to run. 'Come on!'

It was a good job the place was filled with athletes from all nations and of all disciplines, each with their own personal kind of super-power, because nobody took a great deal of notice of a girl in head-to-toe silvery Lycra and a track-suited woman steaming through the alleyways between the tents, the notice boards, the screens and satellites, shouting to each other, 'This way!' and 'Go faster!'

Trent Varley had vanished from view once more, so Janey followed in what she hoped was the general direction he'd been running in with G-Mamma hard on her heels, veering this way and that as trolleys of equipment rolled out into the alleyways or horses backed out of their boxes towards the make-shift stables.

'I've lost him,' cursed Janey under her breath. 'I'm making for the arena now. We'll have to find the others instead and let them know what's going on.'

'Your call, Blonde,' panted G-Mamma, struggling slightly but still managing to keep up with her "athlete" thanks to her Fleet-Feet trainers that she'd plucked from the cell wall, tattered and shredded but still managing to operate effectively.

The arena was to the left, as evidenced by the river of sportsmen and women pouring along the alleys towards it. Janey pounded in the same direction, sticking to the edges of the pathways so that she could get past the crowds, skirting the stragglers and keeping up the pace, powering on through the shadows, rather like Gideon did, or used to . . .

Suddenly her insides contracted as she thought of Gideon Flynn. If Trent Varley had survived that fall, then perhaps Gideon had too. Perhaps, by some miracle, he had also escaped death, escaped Transnordia, and found his way to the World Community Games in Kazakhstan. Right at this moment, however, she'd be happy just to know that he was all right, that he wasn't lying with a crumpled body, lost and alone, among the craggy stones in the foothills of a strange and barren land. The thought spurred her on even more, and she spotted the entrance to the arena not far ahead.

'They're checking everyone!' she called softly to G-Mamma, who was beetroot-red but still only a few paces behind her. 'We can't go in the main way.'

Driving her heels into the dusty red sand that made up the roads beneath their feet, Janey slewed to a halt, with G-

Mamma careering into her back. 'More warning next time!' she snapped.

'Sorry, but look,' said Janey.

The open gateway, the width of a warehouse, was flanked by vast white screens that grew increasingly closer together, funnelling the competitors towards two rows of desks that were slightly staggered like checkouts in a super-market. In fact, thought Janey, that was exactly what it looked like, as the HOST employees sat behind the desks with scanners in their hands, emptying and checking bags before scanning the wrist-band of the athlete at their 'till' and checking them off on the tablet screen attached to their desk.

She watched a few people approach the scanners. They chatted cheerfully with their operators as they first arrived at the desk, grinning and nodding, willingly opening their bags and offering their wrists for checking.

Once the scanner passed over their arm, however, for just a moment they all seemed to freeze. Barely noticeable if you weren't looking out for it as Janey was, it was suddenly everywhere once she'd spotted it. It was like the scanner had hit the pause button, causing the athlete to shut down for a split second while the ruby-studded wristband really got its teeth into them. Then, as if waking from a dream, the sportsperson would stare hard at the operator before grabbing their tennis racquets, skis or running shoes and returning to their previous cheery self.

'They're not checking them,' she whispered. 'They're *activating* them.'

'Activating what?'

'The rubies, I think. The sim cards. It looks as though they're somehow able to control the athletes. Oh! I wish I understood it better.'

G-Mamma smiled scarily at a nearby guard who seemed to have noticed that they weren't moving forward with the crowd, and flung a finger in the direction of the floor. 'Give me twenty, now!' she hollered to cover up their inactivity.

'Twenty push-ups? It's not the army,' grumbled Janey, but she did it anyway, letting her Girl Gauntlet take the strain as she performed press-ups without hesitation, using the opportunity to peer through legs and dangling bags until she could find something useful.

Fortunately, it didn't take too long. She leapt out of the final push-up, to the obvious admiration of the khaki-suited guard, and grabbed G-Mamma by the wrist. 'The last check-out is different. Looks like an enquiries desk. Come on.'

As they jogged across to the operator on the far right, she fished the bracelet she'd taken from the tent out of a pocket and held it up in front of her.

The boy on the check-out looked very taken aback to find it folded in her hand instead of sitting tight on her wrist.

'It broke,' she said, trying to feign concern. 'Just fell off when I was practicing my routine.'

The boy looked around for a supervisor. 'I'm not sure what to do about that. We have to scan in the information for the telethon.'

'How about I hold it out and you scan it on my hand?'

The boy stared at her and then shrugged. 'I suppose that should work.'

Janey knew it would definitely work. She held the bracelet out across her palm, making very sure that the ruby fell between the crook of two fingers and wasn't touching any part of her skin at all. The scanner beeped across the band, as Janey piped: 'Yes, I wanted to go and get another one but they ...' She paused mid-sentence to gaze silently at the boy, counting in her head – one elephant, two elephant, three elephant – and then she continued, '... said each one had been specially assigned.'

'We've had all sorts,' moaned the boy, clearly getting fed up with his job. 'Lost ones, duplicated ones, three people with the same one assigned to each of them. Hope they get it sorted next year.' He waved her through, then shouted, 'Oh! Sorry, no more people. Only equipment.'

'I am her equipment, young man,' blared G-Mamma.

He blinked at her as if he'd just been slapped. 'What ... what sport is that?'

'Human shot-put!' snapped the woman, as if he were an idiot. 'Why else would she be dressed like a ball-bearing? Watch!'

She linked her fingers near her waist and widened her eyes at Janey, leaving her with no choice but to run up to the SPI:KE, plant a foot in her hands and curl herself into a ball as G-Mamma launched her into the arena. She spun over and over until she saw the ground approaching, then opened out to land on both feet, being careful to use her toes so she didn't initiate the Fleet-Feet bounce.

'See?' said G-Mamma, sweeping past the poor boy, whose expression said even more clearly that he just wanted to go home.

Not everybody here was evil, then.

Only a few choice individuals.

They'd made it into the stadium. As Janey explained about the scanner pause, they walked mechanically for a while and then noticed that most people were just moving in their usual way, which often meant fast and determined.

'So, three people using the same wrist-band – do you think that might be our three?' she said at length, looking for Tilly's area which would be labelled by the Union Jack.

'I hope so, or there are other people infiltrating the Games. Which reminds me.'

G-Mamma quickly turned her jacket inside out so that the navy lining transformed it into an official-looking blazer. Kicking off her orange trainers, she walked straight into a pair of black Nikes that some poor athlete – a man, by the looks of it – had exchanged at the side of the athletics track. The Day-Glo tracksuit bottoms were still in full view, but in the same sleight of hand, G-Mamma fiddled with the hem of her jacket and hoisted her trousers up at the waist. The lime green trousers disappeared beneath a cascade of swishy blue material that descended from the jacket's hem, and suddenly G-Mamma was walking around dressed like a perfectly respectable Games official, in navy blazer, dark blue skirt and plain black shoes. Just to finish the outfit off, she inverted her baseball cap into a neat black trilby and shoved all her hair into it.

'Wanted for murder,' she commented, nodding towards a screen with her image plastered all over it. 'Time for a disguise.'

'G-Mamma,' said Janey with a giggle, 'I sometimes forget how amazing you are.'

'How dare you? Don't EVER forget how amazing I am.'

Janey laughed. 'Okay. I won't ever do it again.'

It was actually quite pleasant, strolling about the arena with the babble of excitement and zing of pent-up energy rising all around them. The sportspeople all appeared to be perfectly genuine athletes, and Janey could only imagine that the Games were going to be stupendous. Surely the

HOST organisation weren't planning to ruin that? It would ruin *them* if the Games didn't go ahead!

As if to answer her question, a klaxon rang out across the stadium and an oily voice announced, 'Ladies and gentlemen! Thank you for your attention. It's Henry Wentworth here,' and his face appeared on the many screens around them. 'With only an hour to go until the Games open, we just wanted to wish you all well. What a world-altering, life-changing event this is going to be, with our simultaneous coverage of all the live events from just two outstanding venues like this one in Central Asia. Give yourselves a pat on the back for being a part of this unique and electrifying spectacle. Go on, do it,' he urged with an unctuous grin.

Giggling self-consciously, the athletes around them shook hands, high-fived each other or pretended to pat their own backs.

Then Wentworth continued: 'You all know a very important part of this is the fan-cam viewpoint so that your own army of fans can tune in to your performance exactly as you are seeing it. It's as if they're doing it with you, folks!' He switched his jovial tone to serious and engaging. 'You've all been fitted with your wrist-band. This is state-of-the-art HOST technology that accesses your optic nerves remotely, with no side effects whatsoever, so that the viewer can see what you see. No need to worry – it's not a performance-enhancing drug! In fact, quite the opposite. The fans will see just what a human endeavour this is; what a feat you people are performing as individuals. If you fall, they'll fall with you. If you win, they'll see the finish line as you burst through it. It's all in the technology, and if it's okay with you …' He paused with a hand cupped to his ear, as if anybody would have the guts or the temerity to shout "Actually, I'd rather not, thanks!" Hearing nothing, he grinned and went on, 'We'd like to test the techno stuff. Nothing to worry about – we're just going to send out a little signal that you won't even feel, and we can check back here that the viewers are getting their money's worth. Okay? Great!' he cried before there was a moment to interject. 'Then here we go.'

The enormous crowd, thousands and thousands of people from individual competitors to enough rugby teams to run a three-day knockout tournament, all looked at each other, shrugging a little, murmuring to each other. Nobody looked particularly nervous, and if Janey hadn't known it was coming, she would hardly have noticed the signal go out and the test beginning. It was just as it had been at the gates, only en masse. As a strange, piercing note rang out delicately around the stadium, not loud but impossible to ignore – almost what Janey would imagine a dog whistle would sound like to canines – suddenly all the faces around them froze mid-laugh. As far as she could see, all action had ceased, leaving people with one leg in the air as they ran, parallel to the floor, or reaching out a hand to slap a team-mate across the back; person after person just frozen in whatever activity they'd been involved in, from the stall holders distributing water, to the flag-bearers preparing to display their country's emblem to the world. It was like a scene from Pompeii, without the volcanic ash.

Janey froze too, as did G-Mamma, although their eyes slid around attempting to spot what was going on. The entire stadium stood stock still in absolute silence … apart from three figures on the far side of the stadium, near the tented corridor that led to the screen-testing area. Tipping her head the tiniest fraction in that direction, Janey trained her glasses on the distant gateway and hissed 'Zoom' out of the corner of her mouth.

It was exactly as she'd expected – or feared. Matilda Peppercorn was standing near a team-mate wearing some sort of judo outfit complete with helmet, hands curled into her chest and one leg kicked out to the side. Her face was screwed up in concentration and effort, and Janey guessed that she was either very good at not moving a muscle, or she'd actually been frozen by the bracelet. Just behind her, however, things were not so peaceful. Stein was hopping around her, waving his hands in her face and pointing at the clock, while Jack – oh, poor Jack – was on his knees, hands clapped over ears that were rapidly growing black and furry as his head curled back and forth, and howling at the top of his voice: 'Make it stop! Owwwww!'

So the sound really was exactly like a dog whistle. And Jack was completely unable to prevent himself from giving their location away.

Luckily everyone else was still frozen, and Janey doubted whether they could hear anything through their inertia anyway... but further across the stadium, jungle-geared HOST operatives were making their way through the crowds, straight towards Jack, Stein and Tilly.

'Is that hullaballoo what I think it is?' whispered G-Mamma through her teeth.

'Yes, it's Jack.' Janey cast her eyes back and forth. 'They're closing in on anyone who isn't completely frozen; must be all the broken and duplicate bracelets. They've done this test to ferret us out.'

'Us?'

She'd hoped they'd held their cover, but in the doorway through which they'd come not so long ago, she could see a pair of HOST guards standing shoulder-to-shoulder with a teenage boy - the scanner guy. He was lifting a hand to point at a trio of synchronised swimmers who were all gazing at each other, bemused at what everyone else was doing ... and then to G-Mamma, balanced on one tiptoe with a fixed grin on her face.

'GM, we've been made,' she said urgently. 'MOVE!'

The spymaster needed no second bidding. Spinning on her heel and remembering that the black trainers weren't her shoes, she kicked them off and set off at a staggering pace across the stadium, hoofing innocent athletes out of the way as they posed with their elbows and knees at awkward angles, like human statues. Janey sprinted after her, gaining ground quickly but pausing to topple more athletes to trip up the guards, who were getting closer with every passing second. Across the silent stadium, Jack and Stein had noticed the guards approaching. With Jack still trying to cover one ear, they'd lifted Tilly up between them and were staggering towards the doorway.

'Jack!' cried Janey, cupping her hands together so that the sound echoed around the arena. 'Whooosh!'

It was a good job she'd shouted when she did, because suddenly she heard two sounds in quick succession: Henry Wentworth yelling, 'There! I told you,' and then the bubbling whisper of the crowd, rising like an orchestra warming up and bursting into life as the dog whistle was turned off. All around her, people were melting back into whatever action they'd been carrying out - finishing their step or clasping hands with someone or leaping across a sand-pit - and it was all directly in Janey's way. A little way ahead she could see G-Mamma fronting up to a young basketball player who had inadvertently chucked a ball at her face. 'Leave it,' she screamed at the SPI:KE. The woman shook a warning finger in the man's face and took to her feet again.

Simone Varley's voice penetrated the atmosphere. 'Well done, everyone; that went very well. Your fan-cams are all lined up, and I know you didn't feel a thing. They'd been very well beta-tested with senior officials in your own country, who gave us full permission to expand their usage.'

Tested? Senior officials? Of course! They'd tried them out at the party on the embassy representatives – probably on those security tags that everyone had worn, apart from them. No wonder the Ecuadorian minister had turned on her!

'If anyone is experiencing any discomfort, please let your nearest HOST ambassador know. They're the friendly folks in khaki. And if that experiment didn't work for anyone, well ...' – Mrs Varley let out a gentle laugh which sounded to Janey like the cackle of a mad woman – 'we'll just have to try a bit harder. Won't we?'

Janey almost tripped up, her mind churning ceaselessly through the events of the last few days. Why wasn't Varley more upset about losing her husband? Ha! It must be because she knew he wasn't dead. So what was Trent Varley up to? And what had he done to Gideon? Even more frightening, what exactly were HOST planning to do with all those compliant athletes, frozen on their command, eyes viewing whatever they instructed them to view… eyes viewing whatever they wanted them to view?

That was it!

She side-stepped a stretching marathon runner, evaded a guard and ran on, the realisations crystallising as energy coursed through her. That was what they were doing. They were creating eyes all over the world: eyes that would see the bank accounts fans had used to sponsor them with, or worse still, the presidential suites when they went to collect their special awards. They were creating a secret army, almost like their own spy organisation, with eyes on all sorts of Intel from the most personal to the most destructive, and an unwitting team of strong, nimble, powerful agents to do their bidding, even if they had no idea they were doing it.

It was, Janey realised, really clever.

And also completely unacceptable.

That was why Vance Kettering and Karen Fallows hadn't been allowed to come to Kazakhstan. It wasn't their age, it was their eyes rejecting the implant. 'Oh! Help!' That was what the poor lady in the cell had meant … and the man at the HOST hospital. They were being imprisoned like lab rats.

There was less than half an hour to go. She had to stop the Games.

But then a muscle-bound guard stepped out in front of her and struck her on the temple with an elbow. Her vision darkened and flickered, but not before she'd seen G-Mamma toppled by a HOST guard with a Taser. As for

Jack, Tilly and Stein, she had no idea if they'd even made it out of the Stadium.

She'd failed completely. Failed to save the world. She'd even failed to save Gideon Flynn.

And that was her last thought as her knees gave out beneath her and she crashed to the floor, although she could have sworn that she heard a low voice whisper in her ear. 'Don't give up, Blonde. Don't.'

Chapter 22 – What's in a Name

She opened her eyes with a jump when someone smacked her across the face.

'Finally!' said Matilda Peppercorn, her hair standing out in a steely halo as she leaned over Janey's prone body. 'That's the fourth time I've had to slap you. And I don't usually do slapping, only punching.'

'I'm so glad you didn't punch me,' said Janey with a wince.

'Well, I offered, but they thought I might knock you out again.' She gestured to Jack and Stein who were hovering above her shoulders, both frowning with concern. 'Okay, back off, Creepy and Creepier. She's awake now.'

'Forsooth, the ruby doth have – ahem, does have - a strange chemical make-up,' said Stein in excitement. He scratched Tilly's leather band down a nearby window, and they all watched as a streak of red snaked across the pane. 'A genuine ruby would not do that. This has been alchemically created. Gadzooks, this is all magnificently interesting!'

Janey sat up slowly, feeling tentatively for any parts that might hurt. She was sore all over, and her temple throbbed, but it was nothing that a Wower wouldn't be able to sort out – if they ever got out of here.

She glanced at Tilly's wrist where the bracelet had been. 'How did you get it off?'

'Dogboy chewed it off,' said Tilly a shudder. 'Can't tell you how many kinds of gross that was.'

Jack held up his hands, which were currently normal sized to match his normal teenage boy appearance. 'No, no, please don't thank me. It was no sacrifice at all to have to get that close to your arm even though you reek of cat.'

'You reek of dog,' replied Tilly.

'Do not.'

'Do too.'

Stein was watching them volley insults at each other as if he were a spectator at a tennis match. 'La, are they not fascinating?' he said to Janey. 'The experiments I could do!'

She was almost tempted to let him, but instead she asked them politely to stop fighting as she sized up their surroundings.

They appeared to be in a sealed glass room at the back of some kind of mission control. Surrounding them on the other three walls of the control room were more screens than would be necessary for a missile launch, and each one was broken down into a grid of mini screens, every image growing tinier and tinier as the number of them increased.

Janey went to zoom in with her glasses, only to discover that they'd been removed.

'What's on the screens?' she asked.

'All the athletes.' Jack stared glumly through the glass. 'There are millions of them. That will be a lot of money from fan sponsorships for some very nasty people.'

So they'd worked out some of what was going on – or some of it. She wasn't entirely sure she was right, of course, but it made a horrid sort of sense.

'It's worse than that. I reckon all those poor people will dial in to sponsor their athlete and HOST will take their money, and possibly their bank account, which is bad enough. But think about it: after that, they'll have eyes and ears in every country in the world, attached to world-class athletes who won't know why they're suddenly attacking a political opponent or passing on top-secret information. It's like a spy organisation, in a way. Talking of which…' Janey looked inside the room and then out at the mission control area. 'Where's G-Ma … GM?'

Tilly sucked in a gulp of air. 'Okay. So! They handed her over to the British police, saying that she murdered that Trent Varley character who Jack couldn't find, but he obviously wasn't very dead – not when they thought he was anyway.'

'He's not dead at all,' said Janey. 'We saw him here. He said we only knew half the story.'

'Oh! Anyway, the Big G was shouting that she'd been framed, and I think the local police were a bit scared of her so they arranged for her to be exterminated.'

'Exterminated! What? They're going to kill her?'

With a slow, deliberate step, Jack positioned himself between them. He'd clearly been doing some deep breathing himself and was taking everything very calmly. 'Not exterminated. Extradited.'

'That's what I said,' cried Tilly indignantly.

'It isn't. You were talking about what Daleks do when they zap people. Extradition is what the police do to make criminals face charges in the country where the crime was committed.'

'Okay, Smartypants.' Tilly wobbled her head at him, indicating that his was too big.

Jack shrugged. 'If I'm going to sit in the House of Lords, I might as well know about the law.'

'Zooks and zounds,' cried Stein excitedly. 'That sounds fun!'

Janey let her head sink into her hands. She was deeply worried about everything. It was as if the working parts of her brain were glued together in clumps. For the first time since their new adventure began, she couldn't conjure up a way out. The room was like a hermetically sealed fish-tank, and any of her spy-buys that might help them get out had been confiscated. She guessed the others were being hamstrung, too.

She attracted Jack's attention and pointed to his ears. 'Dog whistle?'

He nodded. 'Every time I've tried to make a move or even change into, you know, Jack BC.'

'It works on cats too, apparently. Sooo much pain,' said Tilly miserably. She flung a leg out towards the tempered glass and her foot merely bounced off it. 'And it's no good for kick-boxers.'

'I, meanwhile, am useless without a laboratory. I can't fashion a glass-cutting instrument from just one small red stone. I have only my pom juice to sustain my good spirits and my undeadness!' Stein extracted the flagon from the leg of his pantaloons. 'They didn't bother taking it off me, or perhaps did not realise I had it with me. I am evidently no threat whatsoever!' he finished with his usual chirpiness.

'Have you always been this cheerful and optimistic?' asked Janey with a grin, glad that one of them, at least, was able to maintain their cheery disposition, even with such a bleak outlook.

'Indeed, no. I was lonely and quite, quite diminished,' he said, 'but then I made a friend, and life – or death – has looked up ever since. I have several friends now.'

For some reason, Stein's words cut through the room like a diamond through glass. Janey could see that Jack and Tilly were thinking the same as she was - firstly, that Stein now had three more friends, but secondly, how they'd all felt that way at some point. Life was pretty pointless without friends. With a sudden pang, Gideon Flynn floated into her mind. There was someone who might have been a friend to her, or who might have needed a friend himself.

Now she'd never know.

She checked the countdown clock, furious with herself for letting her mind wonder, even for a second. Every moment counted. 'There are only six minutes to go until the Games kick off,' she said. 'And we're trapped in here like hamsters. It's infuriating.'

Her new friends trod little repetitive paths across the floor, equally frustrated and exactly like hamsters. It was maddening to be so helpless. Surely with their combined powers, they should be able to do something

'This is ridiculous!' she cried, banging on the window. 'Jack, you're a *god*, for crying out loud, and I'm a spy, sometimes even a super-spy in certain scenarios. Tilly, you're a cat, and a girl and a ... well, magic.'

'You can say "witch",' said Tilly nonchalantly. 'I won't be offended. Especially as I am one, although I'm only sort of witchy.'

'Okay, well, witches are magic, and that surely counts for something. Can't you do a spell?

'I'm not supposed to in NPW – that's Normal People World. Oh, look.' Her silvery hair was intensifying in colour and even beginning to glow. Tilly grabbed a strand and held it before her eyes. 'Turning blue. Oops.'

'What does that mean?'

'Bad jujubes. Nasty baddies. End of the world, that kind of stuff.'

'Just what we need.' Why was she the only one worrying? Janey felt like shaking them all but knew it would lead to no good. 'We must be able to do something though. A god, a spy, a witch, and an …'

'Undead princely scientist,' finished Stein, ever helpful.

But Janey had stopped short, thinking about what she'd just said. A god, a spy, a witch. 'Oh, my goodness! It's an anagram,' she whispered, 'and an acronym.'

'It's a whoey and a whatty?' Tilly sighed deeply and then performed a handstand against the back wall, so her hair fanned out against the floor, looking even more peculiar that usual. 'Doesn't anyone here speak cat?'

'Not cat, but I do speak spy. Which means … puzzles.' Janey wet the end of her finger and traced letters on the glass. 'G for God,' she said, writing G. 'S for Spy. W For Witch. Those are the beginnings of an acronym – a word made up of individual letters that stand for something, like NATO.'

Tilly gazed at the window. 'So … GSW? It doesn't trip of the tongue, does it?'

'WGS. That's like wags – for a dog's tail?' Jack beamed in delight.

But then Janey moved it around. 'What if S for Spy comes first, followed by W for Witch, then G for god last?'

'Swrrrgg,' tried Stein.

'Close, but remember, Gideon brought this team together,' said Janey. 'And at the top of the list with our names on it was a word. SWAG.'

'SWG. That does kind of work. But how does Stein fit in, then?' said Jack.

Janey turned to the younger – older – boy. 'Stein, or rather ... Petroc,' she asked gently, 'is there a special name that describes what you do? Not just science, but turning ordinary metal into gold and life to unusual things?' She thought she knew it, but she wanted to hear it from him.

Stein shifted in rather a guilty fashion. 'I do not know if we are allowed to name it in this century, so I hesitate to say. My mother and father were chased out England for practicing such sinful potion-making. That's why Mother asked if they still hang witches. She has always wanted to go home.'

'Please, Stein. Does it start with ... A?'

They all waited, holding their breath as Stein decided to come clean.

'Yes, forsooth. I am known as an Alchemist,' he said, exaggerating the first letter.

It was as she'd thought, but there was no time for gloating. Instead, Janey inserted the letter A into the writing on the window.

'So that's us. Spy. Witch. Alchemist. God. It all equals SWAG. I thought he'd named the project because of the stuff we were meant to steal, like booty or treasure or what a burglar takes.'

'Or, you know, confidence!' said Tilly. 'Get your swag on.'

Planting her feet back on the floor, she shimmied her way around the goldfish bowl, with plenty of swag.

'It could have been any of those things, but it's not. It's us. It's the team. Gideon's team.' Janey felt her eyes fill with tears, and she brushed them back, angry at herself for getting emotional. 'And we've lost him. What's the point of us, without the person who brought us together? We lost our leader.'

'I don't think we did, Blonde.'

She was just about to ask Jack what he meant – did he mean that someone else was their leader? G-Mamma, perhaps? – when she saw that he was staring past her into the mission control room. It was filling up with people, ready for the hideous countdown and the moment when the Games would open up, along with all the secret information channels, offshore bank accounts and security networks of all the participating countries, if they only knew it. Several of the HOST ambassadors had moved indoors and were now settling down for the excitement to begin, poised in front of the monitors or the phone lines in preparation.

But up on the balcony, high up where nobody was looking as they concentrated on the clocks, the screens, the rubies and the athlete army, two figures were fighting.

Again.

There was Trent Varley, squaring up to the his more slender opponent, striking out with such ferocity that there was no way he could be matched, no way his rival could even survive another attack as vicious, as potent, as deeply personal as this seemed to be …

… especially someone like Gideon Flynn.

He was back.

Then two of the HOST henchmen swung around, alerted to the presence of the two brawling figures by directions in their headsets. In unison, the pair of HOST guards swept towards the balcony, one even lifting a hand to point at the sky-light above Gideon's head … but then they simply held a quick conversation and headed out of the room together, unperturbed by the massive fist-fight going on just a couple of metres from their faces.

It was as if they hadn't seen them at all.

And suddenly Janey's brain cleared with the familiar click that told her that she'd reached some solution, the flashing light in her head that was as spot-on as any gadget that the Big G had ever managed to send in her direction.

The letters of SWAG were still visible on the shiny surface of the glass.

Dampening her finger again, Janey wrote out four more letters.

HOST.

Of course. She should have seen it earlier.

It didn't stand for Helping Others Save Time. It was another acronym.

H. O. S. T.

She wrote the names underneath in lines like the downward clues in her beloved crosswords and search-words.

Henry. Oscar. Simone. Trent. H-O-S-T.

They hadn't just founded HOST – they *were* HOST. A team. A set of friends, perhaps, rather like SWAG.

She stared at it, heart pounding furiously as another clue slid into her brain. It had prodded at her mind since she first saw it, because she'd learned cyphers and codes like this with G-Mamma and the other spies. How could she have missed it all this time?

It wasn't a phone number that she was mapping out on the window now – 0708 151 920. That was just the way she'd heard it, or maybe the way she'd deliberately been told it.

It was *another* type of code, not in phone formation, but in pairs:

07 08 15 19 20.

It was so obvious, now that she was looking at it in the correct way.

H, for Henry, the eighth letter of the alphabet – or 08. O for Oscar was the fifteenth; S for Simone was letter 19 in the alphabet, and T for Trent the letter that came immediately after it, matching the number 20.

Which just left the first pair of numbers.

07

It was ironic that it sounded almost like a famous spy's number, 007, because in this instance, it wasn't a spy code. It was an initial.

G.

G for … Gideon.

Struggling to hold back her tears, Janey wrote the letter in front of the others, above the digits 07. It transformed the letters making the word HOST into something else – something incredibly and horribly appropriate.

GHOST.

Through the damp, scribbled letters on the window, Janey stared at the young man trying to avoid Trent Varley's pounding fists. That was why he couldn't be touched. That was how he could access the dead, the magic, the spy world of old with characters like Garbo. That was why he dressed like he did. Why he'd had to lead them to discover what had happened, because he couldn't tackle it himself. Why Jack could always see him but was surprised they could … which must be because he'd used the Wower and … the VoxPop and … 'Pom juice!' whispered Janey. Why he'd appeared to die, plunging to his death, and yet Jack couldn't find him, and why he had seen Trent before anyone else …

She knew everything there was to know, instinctively and intuitively. He caught her eye, and she knew that he could see she'd worked it all out. Putting a hand across his heart, Gideon gazed directly at her, and in that instant she knew what a fight, what a long and thankless struggle this had been for him. The tears flowed down her cheeks as she turned to the team. His team – the team he'd assembled to put things right, if it could ever be possible.

The team of SWAG.

'So is neither of them dead, then?' said Tilly, following the punches in mime, only ducking rather more effectively than Gideon. 'Only I'm completely confused now. That Trent dude died. But they keep disappearing and showing up again.'

Janey shook her head.

'No, I don't think either one of them is dead,' she said quietly.

'Because it's both of them. They're both dead.'

Chapter 23 – A compound problem

He'd tried to stop it snowballing, really he had. They were just meant to be an innocent science group, pooling resources and interests to move together towards the future. It was a fascinating time, what with men landing on the moon only a few years before, and massive, powerful computers taking up whole rooms in businesses across the country, like Henry's father's company. Working together in this way, they all reasoned – well, they'd just be saving time.

And so they'd created GHOST, a clever acronym from all their names: Gideon, Henry, Oscar, Simone and Trent. He sometimes wondered if the others were truly committed. Both Oscar and Trent were madly in love - not with science, as he was, but with Simone. They fought over her on the rugby field, at their card games, over what video to put in the VCR, so much so that Gideon often suspected that their little club was far more to do with trying to impress the cleverest girl in school.

But then he'd received the ring for his seventeenth birthday, and as he'd never be able to wear such an ornate thing in public, like the idiot he was he'd spent days – weeks, even - researching rubies, poring over the micro-

fiche in the school library, discovering what properties they had, how they were formed, how fake rubies could be created.

It was only at that point that he'd discovered about the different types of waves that emanated from it – long ultra-violet and infra-red. Then Trent and Oscar had really gone into overdrive, setting up companies to patent the testing equipment under the tutelage and encouragement of their business-minded fathers. He had university to look forward to, they reasoned, but they would have to go straight into the world of work. They had to protect their interests. Their creations.

Only they weren't their inventions.

They were Gideon's.

Gideon's parents weren't that way inclined, of course, for which he had always been very grateful. His dad was a history teacher, qualified after the war when not enough young men came back from fighting to fill the positions. His mother was just glad to have been given the gift of a son, late in life when such thoughts and hopes had almost evaporated.

They always thought they didn't understand him sufficiently, seeking advice from the younger, more "with it" parents of his friends, but the fact was, they understood him perfectly. He was an exact blend of the two of them, keen-minded and curious about the truth, about life itself, like both of them, and gently compassionate about mankind, just like his father. A compound. That's what he was. A compound like the chemical combination from which rubies could be produced in a chemistry experiment, precise and flawless – or soulless, in Gideon's view.

But the others had become overly excited, promising each other great success, huge riches, with their families urging them on at every turn. They'd argued over the rights and wrongs of mass-producing rubies to flog to their friends unknowingly, as Henry Snr had done to Gideon's own father, and then they'd argued over the rights and wrongs of creating transmitters with those very same rubies, and then they'd argued over the group, and whether Gideon should remain it if he wasn't interested in the future.

'It's all I'm interested in,' he'd shouted, one night when the five of them were camped out in the tiny kitchen of his parents' cottage, fiddling fractiously with their tea-cups as one or other of them became increasingly agitated. 'Forwards and backwards, learning from history, improving the future with our knowledge. You're talking about controlling people and duping them! That's not right. That's what Hitler was trying to do. The war was less than thirty years ago, guys. Haven't we remembered its lessons?'

Trent stood up, mocking, chest-thumping for Simone's benefit. 'Flynn, it's 1972. Get with the times, man.' And then he'd grabbed Gideon's father's favourite item from

the top shelf – the rifle his own grandfather had used in the
Boer War. 'Come on,' he cried in a poor imitation of
Gideon's voice, 'What about the war? What about guns
and rifles and Hitler?'

'Put it down, Trent,' Henry had said, all smiles and
smooth tones. He'd be a politician one day, like his father
– they all agreed on that. Probably as slimy a character as
well, though Gideon kept that one to himself. 'Come on.
Don't be an idiot.'

'No, I like it,' said Trent, and he'd pointed it at
Oscar's head.

Oscar, his rival in love, and life, and everything.

It was never anything to do with Gideon, really. Or
Henry. They were just hapless by-standers. It was all about
the three of them – Simone, Trent and Oscar. The only
thing was that Gideon wasn't sure how far Trent would
take it. He was always fisty, always the one to fly off the
handle.

And now he was standing in the Flynns' kitchen with
a rifle in his hand – an old unused one, granted, but a
firearm, nonetheless.

So Gideon had done the grown-up thing as Oscar
quivered in the corner of the kitchen, and Simone
attempted to look unconcerned and Henry poured oil over
troubled waters. He'd walked across to Trent, and taken
the gun off him. Then he'd left the house, because he
wanted them out of it, with all their posturing and empty

promises. He wanted them out of his home, so small that his parents had suddenly announced that night that they were going to the pub, which they never did, just to give him some space with his friends. Probably been advised to do that by Harry Wentworth or Paul Varley, both of whom owned mansions with more rooms than they knew what to do with and so much space they'd never notice their own teenage children.

He'd just meant to get it out of sight, then come back and ask them to leave. That was all. GHOST would be over, but he was glad. His father had taken a few shares in it in Gideon's name, prompted by the other parents, but it had lost its meaning for him. Like the ruby, it was meant to be natural. The manufactured ones lost their lustre.

Turning right as he eased out of the front door, he'd loped along to the triangle of grass that masqueraded as a park. Here he'd learned from his parents how the angle of the sun's rays affected the growth of the grass, and many other marvellous tricks and treasures of nature. There was a hollow tree in which he'd hidden his bounty when he was little; the gun could just stay there until this nonsense was over.

But Trent's blood was running high. He had that gleam in his eye that always appeared during rugby matches or other vigorous sports – all the things Gideon avoided.

Suddenly Varley was upon him, wrestling the rifle out of Gideon's hands as the others tumbled through his doorway, crying out to Trent, to Gideon, telling them to stop, put the rifle down, don't be stupid ...

It was an accident, of course. Trent would never have meant to fire the gun. He wasn't to know how ancient it was, and unstable, or that the combination of oxygen, old gunpowder and the violent shaking would make it ... well, not fire, exactly, but explode – explode between their bodies ...

Shrapnel had sliced into Gideon's liver and spleen and he'd gone instantly, right there on the park. For Trent, it was almost worse. Bullet casings and shards of metal lodged themselves in his hip, missing all his major organs by a fraction but causing a great deal of pain, forever, along with the agony of what he'd done. What he'd caused.

They all believed that Simone married him, in the end, out of sympathy.

Gideon had come back on the very same spot, in the shadows beneath the trees where he'd watched nature turn the wheel of time, creating its miracles. He'd sought revenge, of course, for such a long time, but he didn't have the power to cause any damage. He kept a distant eye on the shares that his father had never even gone near, and dreamed of what HOST might have been if he'd still been around.

Eventually he started to hear of the others – others in the half-life, or at least deeply unusual – and finally he understood that the power could be his now, if he chose to organise it. The power to avenge his death ...

Then the Games had been conceived, and he'd discovered what they were planning to do. Trent objected – he'd learned his lesson when he and Gideon fought – but the others were relentless. Bold and diabolic and relentless. Oscar and Simone were plotting again, and Henry was too weak to stand up to them. Poor Trent. He'd rung his own death knell by threatening to leave HOST.

And when he saw what they did to Trent who'd opposed them, paralysing him before putting him into an MRI machine that would rip the bullets up through his body, shooting him for the inside - that was when he knew what he had to do. The money could finally be put to good use, spent remotely and secretly.

It was his money, anyway.

And somehow, he had to finish what he'd started.

Chapter 24 – To Do or Die

'What do you mean, they're both dead?' demanded Tilly.

Janey checked the countdown clock. There was less than a minute to go before the opening ceremony of the World Community Games was broadcast all over the globe. If she started explaining now, all would be lost.

'I'll fill you in afterwards if I can, but for now, could you all just trust me? We have to stop the global activation of the rubies, and that means getting to Gideon. Jack, it's going to hurt, I'm afraid.'

For several precious second, three confused expressions loomed before her eyes. She'd lost them. It was too much to ask, to announce that someone they'd met several times didn't actually exist – not in the usual sense of the word, anyway.

Then she saw the people crowded into this glass cell with her, and, perhaps for the first time, she truly saw them: Jack, a Lord who'd rejected his status in life and ended up helping people through their death experience; Tilly, a weird combination of feisty kick-boxing teenager and a whole host of other inexplicable and magical things, and Stein, the lonely ancient alchemist who created, not just gold, but friends of his own, just to make life bearable.

If anybody (and that included feline, canine and three-hundred-years-old bodies) could understand the need to trust in the unbelievable, it was these guys. If anyone could appreciate that sometimes, nothing was what it appeared to be, it was these three.

'Ready?' she whispered, hoping from the depths of her Fleet-Feet that they would rise up to her belief in them.

And Jack shrugged, his shoulders elevating in the same moment and his jet-black Anubis head soaring up from his collarbones to the tips of his ears in a rush. He shook his head as the dog whistle instantly got louder, obviously in agony, but then looked at Janey.

'What do we do?'

That was it. Janey suddenly started rapping out the orders that formed in her mouth almost before she had captured them in her mind.

'Jack, get us out of here. There'll be uproar and they might switch the sound up, but you'll have to ignore it. Tilly, cut off as many bracelets as you can in the mission control room – we want to be in charge of all the people in there.'

'Aye Aye, Cap'n,' cried Tilly, spinning like a cat chasing its tail until she really did possess a tail, attached to a lean, feline form with sleek grey fur. She whipped out a sabre claw that would have made Trouble weep with envy and dropped into position ready to launch.

Now for Stein.

'What about me, Blonde?' he was saying, but she grabbed him by the wrist and ran towards Jack so that he could transport them all together. 'You're coming with me,' she said, hoping that what she suspected was true.

Trembling with the onslaught that was rupturing his ears, Jack gathered them all together - with Tilly in her cat-form actually daring to perch upon his shoulder - and then he rushed them through the centimetres-thick glass. It melted around them and then closed again, whole and untouched.

In the control room, bedlam ensued as the HOST staff found a dog-headed monster careering through their midst, clearing the way for an evil-looking cat to land on their desks, pinning their arm down with one immensely strong leg and, with the other, ripping their wristbands asunder so that they fell onto the floor or into their coffee cups. Jack ploughed heedlessly through any obstacle in his way that wasn't human – computers, lecterns, control desks, screens – and threw people into a pile, trapping them beneath each other in the centre of the room, ready for the feline cutting machine.

Thirty seconds to go.

While the pair got on with removing wristbands, Janey steered Stein towards the balcony where Gideon and Trent were still engaged in a fight to the death – or so it would seem. Janey suddenly realised how mindless it was for this to go on. How could the result be any worse than their present reality, trapped in spirit bodies and able to touch only each other?

Because she was pretty sure that was the case. It made sense of so much, like Gideon's 'condition', for instance. It wasn't that he had something wrong with his hands that might infect someone else or hurt him if he came into contact with anything - it was that his hands had no corporeal form. It was why he'd managed to slide so easily through the gates around Richmond Park. The bars had gone through him, not the other way round. And it was why Jack, she guessed, had been able to see Trent Varley at the HOST offices as he was accustomed to seeing spirits. And Tilly was a witch, so she'd see him okay. She wasn't sure how she and G-Mamma could see Trent, but luckily someone else was also used to a bit of deadness.

'Up here,' she cried to Stein, and they charged up the stairs towards the battling duo.

Once again, Gideon was bearing the brunt of it, crouching low to avoid the thunderous blows from Trent Varley's angry ghost. Janey ran straight through Trent's torso; he half-stood, outraged, staring at his hands and body and then at Janey and Gideon, before his arm to bring down a crushing blow on Gideon's shoulder.

'Stein, your flagon!'

The boy stopped short, fumbling in his pocket for the flask of pom juice.

'I hope this is as good as I think it is,' said Janey, remembering the strange heat sources that had glowed in her Gogs when she surveyed the castle's laboratories.

'It is a potent unguent,' Stein confirmed with a small smile. Then he handed the flask to her.

Ten seconds to go until the games went live.

Janey flung the pom juice unguent over Gideon's faded, semi-transparent shape, and held her breath.

'Will this work?' she whispered to Stein.

'Gadzooks, I have no idea. I have never tried it without a body before.'

Gideon was gazing at her, half in shock and half in wonderment, his outline shimmering in and out of focus as Trent Varley's fist descended like an anvil, powering relentlessly towards Gideon's crouched body ...

... and then passing right through it. They were no longer made from the same matter – or non-matter.

Gideon gasped, sucking in a great rattling breath as if waking from a dream, then he shot to his feet as Varley stared at his hands, his lifeless, formless hands, and then at Gideon.

They all looked at Gideon, in fact.

His silhouette glowed with a delicate red-gold light, and where his eyes had been sunken and dark, they sparkled now with life and awareness. His skin was still pale, but a faint pink tinge touched his angular cheekbones, and for the first time, Janey could see colour in his lips.

'I ... you've done it!' he whispered, lifting his hands before his face and studying them, eyes round with wonderment and delight.

He turned to Janey, palms upward, showing her the shimmer of light across his skin – actual skin. He was trying to say something when a bell rang behind them.

'You're too late,' said Trent Varley's ghost. 'I told you only knew half of it,' he roared at Janey.

'We can still tell everyone what's happening. Expose the others,' she said. 'Or turn off the control connection on the bracelets.'

He shook his head, his image dimming in contrast to the flickering, flaring light from the multiple screens in the control room, where Jack and Tilly were now rounding up stray employees who had tried to run off and liberating them of their wristbands.

'That's just a fraction of what the bands can achieve,' he said scornfully. 'We were doing things on a mighty scale. All those thousands of athletes, each with a sharp little ruby hovering directly over their wrist – if you do anything else, they'll flip the switch and the rubies will be on transmit.'

'What does that mean?'

Gideon Flynn rose to his full height. It was the first time Janey had seen him when he wasn't hunched over, often with his hands in his pockets, and now he towered above her. 'It means,' he said, his voice stronger as the unguent worked its magic, 'that they've got us over a barrel. They'll send out microwave rays that will damage the athletes' nerve endings, or possibly worse, if we try to stop them.'

'It's all your fault,' said Varley, shaking with rage. 'Why did you let them do this in the first place? You've been advising them, you must have. They haven't the brains to do this themselves!'

'So that's why you've been attacking me!' Gideon moved to grab Varley by the arm, but his hand, so delicately real, drifted through the ghost-man's sleeve. 'Trent, you know that's not true. I didn't want it, any of it. And Simone – well, I hate to say it, but she always had the brains for it, and the beauty, and the ability to make you all fight each other instead of her. She's behind it all.'

'No! You've been guiding them, I know it. And then you got this circus outfit to support you. I knew there was something peculiar when I realised that dog-headed boy could see me. That's why I followed him through that tunnel and found the other freak show in Transnordia. You've been leading everyone! Everyone to carry on with your original plans.'

'Trent, man, I've been dead,' said Gideon with a short laugh. 'How would I have done that when they couldn't even see me?'

'Well, *they* can see you.' Trent glared at Janey and Stein. 'And they can see me,' he added, confused.

It had confused her, too, but then she'd put two and two together. 'The others can see you both because they're not entirely human, and as for G-Mamma and me – I think it must be the rubies that changed our vision. We were both scratched by one.'

Trent winced. 'It'll change your vision for sure, especially when they stick it in your eyeball.'

'That's why your eyes were twitching, even through the curare,' whispered Flynn. 'The control switch?'

'Simone's ring,' said Trent. 'You saw me then? In the surgery?'

As Gideon nodded, Janey watched his face to see if her assumptions were correct, amazed at how alive and radiant it looked. How could she not have understood it before, that there was something about him that wasn't even there most of the time?

'I think Gideon needed our equipment and skills to show up in full form. The emails and so on …'

'Voice activated,' Gideon confirmed.

'Because you'd used the Vox Pop to give yourself a voice, and then the Wower to give yourself form … and the powers that Jack and Tilly have anyway to see things that people normally can't.'

'Gadzooks, and me!' cried Stein. 'I, too, am used to seeing undead beings.'

Gideon sighed. 'Yes, you are. And actually before Trent ran off to Transnordia, it gave me an idea. I thought we could … bring him back to life and scare the others beyond their wits.'

They all fell silent at the thought, before Stein said gently, 'God's truth, I have done some incredible things but never without a body. Did you have your body to hand, Sir Trent?'

'Not one I'd want to use ever again.' Trent looked vaguely sick at the thought. 'Although it would have been a good punishment for the others. So you built this crew from scratch, Flynn? They're all deeply unusual.'

'They're all special. Very special,' said Gideon, his eyes on Janey and Stein. 'But you have to believe me, before I met Blonde and the others, I could only listen. Listen and regret. I had no voice, no presence. Just a growing bank account that my parents don't understand enough to know I've tapped into it. I've been planning how to get back at you all for decades, and now we can do it – together.'

The other three stared at Gideon, his words not making sense. Did he mean they could … get back at everyone together?

'I was going to poison Simone with her own ring,' said Gideon. 'Or rather, the SWAG team was. I planted a letter on Oscar's desk that would cause Oscar and Henry to fight over the rifle. It was primed to go off. But the objects aren't here – they're in the evidence room in the UK. Then

I was going to scare them with Trent, hopefully into heart attacks. We have to think of another way.'

'Another way to what?' said Janey slowly, hardly caring now that, outside the control room, the games were beginning. Her insides were churning as hideously as they had when the super-sized ruby had imparted its evil power on them – for that was what it had done, she was sure of it. It had been getting its claws into her and G-Mamma from simply brushing their skin, until Gideon had instructed her to get rid of it. She was glad she'd listened to him then, but in every other respect she was convinced that she should have stuck with her earlier decision – the one where she'd decided not to trust Gideon Flynn. 'Another way,' she repeated, 'to what?

'To kill them. To kill the others.' Gideon stared at Trent. 'You're already dead, and that's unfortunate, but surely you'd like revenge too?'

Trent shook his head, his eyes sorrowful. 'I was already dying,' he said with a shrug. 'Simone knew that. I'm not sure if the others knew too, but they just sped up the process, really.'

'All the more reason then, Varley!' cried Gideon, his silhouette pulsing with light.

But Janey stepped in between them. 'Gideon, that's not right. That's not what you want, surely. You were setting us up to kill the people who hurt you! Do you know what that would have done to us all? Look at G-Mamma now, sitting in prison.'

Gideon could hardly bring himself to look at her. 'I … I know. That's what it started as, but I didn't know you all then. I hadn't thought it all through. The dark dream just took over. It was what I thought I wanted, for sure, but …'

Wishing she could hold his hand, for comfort or for persuasion or for something, Janey stepped closer to him than she had ever been and lowered her voice. 'I can understand that you'd be angry,' she said carefully. 'You've lost so much.'

'Everything,' he retorted, hardly audible.

Janey felt her eyes burning. 'Everything,' she agreed with a nod. 'But you … you've got some things back now. You've got a … well, sort of a body. You've got us. Me.'

To her alarm, Gideon looked close to tears too. 'You don't understand. This is all that's kept me going for so long, the thought of what I'd do to them all.'

'But … I don't believe that,' she told him. 'The old couple at the cottage, you thought about them too.' Gideon swallowed furiously, clearly trying not to think about the elderly pair he'd watched so affectionately. 'And these people – all these innocent people here, and around the world,' she continued. 'Don't you want to help them? Wouldn't that be a better reason than getting revenge?'

'I see.' Gideon released a mirthless laugh. 'Do you want me to use my power for good, Blonde?'

And Janey nodded. 'Yes. Yes, I do. And I think you'd prefer it too. And I've noticed that ...' How did she phrase this? 'You glow a bit brighter when you're happy.'

There was a deep silence while her words sank in, with Gideon hardly able to hold back tears. The outline of his shape was fading and glowing in an irregular pattern as he battled with his emotions.

Finally, he turned to Trent. 'Would you want revenge?'

Trent sighed. 'I thought I did – against you! But no. No, really I just want it all to be over. It's gone on too long.'

There was a terrible moment while Gideon stared at his old friend in which Janey thought it was over. He wasn't going to alter his plans – and she wasn't going to carry them out, so it had all been for nothing.

But then his shoulders slumped forward. 'It wasn't until I saw what they'd done to you that I started to change my mind,' said Gideon suddenly. 'And I don't want your death to be for nothing, too. Blonde's right. Let's do something positive, Trent. Together.'

Gideon gazed sorrowfully at his former friend, and Trent Varley suddenly crumpled to the floor, hugging his knees as tears rolled down his face. 'I was going to stop them,' he sobbed. 'I told them I was going to the police, to the government, to anybody who would listen. After what happened to you, Gideon, and to me, I couldn't believe they didn't see the danger in what they were planning. I always made them remember you, Flynny – all the things you'd hoped to invent. That's why your initial is still hidden in the code for the HOST name. I insisted! I confess, they convinced me for years that we could rule the world, but I didn't care after a while. Money and power are all well and good, but there's no point in it just for its own sake. What's the fun in playing rugby, say, if you don't have a team that can match you? It all got out of hand, and now we can't stop it.' He broke down again as Gideon attempted to comfort him.

Ever since the shock of discovering what Gideon had laid out for them, Janey had been planning to walk away. It was as she's always said: they weren't thieves, and they definitely weren't murderers.

But they were … friends. Friends like Gideon and Trent had once been, when a tragic accident had altered their realities beyond recognition.

So Janey had been thinking, plotting, listening to what was going on and wondering how they could turn it to their advantage.

And suddenly, Trent's team-talk ignited a spark.

'How about we don't try to stop the games?' she said. 'How about we play them instead?'

It was HOST versus SWAG, and Janey was pretty confident that they had the upper hand.

The control room belonged to SWAG now, which was a very good start, as all the telemetry and broadcast equipment was initiated in there. Unfortunately the staff, while free of the controlling wristbands, were alarmed to come to their senses in the presence of an enormous dog-headed god and a cat that seemed to be shouting instructions at him as it tore at them with terrifyingly accurate claws and teeth. Those who could get out fled the building, running from the central control room as fast as their legs could carry them, and the less fit or the cornered had locked themselves inside the very glass cell from which the SWAG team had only recently escaped. Presumably they hadn't worked out that if Jack could get out of the glass prison, he could get back into it as well.

But what really interested Janey was the fact that the massive monitors lining the walls were all still operating. Right at that moment, Henry Wentworth's foolish face was projected in full colour onto every screen, and only someone watching very closely would notice the slight edge of panic behind his broad smile, plastered firmly across his face so that he looked like a ventriloquist dummy, talking through his teeth – which, Janey thought, was probably about right. He was a puppet, his strings pulled by Oscar Sullivan and Trent's horrible widow, Simone Varley.

'The procession is coming to you from our secret location, where all the world's competitors have gathered for the inaugural World Community Games.' His rictus grin seemed to move of its own accord as he swivelled his head to show the athletes gathering in the stadium, waving into cameras and forming swirling groups with their team-members that ebbed and flowed into the teams for the surrounding countries. They looked so happy, and it truly was an awe-inspiring sight. Janey sighed. If only it was genuine, it might have been quite a world-altering idea. A game-changer, they might have called it.

Well, now they were the game-changers. And this tournament wasn't over yet.

'They're broadcasting from somewhere else,' she said to the group behind her. 'We've got to access the TV station or whatever it might be to beat them at their own game.'

'I … I think I know where they are,' said Trent. 'I even helped set it up – a bunker, you might call it, in case anything went wrong.'

'Can you take us?'

Trent nodded. 'They'll turn the squads on you, though. Won't cause me any harm, but you guys … even you, Flynny, with your new physical presence … you'll be in for a pounding.'

As Gideon shrugged easily, Janey noticed Stein inspecting Gideon and then the inside of his flagon. 'What's wrong?'

'It doesn't last for ever,' said Stein simply. 'That's why we have pom juice every day back in Transnordia.'

'Oh, Stein! We used it all! What will happen if you don't get your pom juice?'

She didn't add 'And Gideon' as she was pretty sure she knew. Gideon would just become half-darkness again, hunched and miserable and not at all this vibrant, glowing being that he'd just become.

Stein tried to look nonchalant. 'Forsooth, I have never had to find out! But I'm sure there's enough left if I lick the bottom of the flagon. Unless you need it, Master Flynn,' he added quickly.

A hundred different emotions flickered across Gideon's face, and Janey suspected every one of them was reflected in her own – loss, yearning, compassion for his friend who needed the unguent as much, if not more than he did, a spark of hope that might soon be extinguished …

Finally, Gideon smiled. 'I'll be fine,' he said firmly. 'You must have it, then you can go home and make some more. No point in both of us disappearing forever.'

'Master Flynn, you are wise,' said Stein. 'And I'd much prefer it if neither of us disappeared forever.'

Gideon nodded, saying nothing and avoiding anyone's eye as Trent hopped uneasily from foot to foot.

'Come on, then,' said Janey, hoping she sounded more resolute than she felt. 'Let's take them by surprise.'

As one, they ran down the stairs into the main control room where Jack and Tilly were

stashing wristbands in waste-bins, their appearance just like any pair of teenagers who'd been sent to do the chores.

'Ready to fight an army?' called Janey.

Tilly whooped for joy. 'At last!' she cried, punching the air. 'I totally am!'

'Gently, though,' said Janey. 'They're only acting under orders, and they won't know what they're doing.'

'Hey, I'm one of them. Injuries are not good for Team GB,' said Tilly with a nod.

'How about Team SWAG?'

It was Gideon who had spoken, and now Stein and Janey moved aside so that the others could see him and Trent.

'You look … different,' said Jack to Gideon. 'Sort of … fuller.'

'Courtesy of some Stein juice. Which may be running out, so we'd better hurry.'

Jack then bowed slightly to Trent. 'And you look – well, dead, I'm afraid. I wondered why I could see you at the HOST offices when nobody else appeared to be able to, apart from Gideon, of course.'

'Guilty,' said Trent, holding up his hands to show his deadness, and then he shuddered. 'Actually, guilty is right. When all this is over, I suppose I'm going somewhere terrible.'

'Don't worry. I'll look after you,' said Jack gently, and Janey wondered, yet again, just what it was that the great Anubis had to do in the "processing" he'd mentioned.

'I was tired anyway, man,' said Trent suddenly to Gideon. 'When I realised what Simone was capable of – well, that's not me. Oh, talk of the devil.'

Suddenly Simone Varley's imperious face swung onto the monitors. 'And now it's the moment, ladies and gentlemen, that you've all been waiting for. Just scroll for the name of your favourite athlete to access your own personal fam-cam. You can run the race and play that game with them. Just add your card details to sign-up, and this truly astonishing experience will be yours for the first time in the history of mankind.'

The names and identity numbers of the competitors began to roll up the right-hand side of the screen.

'Now! We've got to go now,' cried Janey, and SWAG instantly swept into high alert.

Wishing for G-Mamma, or Trouble, or Alfie or even her Ultra-Gogs – just something that would help her as she dragged her new friends out into the path of thousands of the world's most super-fit humans, Janey mustered as much confidence as she could.

'Trent, lead the way, please,' she said. 'Gideon, in the middle of the group. Everyone else, protect Gideon at all costs. He's the ace in our pack.'

And with that, she shoved open the doors to the control room that Trent had just evaporated through and ran on ahead.

The tented tunnel was full of people. Many were the escaping HOST ambassadors who had been relieved of their wristbands. Offering no danger at all, they simply scrambled away as fast as their feet would carry them. As others turned to gaze at them in horror or fascination, however, Janey witnessed that momentary pause as their vision was taken over by the ruby-powered mechanism on their wrist.

'They've seen us,' she hissed. 'HOST will be in control now. Get ready.'

She hadn't spoken a moment too soon. Suddenly a member of the Georgian ballet team whipped around like a spinning top, hurtling straight towards them, gathering speed as he spun and gathering allies as the rest of his team joined in until a whole phalanx of black-garbed ninjas was whistling towards them.

'Ha! Two can play at that game!' cried Tilly, sweeping around with a firmly-extended leg and then disappearing into the fray, punching and kicking and spinning with the best of them. 'I've got this! Keep going!' she yelled, plunging deep into the thick of it.

They didn't have time to stop and haul her clear of the gymnasts anyway. As they emerged from the corridor into the stadium to find that news of their presence was spreading, the athletes were forming terrifying ranks that stretched away across the arena, as far as they could see.

Even with their unusual powers, the SWAG team weren't getting out of this easily.

If at all.

'You don't think people at home are paying to watch us get thrashed, do you?' Jack glanced from side to side. 'Only I think they might get more than they bargained for when they see me.'

'I doubt they've started yet. Back to back! Protect Gideon!'

With Stein and Jack on opposite points of the triangle, they surrounded Gideon, facing out, looking for a chink in the vast army that now stood between them and freedom. Where was Trent? Janey couldn't see him, and she wasn't sure if that was because of the deepening shadows as daylight fell, or because he was so far ahead she'd never find him …

And then Gideon suddenly spoke. 'Blonde,' he said weakly. 'I'm fading.'

She spun back to the centre. It was true: the red-gold track that had highlighted his outline was weaker, pulsing rather than beaming, and the pink lustre to his skin was sinking away to its previous pallor. Stein was also staring at him, reaching for his flask of unguent … but Janey stopped him.

'It's okay,' she said. 'There should be enough time.'

Then Jane Blonde - the spy who had tried at all times to remain invisible, who preferred to work alone to keep others out of harm's way - tapped her new friend Jack on the shoulder. 'Could you lift me up?'

He did it without question. Janey was instantly perched on his broad shoulder, high above the arena floor for all to see. From her vantage point, she could finally see Trent, far away across the stadium, pointing to an enclosed viewing area poised above the athletes. Of course. Where they could truly have eyes on everything.

Well, there may not be enough time to get there now before Gideon faded away completely. But there was time to bring the HOST leaders to them.

High above the heads of even the tallest of the athletes, Janey held her arm up and waved. 'Here!' she yelled at the top of her voice. 'Over here!'

Every pair of eyes in the stadium turned towards her, and she knew exactly what that meant. Simone, Henry and Oscar had pinpointed their position. All chipped eyes were trained on them, so in their glass viewing box the HOST team would be able to see them in great detail. They could plan their attack and bury them in hired muscle – albeit innocent hired muscle – in moments.

Just to back up her theory, the massive monitors situated around them crackled with a burst of energy, and then, instead of a thousand names rolling past the viewers to entice them to share their fan-cam, the image of a strange group of imposters shot up onto the screen. A hulking teenager with jeans and a vulpine head of majestic black fur stared back out at her, beside a smaller boy with long hair, ice-white skin and a strangely old-fashioned outfit. And there was she, Jane Blonde, held aloft by Jack as if she was some kind of mascot, her spysuit glinting as the sun sank.

'Yes,' she hollered, as loud as she could, not daring to see how weird it would all look as she was projected all around the arena and possibly all over the world. 'We're here. We are SWAG.'

Now she could deduce from the camera angle exactly where the HOST exec were. Glad that the athletes were all slightly dazed from the ruby-powered manipulation, Janey instructed Jack under her breath. 'Throw me as far as you can, and keep Gideon safe.'

'Hope you know what you're doing, Blonde,' said Jack.

Simone Varley's vile cackle rang out across the Kazakhstan landscape. 'SWAG? What errant nonsense. You hold no threat for us, dear.'

'Now,' said Janey.

And Jack pushed upwards with his shoulders, launching her out cross the enormous field of confused but powerful competitors. Not even stopping to apologise, she jumped from one to another, landing on heads and shoulders and arms that reached out to grab her, occasionally on the ground in a space between athletes and then up again, across the top of the crowd, the cameras following her the whole way, showing her the distance she needed to navigate. Two hundred metres – and a sprint across the rooves of the horse trailers near the polo field. Yes, there was Senor Litardo, advancing on her with the same evil intent he'd shown at the party – not that he could help it with the lanyard controlling him. A hundred metres, just in time to race along the athletics track in a quicker time than the world's best would ever manage. Fifty metres, then forty, then thirty, all the time with the cameras focussed on her face, for all the world to see as she sprang up the bleachers towards the executive boxes.

That was where they were, hidden in plain sight in a glass box above the stadium. Reaching the side of it, Janey ejected the special smash gas, balled her fist and obliterated the frozen pane with her Gauntlet.

They were all there – Simone, Oscar, Henry, all surprised but all looking remarkably unconcerned at what was going on. It looked for all the world as if they were simply having a board meeting, clustered around the end of a long maroon table with a simple console in front of them, operating the myriad cameras and sound recording devices from their fingertips while two larger TV cameras were trained on them, operated by HOST ambassadors.

Janey grinned. 'Hi. We've got something of yours. Of HOST's, I mean. Or should I say … GHOST.'

'What is the girl blathering about?' snorted Henry Wentworth, unaware that his voice was being broadcast to the world.

'What are you?' Simone Varley's voice was venomous. 'Some kind of traitor or a terrorist? Stopping the games for your own ends?'

'Interesting choice of words,' said Janey, running along the boardroom table. 'Because talking of traitors, here's someone you'll remember.'

Knocking the cameraman out of the way so that he staggered to the edge of the box and fell out of it, she grabbed the camera that had been trained on their faces and pointed it out onto the grounds.

'Jack and Stein, would you move apart?' she cried, hoping the microphone would pick up her voice.

The two boys did as she asked, with the world's cameras trained directly on them … and for the first time in forty odd years of the existence of HOST, their first member appeared.

'Hi, guys,' said Gideon Flynn pleasantly. 'Long time, no see.'

Janey glanced into the monitors. Someone was still activating the camera inside the room. As the split screen showing Gideon in one half, in the other, Henry Wentworth's vapid grin was rotating slowly, alighting upon a man's suited knee, the sleeve of a white shirt lying across a gleaming table, and then onto the formerly handsome profile of Simone Varley.

Her glamourous demeanour had completely disappeared. It was as if she'd aged ten years in a single moment. Every carefully powdered wrinkle was amplified by the camera, and the horror in her eyes bore through the lens, naked and terrified.

'Gideon,' she whispered. 'How … you're still …'

As Janey hoped they wouldn't notice that his silhouette was becoming increasingly indistinct, Gideon unleashed his quicksilver smile again. 'Seventeen,' he replied. 'Like when I died.'

'I don't … we're not …'

'Oh, I think you are,' said Gideon with a laugh, clearly enjoying himself, but as the word 'are' was released from his lips, it tailed away to nothing. The effects of the pom juice were evaporating, and so was Gideon.

This had to end now.

'Simone Varley, Oscar Sullivan and Henry Wentworth,' cried Janey. 'You are the people responsible for the deaths of Gideon Flynn and Trent Varley. Gideon, as you can see, is back amongst us, and we – SWAG – have the means to bring back Trent Varley too. He led us straight to you, and we can prove that you murdered him, not Rosie Biggenham.'

'Yes,' called Jack cheerfully from down on the field, 'we're going to have you *extradited*.'

'You can't know this!' cried Simone Varley. 'It's impossible!'

'Ask if it's as impossible as controlling the combined athletes of the world with ruby-powered infra-red rays,' said Gideon, his voice hoarse, fainter by the second.

Janey repeated what Gideon had said. The camera moved jerkily away from the woman's horror-struck expression, and finally Oscar Sullivan spoke.

'What do you want, Flynn?'

He rallied for one last comment, the power of his intention and resourcefulness illuminating his body and face.

'I want it to stop.'

'It's over, HOST. You're over. Turn the rubies off,' Janey ordered when nobody spoke within box of glass. Could they possibly ignore Gideon?

Then a familiar voice echoed across the arena. Janey whipped around – it was penetrating the outside air, but it actually came from within the room. 'You heard her.'

Tilly. Tilly had been operating the other camera. For a second, Janey's heart plummeted. Perhaps it had been a trick. Peppercorn had lured her up here. She'd been in it with Simone Varley from the beginning, and now they were going to end it together. It would make sense of why she was able to get the ring off her so easily. Of how the incriminating objects had ended up in G-Mamma's lab. Of how Matilda Peppercorn had turned up, one step ahead of her, the whole of the way through this mission … Or maybe she'd done it unwillingly, controlled by her athlete band …

But then Tilly's eye winked at her beside the camera lens. 'Get on with it, then, Janey, or I might have to practice my kick-boxing in here. Or we could call Gideon and Trent up for a little reunion while we tie these smugly smuggertons up?'

'You're not being controlled by your wrist-band?'

'Only partly. The part of me that's human. As for the other bits …' Tilly pretend-punched herself in the head. There was no doubting what would happen to the human element of her if Tilly thought something was trying to control her.

Tilly was on her side. So on her side. She had an ally – and possibly even a friend. Not a BFF, as the cat-girl had said herself, but certainly someone to share adventures with. Missions. More heists and toppling of world-class criminals like this …

'Thanks, Matilda,' said Janey happily.

'No problem, Blonde. Actually it's quite a lot of fun watching guilty people squirm. Shall we take a selfie with them? Oh, better not. We're supposed to be at school.'

As her friend prattled on, Janey walked the length of the boardroom table almost as Tilly had done in the lab. Not a catwalk, this time. A spy walk. A Blonde walk. She halted in front of Simone Varley.

'Stop it now,' she said firmly.

'I don't answer to little girls,' snapped Varley.

'Good job I'm not a little girl then,' said Janey bravely, although the woman's brazen, commanding presence unnerved her a little.

She advanced along the table towards Varley, preparing to take her one-on-one if needed, but then the woman reached out a hand. She was going to poison her! But Janey checked, and there were no rings on her fingers. What was she doing? Stretching out a wizened but beautifully manicured finger, Simone Varley pressed a button on the console before her, and Janey suddenly realised why she didn't need a ruby ring of her own …

With a horrible, nauseating vibration pulsating throughout her entire body, Janey staggered to her knees. The whine in her ears was unbearable; she clapped her hands over them but even with the Gauntlet blocking it out on one side, the noise seemed to increase inside the cavities of her own head. The BUDS! Feeling sure she was about to vomit, Janey scratched at the latex ear pods out of her ears, but her arms felt weak, too feeble even for her to lift them up. She collapsed onto the board table, the whole surface vibrating and humming like the vile super-sized ruby, only worse, more intense, stripping out every atom of power in her body as if the oxygen was being sucked out of her through her skin. And then the pins and needles began, amplifying second by second until the pain seared through her as if they were actual pins and needles, and then knife-points and skewers, and then … agony such as she'd never experienced, not stopped in its tracks by her spysuit as a bullet would have been, but pulsing across and inside and through her body as if her veins had been set alight. As if, in fact, her nerve endings were being fried alive …

She hardly had the strength even to gasp, to register this information, but somewhere in the depths of her brain the thought crystallised and Janey knew what was happening. It was the reversed power of the manufactured rubies that Trent had warned them about. All over the stadium the athletes would be experiencing this same terrifying pain from the band on their wrists − but she wasn't wearing a band, so why was this happening to her? And covering her entire body?

Her fluttering eyes focussed for a second on the surface beneath her, and she groaned. How could she have been so stupid?

'Tilly,' she managed to say, hoping her friend could rescue her, but Tilly herself was writhing on the floor, her head gripped between her fists.

It was the table. The very board table on which she'd so casually walked was the cause of it all – the most enormous, lozenge-shaped, super-sized ruby of all. 'The table is a massive ruby,' she gasped, unsure if anyone could hear her. Pain washed across her in a tide of misery, convulsions now rippling from her fingertips, across her outstretched body to her other fingertips, and from the cheek which lay on the evil, cold crimson surface to the tips of her Fleet-Feet. Even her gadgets were no good if she couldn't operate them, and there was no power in her limbs to slam her feet or press a Gauntlet finger.

Then suddenly she saw him – not down in the stadium where she'd left him, but right behind Simone Varley. He seemed as solid and alive as the HOST execs, which could only mean one thing.

If Gideon Flynn looked completely alive to her, then it must be because she was almost in the same state. Jane Blonde was close to death.

And Gideon knew it too. 'Come on, Janey,' he said. 'Fight it. Don't become like me.'

But what could she do? She had no strength left in her, no gadgets that might work …

Apart from one or two.

It was a slim hope but the only one she had. The only one they all had. If this continued, Janey would die, the competitors would all be damaged and HOST would have control of all they desired.

She just had to cross her fingers and believe that they could all still be shocked. Because it wasn't just her arm this time. This time, she was in her spysuit.

With the last strands of energy that she had in her body, Janey leaned her chin down towards her chest and whispered one word:

'Invisibubble.'

She watched as her body vanished, and then turned her eyes towards the remaining HOST leaders. Just a head. Just a head staring at the three evildoers with eyes framed by Ultra-Gogs. Varley screamed and clutched Oscar's hand, and they all moved together involuntarily as Janey shook the glasses from her face so that they lay on the ruby table top before her. She had no idea if this would work, but she had to try.

'Gogs,' she whispered hoarsely, 'target the console.'

The lenses flickered before her, zooming in on the machinery in front of the trio.

'Reverse,' said Janey. 'Reverse the ruby power. Light it up.'

The Ultra-Gogs took her instruction and tried to make it work; this wasn't a function it was set up for, but it did, at least, activate its laser-powered lights. With a blinding shock like lightning, a searing beam with a spectrum of red from pink to deepest, darkest blood colour sliced towards the console, shot through. The console hissed and smoked and then burst into flames.

Immediately Janey's pain eased. In seconds she was able to prise herself off the table surface and clamber towards the end, removing the Invisibubble shield and allowing the agony to dissolve. Simone and Oscar were shouting at each other, batting helplessly at the flaming console to prevent the flames reaching a particular button … the one corralling the athletes, no doubt …

But then, Henry Wentworth reached across them. It was the first time Janey had seen him without a fatuous smile on his face.

'No. I'm done with it too,' he said. 'You two are … impossible.' Shoving Simone's hand out of the way, he pressed the button even though flames were licking at it.

And suddenly a high-pitched whine sliced through the air. Every athlete around them froze momentarily, and Jack dropped to the ground as he clutched his hands to his ears, howling, begging for the pain to end … and then it stopped, just as abruptly as it had begun.

As police sirens wailed across the dustbowl, the competitor army before them stood down, athletes staring at each other in surprise as they discovered they seemed to have been lined up in military formation for some routine they'd never practiced.

'We've done it,' she said breathlessly, staring through the monitors as a Georgian competitor inspect his ripped shirt with bewilderment, and the synchronised swimming team checked each other for bruises. 'It's over, Gideon.'

But when she looked behind Wentworth, Gideon Flynn was no more. Where he had stood there was just the faintest eddy of red-gold dust, exactly like the earth beneath her feet.

Chapter 26 – The School of ICE

'Perhaps,' said Matilda Peppercorn, in as comforting a fashion as she could manage, 'Gideon's absence is like a ghost disappearing from this mortal plane when he's completed his good deed, like Trent did. Or that other famous dude. Scrooge.'

Jack threw a peanut at her. 'Scrooge wasn't a ghost. Marley was a ghost.'

'Who's Marley?'

'The ghost! In Scrooge! Have you even read A Christmas Carol?' howled Jack in frustration.

'Of course not,' Tilly retorted. 'I did see the Muppety film version, though.'

'Okay, well, was Scrooge a ghost or a man?'

'I think he was a frog, wasn't he?'

Jack shook his head. 'Woeful. I give up.'

'Actually,' said Janey, 'I'm rather glad. I keep hearing the word "ghost" and it makes me …'

She didn't even finish the sentence, as she couldn't find the most appropriate word. It made her all sorts of things, really. Sad, mostly, because that was what both Gideon and Trent had been – actual ghosts - and now Gideon was gone. Then her mind would wander over GHOST the organisation that lost Gideon in some hideous accident before becoming plain old HOST, and then Gideon was gone from them too. And plain old HOST was a complete misnomer, as was 'Helping Others Save Time'. Helping Ourselves Shoot Trent, more like, and generally helping themselves to anything they wanted. And Gideon was gone.

Jack and Tilly were staring at her, their eyebrows furrowed in such a similar way that they would have hated it if she'd pointed it out to them.

They were lined up along the fountain in the grounds of Jack's castle, waiting for G-Mamma to call them in for her surprise.

It was just one of the several extraordinary circumstances that had evolved around the surprisingly sudden collapse of the World Community Games. To the outside world, it appeared that the police had discovered the role of H, O and S in the recent death of T in the HOST organisation and had pulled the plug on their management of the Games. Simone Varley was being charged with murder as she'd administered poison to her husband which rendered him incapable of avoiding a trip to an MRI which was mysteriously jammed – by a minion controlled by a ruby ring, Janey guessed – and where the metallic remnants of a past accident ripped out of him, shooting him, as it were, from the inside out. Wentworth and Sullivan were both named as accessories, and Miss Rosie Biggenham was cleared of all charges as she'd clearly been framed with evidence hidden in grocery boxes. Jack had read all this out to them with considerable glee, taking special care to explain all the legal terms that might otherwise be lost on them, especially to Matilda.

So that was what the world at large believed. Like Janey, many people had expressed regret that the World Community Games weren't actually going to happen, as it was a pretty stellar idea (and some new consortium had stepped in to take over for the next year).

What few people had seen, though, was the other set of … well, non-people, clearing up after the event.

Stein had swigged down the last of his pom juice just as soon as he could, sent an email to his friend Moose requesting "immediate supplies via Ambro Flight, gadzooks and forsooth!", and then helped Jack to process Trent who was still roaming the arena, rattling his head.

'Can't believe my own wife would have me killed,' he repeated. 'My own wife!'

Jack smiled benignly. 'You'll have some great stories to share with my rellies, and they'll have some for you!'

'Why? Where am I going?' said Trent, backing away from Jack suspiciously.

'Well,' said Jack, squatting like a teacher explaining some complex maths to a toddler, 'I think your time here is done, and you'd be much better off if I passed you through to the Field of Rushes. You can meet all your old family there, and my dad, grandparents, great grandparents and so on, and … you'll have fun. They love rugby! All sports, actually.'

'You can do that?'

'God of death,' said Jack with a nod. 'That's me.'

And so it was decided that Jack and Stein, who wasn't too freaked out by death either, should take Trent to the rugby pitch on the peripheries of the stadium and usher him through to his final destination, beyond the Field of Rushes.

'Thanks,' he said awkwardly to Janey and Tilly. 'And sorry if I was a bit of a loon.'

'We completely understand,' said Janey. 'Say …' What was it? Goodbye? 'Say hello to Gideon for me. Us, I mean. If you see him.'

'Bye, Trent. I'm going to take up rugby in your honour,' Tilly announced.

Trent frowned. 'Girls can't play rugby.' Then he met Tilly's glare. 'All I mean is that they didn't in my day. But you … you'll make an unbelievable prop forward. Good luck!'

'Thank you,' said Tilly primly.

They'd left them to it, and then Janey had asked Tilly for a favour. 'I know you're not meant to do magic to Normal People,' she said, walking with Tilly towards the control room, 'but can you magic them by SPIV? I mean, Skype?'

'Never tried it,' said Tilly with a shrug. 'But I'll give it a go. Is it the parentals?'

Janey laughed. 'Yes, my mum and dad. They were expecting me home hours ago, even with the time difference.'

'Mine too. It's weird having normal parents when you're not normal, isn't it?'

Janey couldn't help but agree, especially as hers had once been quite extraordinary, really. And they still were, she decided, as their worried pixilated faces swam into view on the large screen before them and she introduced her brand-new homework buddy, Matilda Peppercorn.

'I'm SO sorry to KEEP Janey all to mySELF,' crooned Tilly in her mesmeric voice. 'I'll have her HOME by TEN, oKAY?'

Boz and Gina stared at her blankly in a way that reminded Janey of the athletes when the wristbands were activated. Then they nodded enthusiastically. 'Great!' said her father. 'You'll have to come over at the weekend, Matilda.'

Gina beamed into the camera. 'We'd love to meet your parents. How about a barbecue?'

'PURRRRfect,' Tilly sang, turning to Janey as they ended the call. 'Wow! That was outstanding. If I can do that by Skype I can pretty much magic anyone, anywhere!' She stroked her chin thoughtfully. 'Hmm. I should turn that big camera on myself and induce everyone into forgetting about the Games.'

'Careful. That sounds a bit like HOST.'

But Tilly had just laughed, then called her own parents with Janey peering in from the side of the screen, introduced as Tilly's new homework buddy …

With all that excitement behind them, Janey had returned home with the distinct feeling that she'd developed a split personality. One half of her was thrilled about having met the others, but the other part simply felt bereft. With Gideon gone, SWAG was no more. Her new adventures had been short-lived, and she felt almost as if she'd failed as they hadn't brought everyone home, even if they had managed to thwart HOST's plans.

It was the thought of 'home' that gave her the idea, though, and that was how she had found herself crossing Richmond Park in her normal clothes on a sunny Saturday afternoon. Once the trial of the three HOST members was over, Jack had worked his legal 'I'm going into the House of Lords' angle and helped Janey out with her own personal mission.

Before going to the house, however, she continued along the path to a triangular piece of parkland. Around it, the horse chestnut trees were turning red and gold, shedding their prickly shells onto the ground to reveal the delicious gleam of the conkers within. How appropriate, thought Janey. It was pretty much what Gideon had done too.

She understood, now, why he'd always stayed in the shadows. He wanted to stay under the trees, soaking up the nature around him. It must have given him some sort of power, some sort of energy. Then he'd discovered spy-buys, giving first his voice and then his whole body a physical presence in the Wower so that he could gather his team, each one of whom had even more ability than the previous one to help him become … what was the word? Whole? Real?

Embodied, Janey decided.

In her case, he needed her spy instincts and SPI gadgetry. Tilly had a magic animal instinct to perceive him wherever he was. Jack saw spirits anyway; that was why he'd checked that she and G-Mamma could also see Gideon and Tilly when they first met, to ensure they weren't dead – although he must have had his suspicions. And Stein, the little rock, three hundred years old and able to turn base metal into gold. An ancient boy turning gold. But that wasn't the limit of his talents. She'd looked it up as soon as she got her Gogs back, and alchemists didn't simply create ingots. They could also create immortality – and life.

Well, he might not have life, but now she was going to honour him by doing something for the people who'd had no control at all over what happened to him.

'I'm going to see them now,' she whispered into the air, feeling only a tiny bit foolish. 'I wish you were here too.'

Then she knocked on the door, finally, and smiled at the elderly couple who opened it.

'Mr and Mrs Flynn? I'm Janey Brown. I've come to return some items to you from the recent trials.' She handed them the ring and the rifle. 'I believe they belonged to your ... your son? There's a sitar, as well, but I'm going to need transport for that.'

The woman's face crumpled for a second, then she gathered herself and nodded. 'Thank you. It means so much to have his things around. It makes him feel closer, somehow. Even after all this time ...'

She wasn't able to finish, but Janey knew what she'd been going to say. Sometimes, they were able to sense his presence. It wasn't strange to Janey ... because on occasions, she felt his presence around her, too.

'Would you like to come in, Miss Brown?' said Mr Flynn suddenly, with the flash of an extraordinary fleeting smile. 'You've been so kind, bringing this to us. We can show you some photos. And the least we can do is offer you a cup of tea.'

'I'd love to,' she said. 'In fact, if you're willing, I'd love to hear all about him.'

When the time had come to part company after the Games, they'd all found it hard.

'You could all come and live with me, you know,' cried Stein. 'Gadsbudlikins, what fun that would be!'

'Actually, I've been thinking about that,' said Jack. 'I've got a castle too, you know. It's big and empty, and…' He mouthed "with fewer vampires" to the girls, 'and we could use one or two wings without my mother even knowing. Or caring!'

'For what?' said Tilly, always the first to leap on Jack's suggestions.

'Well, for SWAG HQ. You'd have to come back to England, Stein, but it might be nice for you to see the old place again.'

'What about the Spylab? And G-Ma … GM?' Janey felt disloyal even thinking about setting up headquarters anywhere else, even though it did kind of make sense, and there'd be much more room for every … for everything.

'We could set a spy depot up at Lowmount, and a posh place with a massive desk for the Big G to vet all our clients. And a … freaky Stein lab, for whatever it is you do behind closed doors, and a cauldron cat room for Tilly, and I've already got a museum with all my bits and bobs in it. I've been planning to set up a school there anyway – for special people. Like us.'

It was almost an exciting idea - but they were dreaming.

'You've forgotten one thing, though, Jack,' said Janey sadly. 'There is no SWAG. We were set up by Gideon, for Gideon. Without him we're just like a kids' club, hanging out in the shed.'

Jack frowned. 'I … I think we could still do something, couldn't we? Something useful.'

'Zooks, I for one would love a kids' club, hanging out in the shed! I'll ask Mother and Father if I can come,' cried Stein.

'Can I think about it? It is a good idea, but I just need to come to terms with a few things.'

That had been a while ago; now here they were together again as G-Mamma threw open the vast creaking door that they'd knocked on to summon Jack, all those months before. She could hardly bear to hear it all, if she was honest. Even as Jack beamed and G-Mamma chattered about the tremendous facilities for witchery, alchemy, Egyptology and spycraft, Janey knew she was going through the motions, peeking through doorways and joining in laughter.

Hardly able to bear Jack's disappointment that she wasn't enjoying it wholeheartedly, Janey peeled away from the main group. SWAG had ended so weirdly that she wasn't sure what she wanted any more. She'd revved up all her spying activities again, and the end of the team felt so anti-climactic that she wasn't sure she could stand to establish a business headquarters that was also a school

for misfits, waiting again for something exciting to happen
...

She found herself beside a laboratory built exactly to Stein's specifications, and smiled to herself. It really had been quite an adventure. More out of habit than anything else, she fixed her eyes on the doors of each laboratory and instructed her Gogs.

'Zoom,' she said in a flat tone of voice, hardly bothering to look into the room.

And then her throat closed over.

This lab was exactly like the one in Transnordia had been, with just a faint sheen edging the tables and shelves. The second one, however, had little bursts of life pulsating from its peripheries. Then, in the middle, standing by the main bench, was a clear outline.

Of something.

Someone.

She pushed the door open slowly.

'*A story once told. As an ancient boy turns gold, the truth emerges,*' said Gideon Flynn, glowing gently with whatever ran across his pink-tinged skin. 'You were right – it is a haiku. I eavesdropped when you were learning about them at Everdenn. I'm not sure you'll cover them here at the School of ICE.'

'ICE?'

The tiny grin flashed across his face. 'Jack's idea. Inter-Connecting Energies.'

Hoping she could be heard over the hammering in her chest, Janey nodded slowly. 'I like it.'

'It's very Jack. Very all of you, actually.'

Janey hesitated before asking as she always would, so as not to hurt feelings, jump to conclusions. But then she took a deep breath. 'You knew such a lot about us. About all of us. How is that possible?'

'I've hung around for a very long time, in the shadows. The half-light, you might say. I've met a lot of interesting people, there in the half-light, and they led me to all of you. To special people with their own unique talents and gifts.' Gideon stared down at his hands – hands that sparkled with life. For the moment, at least. 'Actually, I was thinking that we should probably put another G on the name of SWAG. Spy, Witch, Alchemist, God, and … Ghost.'

'Gideon.'

'Yes?'

'No.' Janey laughed, blinking back tears. 'The G should be for Gideon. Meaning pure positive energy.'

'Not sure I'm all that positive.'

She moved further into the room. 'You're getting there,' she said, 'and I've learned some more things at Everdenn - something interesting in physics. Energy can't be destroyed. Especially if it's inter-connected.'

They both gazed down at his hands. Hoping.

'I've heard that too. Either way,' Gideon said, his crooked smile flaring suddenly across his thin face, 'it sounds as if we're agreed. It will be SWAGG, with two Gs. And we'll operate from this head office stroke school type thing in Jack's spare castle wing, and, you know ...' He shrugged. '... Fight crime.'

Janey nodded mutely, hardly daring to believe that her friend was here again – dappled through with light and not completely solid throughout, but definitely opaque and visible, and definitely here.

'This is the most body I've had in decades.' Gideon stared at his hand. 'Apart from ... well, I sort of agreed with an undead person that I could borrow his for a while.' He grinned in a fangy way.

'Ambro? You were Ambro?' No wonder he had gazed at her so intently.

'Just for a while.'

Janey stared at him, so many feelings zipping around her chest that she couldn't speak.

'Oh, hey,' said Gideon suddenly, holding out his arm. 'Try this.'

She held her breath, watching what he was doing. What was he trying to give her? Then she realised how unlikely it was that he should pass anything to her, and stared again.

The hands stuffed in pockets were a thing of the past. His condition had been revealed to be a cover story.

And now he was stretching his arm out towards her.

'You're not a solitary spy any longer, Jane Blonde. You don't need to go it alone. You're leading an incredible team.'

'No, you are.'

Gideon laughed. 'No, it was always your team, and you stepped up admirably.'

And somehow she felt the truth of that. There she was, the most human, the least amazing, taking charge of this extraordinary mission with these incredible team-mates.

'Stein has refined the unguent,' he said. 'So if you're willing to have me on board, I'm here and … I'm in.'

She held out her own hand. Just for a moment until his energy dipped, their fingers touched.

Janey caught her breath. He felt whole. Real.

It – the whole of it – was real.

And even as his outline gently faded, Jane Blonde knew that whatever happened next, there was no going back. They all existed, now, in this new form.

From this moment on, they were SWAGG.

The End

ABOUT THE AUTHOR

Jill Marshall is a proud mum, nana and communications consultant, as well as the author of dozens of books for children, young adults and (old) adults. When she's not doing any of those things, she loves singing, dancing and theatre and going to see other people do singing, dancing and theatre. She divides her time between the UK and New Zealand, and hopes one day to travel between the two by SatiSPI.

Look out for the next in the SWAGG series: School of Ice – coming soon

SWAGG 2, School of ICE

Look out for the next book in the SWAGG series – coming soon! Pre-order now, or sign up for <u>*Jill's newsletter*</u> *to receive it before release date.*

Jack Bootle-Cadogan crept through the halls of his stately home, admiring the handiwork of his leader and mentor, Gideon Flynn. He stuck his canine head through the nearest wall. Spylab – nice. The kit was lined up along the walls like the armour ranked along the corridor, sparkling and inviting. Jane Blonde and Trouble were doing a double act, checking off inventory. Scenting his presence, Trouble whipped around.

Jack withdrew his head hastily. Wouldn't do be found peering in on the guests, uninvited.

He passed the next two SWAGG Sector Rooms without investigating. Tilly's area was a mystery to him, full of witch and warlock training rooms, broomstick stables and, of course, Matilda Peppercorn herself. Whatever she was doing she was building up a sweat – he could see the blue glow through stone walls a metre thick.

She scared him a bit at the best of times. Doubting that this was going to be the best of times, he slid past noiselessly.

Stein's laboratory lay off to the right, down the half-flight of stairs. Through the tiny window, Jack could see that Stein was entertaining Jack's own sort-of cousins, Joe and Mindy, by animating one of the mummies from the museum. Mummies were a very familiar sight in Jack's weird life, so he didn't stop to watch other than to take in the thrilled expression on Stein's sallow face – thrilled that he had these powers to make new friends. There was another reason he moved on quickly too, though. The mummy reminded him of someone very dear to him. His oldest friend. The whole family's oldest friend. With a sigh, Jack shook his head and pulled back from the door.

Then he shook it again. What was that?

His canine hearing kicked in. Someone was in his museum. He'd given it over to the School of Inter-Connecting Energies when they were setting it up, but it was still meant to be locked while it was transformed into a centre for learning about Egyptology and all Jack's background. Jack himself had the only key, and he hadn't used it as he'd just stuck his head through the plasterwork from time to time to check in.

Last time, there'd been very little progress. All his Egyptian artefacts had been carefully set aside as space was cleared for some impressive turntables, library shelves and state-of-the-art imaging technology.

Judging by the clanking coming from the castle's cellars, though, it wasn't empty any longer.

Not even stopping to think that he might be putting himself in danger, Jack Zipped through several of the rooms reserved for the public and straight through the earth to the tunnel that led from the museum to the crypt.

He entered the room from the back, silent as the ghosts he processed, planning to surprise whoever – or whatever – had sneaked in there.

But instead, it was Jack himself who got the surprise. Something he could never have imagined was taking place in the Lowmount museum. Never have imagined at all, in a million lifetimes …

Want the full SWAGG experience?

Immerse yourself in the origin stories.

The Jane Blonde series
Jane Blonde, Sensational Spylet
Jane Blonde Spies Trouble
Jane Blonde, Twice the Spylet
Jane Blonde, Spylet on Ice
Jane Blonde, Goldenspy
Jane Blonde, Spy in the Sky
Jane Blonde, Spylets are Forever

Jack BC in the Doghead trilogy
1 Jack BC, Doghead
2. Jack BC, Dogfight
3. Jack BC, Dogstar

The Legend of Matilda Peppercorn
TLOMP, Witch Hunter
TLOMP, Toadstone
TLOMP, Questioner
TLOMP, Trinity

Stein & Frank: Battle of the Undead People-Eaters

Also by Jill Marshall
Available in print, mobi, epub and audio.

For Young Adults
Pineapple
Fanmail
Lena's Fortune

For Adults
The Most Beautiful Man in the World
The Two Miss Parsons
As It Is on Telly

For younger children
Kave-Tina Rox

For more adventures and

information,

visit www.jillmarshallbooks.com

Follow Jill Marshall Books

on Facebook

Email jill on

info@jillmarshallbooks.com